CURSED

One, two, the witch is due.

Richard Schiver

Abis Books
Cumberland, Md.

Cover art by Dean Samed

ISBN: 978-1-951552-04-6

Dedication

For my wife, Dena, who manages to keep my feet firmly planted on the ground while my mind soars. I love you.

Acknowledgement

I want to thank the Horror Writers Association for their help in making this book the best it could be. When I finished writing the first draft more than two years ago I figured after a couple of rounds of editing it would be ready. Boy was I wrong. That was the year I joined the HWA. I know I've always said I never wanted to be a member of any group that would have someone like me as a member, but in 2018 I bit the bullet and paid my dues.

In the HWA I learned about their mentor program. New writers such as myself could ask to be paired with a writer working in the field for some intense one on one editing of a manuscript I felt was ready to go. I really wish I would have done this years ago. I learned so much about what to do, but more importantly I learned about what not to do. I was paired with Lee Allen Howard and at first I was afraid our styles would not mesh. Again, I was wrong.

Thank you HWA and thank you Lee, for opening my eyes and helping me along the path to creating compelling fiction. The journey is far from over, but I find myself on the right path now.

I would also like to extend a heartfelt thanks to everyone who contributed to the completion of this book. My beta readers, Wendy, Sherri, and Danielle.

My editors Patricia Russo, and Brieanna Robertson. My co-workers who listened to my ideas and offered encouragement. My friends on Facebook who are always ready to offer insight into the craziness that is writing, and a special thanks to Dean Samed for the killer cover.

1

At night, the world slips on a different mask as the shadows grow long and deep. Moonlight washes away the colors of the day. Replacing them with varied shades of gray that transform the most innocent objects into nightmare apparitions. The dresser in the corner had become a towering beast that threatened to devour him. The shadow of the lamp on the desk reached out with slender fingers of night.

Bobby slept. Unaware of the terror that lived in the shadows around him. Lost in a dream of a time and place that lived only in his imagination. The aroma of fresh popcorn, hot dogs, and beer assailed him. Vendors carrying trays of assorted snacks and drinks balanced on one hand, ran up and down the steps, hawking their wares.

"Get your popcorn, cold beer, and soft drinks," they shouted, their voices mingling with the roar of the crowd.

He was in the cheap seats, the nosebleed section. High above a bright green field as the noonday sun rode across a cloudless blue sky. His dad sat next to him, a dark silhouette whose features remained hidden. His arm rested lightly across Bobby's shoulders, the weight of its presence filling him with a sense of security. As long as he was with his dad, nothing could hurt him.

Around him the crowd was a multi-colored beast that moved of its own accord, speaking in a variety of tongues and tones.

From the field came the crack of a bat. The crowd jumped to its feet with a roar. Yet he remained seated, another sound having captured his attention. A sinister whisper that came from the shadowy space beneath his seat. Close to the floor where the scent of spilt beer mingled with the odor of past disappointment.

Bobby leaned forward and peered into the shadows as that soft whisper filled him with growing terror.

He looked up for his dad, but he was gone, and bitterness filled his heart. The stadium was gone, as was the crowd that once surrounded him. Shadows danced with a life of their own against the blank wall above his bed as dark clouds slid across the face of the moon, plunging his room into a nighted abyss.

His disappointment grew as cold reality settled around him. He was dreaming about his dad again. A man he never met.

His mother told him his father left after Bobby was born. Bobby's older sister Twila said their mother threw Dad out because he refused to give her money to waste on booze. Bobby suspected Twila was lying to protect his feelings. He believed his father left because of something he'd seen as Bobby lay in his crib. Some unfathomable truth that told him his only son would be a big disappointment, and to get out now, while the getting was good.

The sound came again, a soft murmur from the other side of his bedroom's only window. He slipped out of bed, and crossed the room, the floor cold under his bare feet.

From beyond his closed bedroom door came the muffled voice of his mother as she entertained one of her friends. His name was Jerry, a young, brash, blond guy with a small pointed beard that reminded Bobby of the devil. He called Bobby "Sport," which he detested.

When Jerry tried to tousle his hair, Bobby moved his head aside at the last moment, leaving Jerry's hand hanging in mid-air. It was his way of showing Jerry that he was no pushover, no sport.

Jerry was auditioning for the role of Bobby's father, a job that opened up once again. His mom caught David, the previous applicant, stealing money from her purse. Money she worked hard to earn as a bartender at a small tavern in town. Money that should have been spent on food but ended up being squandered on booze to make it through another day.

"You don't know how hard it is. I could have been a star, I could dance." She told him one day as she sat at the kitchen table, downing shots of cheap whiskey. To Bobby it looked as if it was a task to keep her head upright. *"I could have had everything I wanted, but what do I do? I work my fingers to the bone to pay the bills around here, then I come home and work even more to make a home for you and your sister."* She wiped her mouth with the back of one shaking hand, smearing her lipstick, before reaching for the bottle.

Bobby disagreed with her statement. He wanted to point out that while she was working, Twila was taking care of the trailer they called home. But he'd learned early not to argue with his mother when she was drinking.

It's out there. The thought whispered, drawing his attention to the window as the memory of his mother faded. He felt its presence in the cold chill of a winter's night that nipped at his face and sent fear rippling down his spine.

He hated the long emptiness of the night. The wind calling to him in a mournful voice as the shadows of the trees danced against the wall. The isolation as he waited impatiently for the first fingers of dawn to push back the gloomy depths that carried the essence of nightmares.

Another sound came from outside, soft, sinuous, drawing him to the window. Beyond lay a moonlit night whose long shadows crossed barren fields that were slowly emerging from their winter sleep.

She was out there, the Witch of Porter Mines, coming to take her due.

He spotted her, and took a step back, afraid she might see him. Her black shape pulsed and shimmered in the moonlight, yet she cast no shadow. She stood in the center of the field behind their mobile home, watching him with a peculiar stillness that stirred the short hairs on the nape of his neck. He recalled the song the children sang at recess when the teachers weren't around.

One, two, the Witch is due.

Three, four, she's at the door.

Five, six, who will she pick?

Seven, eight, at night she waits.

Nine, ten, don't let her in.

The Witch of Porter Mines was an old legend. Everyone who grew up in the area had been threatened by their parents the Witch would take them if they didn't behave. Bobby's own mother promised it would happen to him if he didn't listen.

He tried to be good, but sometimes it was so hard. His desire to do right was there, but the ability was absent. He tried to listen to the babysitter, one of their neighbors, a young mother herself. Cathy would sit before the television instead of watching them, chain-smoking cigarettes, talking on her cell phone, yelling at him and Twila if they made any noise.

One, two, the Witch is due.

The sound came again, drawing him from his thoughts, back to what was waiting outside. She stood at the edge of the field. A young girl glowing in the pale moonlight, and with one crooked finger, she beckoned for him to follow.

Three, four, she's at the door.

"I have a secret," she whispered in his mind.

Bobby didn't like secrets. Secrets were painful. One of his mother's boyfriends stumbled drunkenly into his room one night while he slept. He'd awakened to rough hands touching his body in places that weren't meant to be touched.

"We have to keep this secret," his mother told him the morning after, threatening to send him away if he told anyone.

He didn't care if he never saw his mother again, but Twila was different.

He loved Twila. She took care of him and protected him from all the bad things in the world. She always made him what he wanted for dinner, no matter how strange his request.

He wished Twila was with him as the girl drifted closer to the window.

Five, six, who will she pick?

The girl was no taller than Twila, who was twelve, probably no older as well. He glanced at his door, afraid his mother would catch him staring out the window. When he looked back, the girl was on the other side of the glass, staring at him with fathomless black eyes.

"I have a secret," she whispered in his mind.

Seven, eight, at night she waits.

A shadowy apparition danced in the wind behind her. It looked like the tattered edge of an ancient shawl. Fading in and out of focus, it was a part of the girl as much as the girl was a part of it. Yet they were two separate entities, that shadowy presence wearing the girl like a mask.

Bobby would have stepped back from the window, but his feet had taken root in the floor. Hot urine dribbled down his leg as an acrid odor rose from below. Her presence blocked the moonlight, blanketing his room in a chilled darkness that wrapped itself about him like a snake seeking warmth.

Nine, ten, don't let her in.

"Open the window."

He felt like he was falling into the nighted abyss of her unwavering gaze. His actions no longer his own as he reached for the lock, unable to stop himself, unable to scream. A whimper was all he could manage before his fingers closed on the brass latch, and against his will he turned the lock. A cold blast of night air washed over him as the window slid up. That primitive shadow slithered into his room and surrounded him with the icy depths of hell.

He realized then he was no longer dreaming.

2

Susan moaned as John's callused hand slid across her bare belly and dropped into the dark region between her thighs. She shuddered as his fingers caressed her and his warm lips closed over her erect nipple. His body radiated a warmth that wrapped her in its loving embrace. She reached out for him, her fingers finding only cold, empty sheets.

"No," she whispered as she struggled to recapture his warmth. A chill slithered along her side and she recoiled from it. For a moment she teetered on the line between deep sleep and semi-consciousness before slipping into a nighted abyss.

Images flashed through her mind, snapshots from her past. John at the lake, grinning at the camera with a devilish smile, a vast expanse of water spread out behind him. John in the hospital holding the tiny bundle that was Christine as he gazed at his daughter with rapt wonder.

With each image, her longing became more pronounced and her sorrow deepened as the images became somber reminders of her loss.

A copper-colored casket, its surface gleaming in the bright sunlight. A folded American flag presented by a soldier too young for such serious matters. A row of soldiers in full dress uniform standing at attention as the distant notes of a single trumpet echoed with a forlorn voice.

She awoke with a start, panting, looking around the room as her awareness grew. A child's scream sliced across her consciousness and she snapped fully awake as the last vestiges of the dream faded into the night around her.

The scream came again. She threw back the covers, swung her feet to the floor, and raced for the door. Tripping over a stack of boxes she had yet to put away. The coarse fibers of the Berber carpet rubbed against her bare flesh. She was wearing only a pair of panties. Snatching her robe from the chair beside the bed she slipped it on and raced from the room as Christine cried out again.

In Christine's room, Susan flipped on the light switch to find her daughter curled up in the corner, her stuffed bunny clasped to her chest. She was staring at the window with vacant eyes through strands of hair plastered to her sweaty face. The tip of her tongue peeking out from between slack lips.

What the hell!

Susan crossed the room, knelt before Christine, and gently touched her shoulder. Her daughter shivered beneath her sweat-drenched nightgown.

"Christine, it's okay. Mommy's here."

Christine glanced from the window to Susan and back again. Susan was struck by the expression of hopeless terror on her face.

"Mommy?" Christine's voice quavered.

"It's okay, I've got you." Susan wrapped her in her arms and lifted her from the floor. The stuffed rabbit slipped from between them and fell to the carpet.

"Don't forget Puddles."

Susan picked up the rabbit. The argument she'd had with John over the cost of winning it filled her with guilt. What was twelve dollars compared to the comfort it provided? But hindsight was a double-edged sword. Had she known then that he would never come home, she wouldn't have let him go.

"Let's get you back into bed."

"No," Christine moaned, tightening her grip around Susan's neck.

"But sweetie, you have to go back to bed."

"She'll get me if I do."

"No one's going to get you."

"She said she was coming to get me."

"Who said that?"

"The witch."

Susan pried Christine's hands from around her neck and lowered her to the bed. She looked around the room. "I don't see a witch."

Christine pointed at the window. "She's outside."

Susan crossed to the window and Christine slipped out of bed to follow. Susan leaned against the sill and peered out at the night, her breath fogging the glass. In the light of the moon she spotted a tree limb lying across the shattered remains of an old shed. The wind must have knocked it off. She'd have to clean that up in the morning.

"I don't see any witches," Susan said.

"She's out there," Christine said. "I saw her, on the other side of the window."

"But we're two stories up, sweetie. She couldn't have been out there unless she was flying." Even as she said it, she realized she should have kept her mouth shut. It would only fill Christine's head with things she needn't think about.

"Marjorie said--"

Susan held up her hand. She had to nip this in the bud.

"I don't care what Marjorie said." She led Christine back to bed and helped her under the covers. "You know, sometimes, when you're in a new place, and you hear stories from your friends, you might think you see things that aren't really there."

Christine shook her head. "But I saw her, Mommy. She was right outside my window."

The conviction in Christine's eyes sent a chill down Susan's spine. She was filled with the unmistakable sensation that someone, or something, was watching them from the shadows. She looked around the small room, from the pile of boxes stacked in one corner to the stuffed animals occupying the Little Princess table in the opposite.

In the light they were harmless inanimate objects. But at night, with only a nightlight to hold the shadows at bay, they could take on more sinister forms to a child trying to sleep in an unfamiliar room.

Susan pointed at the pile of boxes. "I bet you thought that was the witch."

Christine seemed to be considering this and shook her head.

"She was on the other side of the window, Mommy. Can I please spend the night with you?"

Susan stroked her hair. "We've talked about this before. If I let you spend one night, you'll want to spend another, then another. Before you know it, I'll have to find a different bedroom."

"I promise, it will just be one night."

"Remember what we talked about before we moved here?"

Christine scrunched up her face.

"We talked about how a new house will feel strange at first. There will be unfamiliar sounds and we might see things that aren't really there."

"But she was real, Mommy."

"Are you sure?"

Christine looked from the window to her closet door, which stood ajar.

"Please, Mommy, just one night, I promise."

Susan hated to see her so frightened, but it was time for her to be the parent instead of her child's best friend. Letting Christine sleep with her would only lengthen the time it took for her to get used to the new house.

"I'm sorry," Susan said, "I'll leave the hall light on for you, but you can't sleep with me."

"But the witch will get me."

"We've talked about this before. People make up stories about witches to scare other people."

"But Marjorie said--"

"I don't care what Marjorie said." Her tone reflected her exasperation. She didn't want to argue. Christine's refusal to listen was pushing her to the point where she would simply put her foot down. Of course, once she did that, Christine would sulk for a few days, and Susan would become the bad guy. She wanted Christine to have something Susan lacked while growing up. A strong, loving, relationship. The opposite of what she'd had with her mother.

Slipping off the side of the bed, Susan knelt on the floor, the carpet coarse against her knees. Level with Christine, she looked her in the eye. "I'm not going to let anything happen to you."

"You promise?"

Susan drew an X across her own heart. "Cross my heart and hope to die."

"Stick a needle in your eye," Christine said, a faint smile curling the corners of her lips.

Susan slapped her hand over one eye. "Eeewww, no. I'm right down the hall. If anything comes to get you, just yell, and I'll be here so fast it'll make your head swim."

"Promise?"

"Anything for you."

"Can I sleep with you?"

"Now you're pushing it." Susan tickled Christine, who laughed.

Christine burrowed deeper into the blankets and gazed up at Susan with a smile. "I love you, Mommy."

"I love you too, Baby Doll."

Susan turned off the light next to the bed and backed across the room to the door.

"Will you leave the hall light on?" Christine asked.

"Sure."

"Good night, Mommy."

"Goodnight, sweetie." Susan stepped into the hall, leaving the door ajar.

She rubbed her arms as she walked back to her room. She'd heard the rumors after buying the old Jenkins place. An old wives' tale that was tied to Porter Mines as snugly as the names of the inhabitants that lived there. A legend that failed to reach beyond the borders of the small, unincorporated town. A ghost story that many of the parents used to keep unruly children in check. At its core, she later learned, the story contained a nugget of truth.

Had she known about the witch prior to moving here, she would have looked elsewhere, for no other reason than to protect Christine from the rumors. It was too late now as she'd already invested her savings in the house. The only thing she could do was try to counter any talk of the legend with reasoned arguments.

At the top of the staircase she stopped when a sound like a child crying came from the darkness below. She stood at the top of the steps with her head tilted to one side, listening. From below came a thump, followed by the faint whine of the heat kicking on.

It's only the heat she decided, before turning down the hall to her bedroom.

3

Old Man Watkins, Andy to his few friends who remained, sat up startled. He'd been sleeping again, his dreams filled with memories of a better time that lay in the distant past. He'd fallen asleep in the overstuffed chair on his front porch as the full moon marched across the night sky. The air still carried a hint of winter's recent passing.

His neighbors thought he was crazy for putting such a fine piece of furniture on the front porch, unprotected from the weather. As far as Andy was concerned, he would do what he damned well pleased. He'd earned the right. He'd worked his whole life to give his family all they needed. He'd paid his taxes on time and owed no one. He brought his kids up right, protecting them as best he could from the evil in the world, and sent them out to prosper knowing they were prepared for whatever came their way.

Now he was alone. Wilma died four years ago, and the hole left in his soul ached with the memory of her. She'd been by his side so long he felt like a part of his physical being passed with her. They shared so much in their time together, so much joy, so much happiness, as well as a few moments of despair. But that was life, you took the good with the bad.

"Jacob," he moaned, and rubbed his arms with his hands as he looked around, blinking rapidly, still groggy from his nap. His dreams had taken a brief detour into the shadowy realm of nightmares, touched by something passing in the night.

He leaned forward and grabbed the railing with arthritic hands, staring into the yard as the last of the nightmare dissipated. He'd been dreaming about Jacob again and a small part of him felt his presence in the shadows gathered around the house.

The first dark period in their lives started the day the olive drab sedan pulled into the driveway in 1971. Andy had stopped by to refill his Thermos when the car pulled in behind his coal truck, and two uniformed soldiers emerged. Having served in World War II and with William, their oldest son, in Vietnam at the time, the moment he saw them he understood what happened.

Afterwards, when they were alone, he held Wilma close as her sorrow overwhelmed her. Together they cried as they reminisced about their oldest child and began their journey through the sorrow. At the time they didn't know it could get any worse. After all, what could be harder than outliving a child?

Four years later, Jacob vanished. Born a year before William's passing, he was their miracle child. Wilma was on the wrong side of forty to be carrying a pregnancy to term. Only five years old, Jacob was playing in the back yard while Wilma hung out the clothes. She'd gone in for another load, and when she returned, he was gone. In a panic she searched the yard, then the house, calling his name. Crying out for him to come to his mamma.

It was the only time she ever called Andy at work.

At the time he was halfway between Oakland and Morgantown, returning with an empty truck to pick up another load of coal. Because of the ridges and valleys around them, CB radios were unreliable, so his dispatcher, knowing his routine, called every stop along his route until he found the one he hadn't reached yet.

When he received the message that his wife called, he knew it couldn't be good. Wilma wouldn't bother him at work unless it was a dire emergency. With his dispatcher's blessing, Andy drove straight home, pulling into his front yard with hissing air brakes that scattered the few chickens they kept.

Wilma sat on the front porch, sobbing Jacob's name. It took a bit, but Andy got the story out of her and called the Sheriff's office, which mobilized a small army to look for the missing boy.

For two days they searched the woods behind the house, beating the brush, using dogs to follow what little trail he'd left, one that vanished completely a hundred yards into the trees. It was as if Jacob ceased to exist, and this soon fueled the rumors that whispered through the community.

The Witch had taken her due. At the Green Lantern Diner, on Widows Hollow Road, just off old Route 40, the topic of the Witch held sway over all other subjects. Even the recent ending of the Vietnam War took a back seat to the legend of the Witch of Porter Mines.

In the late seventeen hundreds, Porter Mines was an outpost at the edge of a vast wilderness that was today western Maryland and southwestern Pennsylvania. During a particularly bad winter, a severe epidemic of dysentery ravaged the small community, killing old and young alike.

While the voice of reason asserted that the problem lay in the inhabitants' sanitary measures, many believed the deaths were the result of someone dabbling in witchcraft. That particular someone was the Widow Jenks, who lived alone at the northernmost edge of the hamlet.

Fueled by anger, and a healthy dose of whiskey, a mob formed in the widow's front yard. Legend had it she attempted to cast a spell to cover her escape but failed to complete it before they broke down her door and dragged her into the muddy street. There she was tried, found guilty, and sentenced to death by burning at the stake. With her dying breath, she swore vengeance upon those who participated and their descendants, vowing that for every generation that tainted this land she would return to take her due.

Andy was as familiar with the legend as anyone else who was raised there. Many had grown up under its threat. His own mother used it to keep him and his siblings in line.

Two days after Jacob vanished, a girl on the other side of the valley disappeared. The results of the ensuing search were the same as for Jacob. A week later another boy went missing.

The sudden flurry of disappearances lent new weight to old legends. Parents watched over their children as they glanced towards Fiddlers Pond where a French outpost once stood next to the pond in the turbulent days of the country's birth. During the course of the summer the sounds of children at play was replaced by a nervous silence.

Another child vanished, a girl, and the Sheriff's office picked up Adam Tasker, a local electrician who'd done work for practically everyone in the area. He was seen talking to young Regina Forrester the day before she vanished. He'd also spoken to Regina's mother and father, as he was at their house to repair a faulty outlet. That last little tidbit of information was overlooked by everyone as word that Adam had been taken in for questioning spread through the community.

The police only wanted to know if Adam had seen anything out of the ordinary when he was at the Forrester household. He wasn't even a suspect. But the locals didn't know this. They thought he'd been taken in because he was involved in the actual disappearances.

It didn't take long before talk turned to action and a mob formed outside the Sheriff's office in downtown Porter Mines.

Andy wasn't proud of what he did that day and would rather forget all that happened. But the guilt he felt for being involved in another man's unnecessary death ate at him. Over time it turned him from a loving, caring father into a bitter old man. It was no surprise that as each of their remaining two children reached the age to leave home, they fled to the four corners of the country, until it was only he and Wilma, alone with the memories of their loss. With Wilma's death, his bitterness deepened.

As the night settled around him, Andy pushed away the memories clamoring for his attention. It still wasn't warm enough to sit on the porch, and the cold was eating into his bones. He'd better get inside, turn on some lights, and fix something to eat. He didn't feel like eating, but old habits die hard. If Wilma were still alive there'd be a full meal waiting on the table for him. He'd probably warm up something in the microwave and eat in front of the television again.

With a confidence born of familiarity, he moved through the dark living room to the kitchen. A nightlight over the counter offered some illumination. He was reaching for the light switch when a sound in the deeper shadows stopped him. Someone else was in the house with him. He felt their presence. He smelled them. The odor was an odd mixture of sweat, leather, and a strange aftershave that stung his nose, and made his eyes water.

"Who's there?"

No answer came save the ticking of the clock above the kitchen sink. From his right a whirring sound forced him back a step before he realized it was only the refrigerator kicking on.

"You foolish old man," he chided himself as he reached for the light switch. He'd survived the taking of Iwo, and here he was acting like a frightened old lady.

Soft light filled the kitchen, glowing dully from the surface of the table in the middle of the room. Six empty chairs sat around it, occupied by the ghosts of the past. He'd sit at one end with Wilma at the other, and between them their four children, three boys and a girl ate every meal together. As he stood staring at the table, reliving the happiness it once knew, he detected that odor again. Someone was here. The odor was even stronger, a mixture of sweat, leather, and aftershave that wasn't his brand.

He'd quit using it after Wilma passed. There was no one he wanted to smell good for anymore. He'd quit doing a lot of things after she died. Sleeping in the bed he'd shared with her at the top of the list.

He doubted the sheets still carried her scent from her last night before the stroke took her. But he couldn't bring himself to change them or mar them with his own odor. It would be like washing away her memory once and for all. After her death he made himself a bed on the couch in the living room. No one visited anymore so it didn't matter. From the second floor above, a board creaked as someone shifted their weight.

Had Wilma come back?

He pushed the thought away with a shudder. She was never coming back. She was six feet under at Holy Park

Cemetery in Grantsville. And if she did, he didn't want to see what had become of her after four years in the earth.

The creaking came again, and he had to admit that someone was on the second floor. His first thought was to call the police and let them take care of it. But this was his house, and he'd be damned if he were going to let anyone walk all over him.

Turning back to the living room, he crossed to his gun cabinet and took down the twelve-gauge pump shotgun. After inserting four shells of double ought buckshot, he jacked one into the chamber and felt the reassuring sense of power that came with being well-armed.

If anyone was still around after hearing that, they were a damned fool. He used a twelve-gauge on Iwo as they cleared the caves on that hellish mountain. He'd seen firsthand what it could do to the human body. It wasn't pretty, especially at point blank range.

He returned to the kitchen and crossed to the bottom of the narrow stairway leading to the second floor. The stairs vanished into the deeper shadows above. Flipping a light switch filled the stairway, and the hallway above, with a comforting yellow glow.

He started up the steps but stopped halfway, winded. As he caught his breath, he listened for any sound from above. Silence shrouded the hallway.

Cautiously he moved up the remaining steps, the shotgun resting easy in his hands, the muzzle aimed at the stairs, ready to be brought up in an instant. Above his head a railing protected two sides of the opening down which the stairs were built. One step below the upstairs hallway, he stopped.

He'd been foolish to come up and now wished he'd called the police. Who cared if they laughed at him, or called him a frightened old lady? It might be better than what was waiting for him in the hallway above.

With a fear born of the unknown, the shotgun very heavy in his hands, he eased himself up for a quick peek down the hall and breathed a sigh of relief.

It was empty.

Stepping into the hallway, he heard movement from behind the closed door of the bedroom he'd once shared with his wife. With the shotgun in one hand, he crossed to the door, and placed his free hand on the knob.

He twisted the knob and shoved the door open. "I've got a gun."

The room was dark, but the raised shade of the room's only window allowed the moonlight to illuminate the object hanging from the center of the ceiling. The object's shadow was imprinted on the wall next to him, and as he gazed up at the hangman's noose. He understood then that what goes around, comes around, and it had come around for him.

He didn't see the figure step out from the deeper shadows of the corner on his right until it was too late.

4

A half empty bottle of Johnnie Walker Black stood next to a pile of seven slender files. Sheriff Paul Odenton sat at his desk with a glass in one hand as he gazed at the files with the expression of one who carried the weight of the world upon his shoulders. In the kitchen, his wife Maggie was gabbing on the phone as she washed the supper dishes.

He reached for the top file, changed his mind, and snatched the bottle instead. Pouring himself another three fingers, he sat the bottle down and proceeded to sip at the amber liquid.

Johnnie Walker was some good sipping whisky. The best, in fact, if his father and grandfather were to be believed, but Paul had known better. In his younger days, when he still had the energy to moonlight, he could sometimes afford a good bottle of Lagavulin sixteen-year-old single malt. But not anymore. His future was pretty much set in stone and his past refused to offer any solace. He'd work as long as it was physically possible, or until the county commissioners replaced him with a younger man, though that would not happen for some time yet. He knew his job, he knew his people, but most of all he knew his place.

He would forever and always be the sheriff of a little backwater county in the rolling hills of western Maryland. He had no aspirations for greater things in his life. He had no need for the glamour of a public office. He had only his job and his record. No crime had been committed in his jurisdiction without being solved, except one. Which drew his attention to the files on his desk.

Such a small stack to represent the hopes and dreams of seven young lives. None of the files contained much information beyond the usual name, address, and date last seen, for there was no other information. It was as if these seven children vanished into thin air. No bodies were recovered, though he knew in his heart of hearts that each of them died shortly after their disappearance. He never shared this information with anyone, not even his wife.

Now, as a sixty-year-old sheriff, he found himself searching for the ghosts of the past.

With a sigh, he pulled the first folder from the pile and flipped it open on the desk. Inside lay a single sheet of paper, a missing person's form, the entries typewritten. His gaze slipped to the small photo stapled to the corner. It was a school picture of a black-haired boy who smiled with open innocence.

Jacob Watkins. Paul remembered how distraught the boy's mother was when he went missing. She was so hysterical Doc Miller had to sedate her. Her husband Andy, on the other hand, had been calm, but his eyes were clouded by a smoldering rage that frightened Paul at the time. With the intervening years between then and now to contemplate what happened, Paul understood the reason for his rage. But at the time, that look sent a cold chill winding down his spine.

Maggie stepped into the door of his study. "Are you gonna beat yourself up all night over those?"

He looked up at his wife. They had tried, a number of times, to have kids, but it wasn't in the cards for them. The doctors explained it away with a bunch of mumbo jumbo about low sperm count and maintaining a viable environment. He and Maggie quietly accepted the fact children would not be in their future.

"You getting ready for bed?" he asked, purposely changing the subject. She knew how he felt about these missing kids, and he supposed she was worried that he'd let it eat at him until there was nothing left for the memories to feed on.

"Heading that way now. Are you coming up, or are you gonna sit down here and feel sorry for yourself?"

"It's my right," he shot back. They'd grown comfortable with one another over the years and the nightly banter before bedtime was an expression of that.

"Well, when you do come up, be quiet." Maggie turned from the door, leaving him with his thoughts.

"As a church mouse."

"More like a bull in a china shop," she shot back from the bottom of the stairs.

Paul chuckled and returned his attention to the folder lying open before him.

Andy was a tough one. Most everyone in their little town knew he'd been in the Marines. They knew he fought on Iwo. But what many didn't know, outside of the police who periodically responded to his outbursts and the few neighbors close enough to see what was going on. He was still fighting the demons from that war.

Every so often he'd get into the drink, and the memories would have their way with him. The rest of the time he was an upstanding, law abiding citizen. Except for when his son vanished.

Paul had been on the force for a couple of weeks, freshly graduated from the local community college with a degree in criminal justice that armed him with just enough book learning to get into trouble. Three children were already missing, and the tongues in town were wagging about the Witch taking her due.

He was familiar with the legend. Had been threatened by his parents that she would take him if he didn't listen, but he refused to put any stock in it. As an officer of the law, he dealt in absolutes, where physical evidence took precedence over ghostly legends.

During the course of the investigation, they learned Adam Tasker was last seen with one of the missing children. He was brought in, not as a suspect, but to interview him with the hope of learning more than they already knew. It was how most cases were really broken. By putting together random, unrelated pieces like a jigsaw puzzle until a full picture emerged.

Adam Tasker agreed readily enough. After all, he wasn't a suspect.

Word spread among the parents the law was talking to him and before long a crowd gathered outside the public safety building where the Sheriff maintained his offices.

Andy was the most vocal member of the group, demanding they release Adam so they could settle matters themselves since the police seemed unable to do so. As the day wore into the night the crowd outside grew larger, and more brazen. Conversations among the deputies questioned Sheriff Preston's ability to perform his job. He was old, nearing seventy, refusing to relinquish his grip on the power he held. Little did he know the council had already stripped him of much of his power.

Adam was terrified, begging they protect him from the crowd, and for his own safety Paul placed him in one of the holding cells. Not that it would do much good. If the mob wanted to, they could have stormed in and taken Adam at the very start. Preston refused to call in the state police, clinging to the belief the crowd would listen to him.

For what it was worth, he did try to reason with the mob, but to no avail. He waited too long to face them, and when he did, it was viewed as a last-ditch effort to dissuade them.

To the mob, Adam had already been tried and found guilty. All that remained was to carry out their sentence. Someone picked up forty feet of sturdy three-quarter-inch rope from the hardware store on Main Street. In the end they forced their way into the police station and hauled Tasker outside, where they hanged him from a streetlight.

Paul was ashamed of Sheriff Preston's actions that day. He'd always looked up to the man in the past, but after he fled in the face of the mob, Paul's estimation of the man diminished drastically. The other deputies were evenly divided over what to do. Some wanted to stay and do their job while the rest chose to ignore what was happening on the street in some misguided belief that if they ignored it long enough, it would go away.

Paul poured another three fingers into his glass as the memories faded into the past. *There was no sense crying over spilt milk*, his mother would say. It was a shame to liken a man's death to the spilling of a drink, but in the end, what more could be said?

One thing stood out that made Paul shudder when he thought about it. Donnie, Adam's son, watched his father's death at the hands of the crowd. He'd been with him when he came in for questioning and, though they tried everything they could to distract him, in those final moments as his father hung ten feet above the pavement, his feet kicking at the air, Donnie watched through the front window.

When they were done, when justice in their mind was served, the mob disbanded. Each went their own way, leaving in their wake a grisly reminder of man's inhumanity to his fellow man.

Afterward Paul tried to keep an eye on Donnie, to help him through the sorrow he must have been feeling. Unfortunately, the boy was sent to live with his mother in California. At the airport Paul watched him boarding his flight, a lost little boy heading into an uncertain future. Paul hoped he made something for himself out west.

Closing the file on Jacob, he slipped it aside and opened the next. He scanned the enclosed form, his gaze settling on the date last seen.

April twelfth, 1975.

Thirty-two years ago, to the day. He remembered its significance. Julie Philips was the first to vanish. Her folder was a tad thicker than the others only because Paul did a little research when she disappeared.

At the library he found microfilmed copies of the local paper from 1937 to 1942. In the spring of 1943, seven stories appeared that did not deal with the ongoing battle in the Pacific.

The Witch had taken her due thirty-two years before Julie Philips went missing. While American forces in the Pacific pushed the Japanese back toward their homeland, seven children disappeared in Porter Mines.

By his calculations the Witch, be she fact or fiction, was about to take her due again. He shuddered and as he reached for the bottle, the phone rang. He snatched the receiver from its cradle before it could disturb Maggie.

"This is Paul," he answered, already aware of the message he was about to receive. He gazed at the bottle with longing. It was going to be a long night, and there would be no place for drinking anything but coffee.

"I'll put a pot of coffee on," Maggie said from the door of his office. She had come back down after hearing the phone ring. Paul nodded his consent.

As he hung up, she said, "It's happening again, isn't it?"

"Now don't go getting yourself all worked up over this. You know what the doctor said about your blood pressure."

"Who is it?" she said.

"Bobby Carr from the trailer park."

"Oh dear." Tears filled her eyes, and she covered her mouth with her hands. "Such a sweet little guy, it's a shame." She turned and vanished into the kitchen.

Maggie had been driving the school bus for over thirty years, fulfilling her maternal need by nurturing the young children who rode with her daily. Paul knew the loss of any child to her was like taking one of her own. He followed her into the kitchen as a sour ball settled into the pit of his stomach. He'd have to keep a close watch over her. It was going to be a long summer, and he was worried her heart wouldn't be able to take it.

5

From the basement came a muted thump and Susan jumped at the sound, her heart skipping a beat.

Was it a footstep? She mustn't let her thoughts wander in that direction. There was no coming back from where John had gone. It's been three years since she saw him, the last image of him burned into her memory. That damned cocky smile that said he was ready to take on the world, yet she noted a hint of worry at the edges where his lips turned down slightly. He knew what he was walking into, just as she knew the risk of becoming a widow at a young age when she accepted his proposal.

She pushed the thoughts away and busied herself at the kitchen counter, alone, the house around her silent as dawn pushed away the night with the promise of a new day. She considered how far they'd come in the past three years, and she marveled at Christine's resilience to all the changes that happened since her father's death. She was worried about her recent nightmares and hoped they would go away so she could settle into their new home.

Last spring, they escaped the cramped apartment in California filled with memories that clamored for Susan's attention, and moved across the country. Up until last week she'd been renting a small two-bedroom apartment over a garage in Oakland. Using the insurance money from John's death, and with a little help from her in-laws, who were all too happy to have their grandchild living so close, she purchased the old Jenkins farmhouse. They just moved in this week and she was in the process of turning their new house into a home. She was far from done, but in a little more than a month a lot was changing for the better.

Full boxes were still scattered about the house. They'd been delivered two day ago from the storage shed she and John rented after their wedding. They wanted to keep their presents safe until they could put down permanent roots. Base housing didn't offer much room, and neither of them felt like dragging everything all over the world as John followed his career in the Marines.

The farmhouse had undergone a major facelift. There was a lot yet to do, but they were making progress. With two weeks left before she returned to work, they might make it. She was eager to get back. She'd been so busy on the house there was little time to think about the Real Estate exam she'd taken before her leave.

Did I pass?

For the past six months she worked as a receptionist at the biggest real estate office in Deep Creek Lake, a tourist attraction many in the business were comparing to Lake Tahoe. It was spring of 2007 and business was booming, real estate prices were skyrocketing, and she wanted a piece of the pie.

Coached by Marie, an older agent who had become her friend, and with the owner's blessing, Susan studied for the exam, taking it the Friday before her vacation. She was confident the test results were back but quelled the temptation to call. It would be better to wait until she returned to work to find out the results.

If I failed, the thought teased, and she pushed it away. If she failed she'd take the test again, and again. As many times as necessary till she passed.

After getting Christine settled last night, she tried to recapture the moment she'd experienced right before she was awakened. It was no use. Her dream had tormented her with a glimpse of what could have been, and for the first time in more than a year she allowed her sorrow to wash over her.

John was gone. Nearly a year had passed since his death, two years since she last saw him, and it was time she got on with her life. After all, how long were you supposed to grieve over a lost loved one? How long was she supposed to remain true to the promise she made when they married? And didn't the vows say, "Until death us do part?"

Yet she couldn't shake the guilt that filled her whenever she thought about getting on with her life. She felt like she was trapped in a time warp where everything and everyone around her was moving forward while she remained locked in the past. Trapped in the memories of what could have been.

A door closed upstairs. Soft footsteps thumped down the carpeted stairs, and Christine entered the kitchen with Puddles held close to her chest. She rubbed the sleep from her eyes as she climbed into a seat at the kitchen table.

"Cereal," Christine said, sitting her stuffed bunny on the table in front of her. "Now, you stay."

Susan placed a bowl before Christine and poured her a glass of orange juice from the jug on the table.

"Good morning, Mommy." Christine twisted around in her seat to watch as Susan retrieved the cereal from the cabinet.

Susan poured cereal into the bowl. "Did you sleep all right?"

"Yeah," Christine replied before slurping the orange juice.

"No more dreams?"

Christine shook her head. "Will Eric be coming over?

Susan glanced at the wall clock above the stove. It was almost six. "He should be here any minute, why?"

"I want to ask him a question."

As if to confirm Susan's answer, there was a knock at the front door.

"I'll get it." Christine slipped down from her chair and raced into the foyer. A moment later she returned with Eric in tow.

Eric was tall, six two, with a narrow waist flaring out to broad shoulders topped by a handsome face that carried a close-cropped beard. His rugged features caused women to become weak in the knees and Susan experienced a hot flash as his gaze found hers. Though he was nearing forty, Susan learned, in a roundabout way, he'd never married. It was obvious he had yet to find the one he wanted to spend his life with, and she hoped she could measure up.

They'd been on a few dates, and you could say they'd become an item. They had many things in common, and Eric was far more intelligent than he let on. He held an MBA in business administration and could have been the CEO of any Fortune 500 company. But he preferred the slower pace of being a local contractor.

It was one of the things she found intriguing about him. Yet she couldn't help but feel like she was cheating on John.

Guilt was keeping her from pursuing a deeper relationship with Eric.

"Good morning." Eric settled into a seat across from Susan and Christine climbed onto his lap.

"Good morning," Susan answered. Their eyes met, and a spark shot between them.

"You're looking good this morning," Eric said.

Susan wasn't sure if he was being kind or honest. She was self-conscious about the way she looked and how she was dressed. Old sweats and an oversized tee-shirt, her hair was a mess, and she hadn't put on any makeup. She turned away as an all too familiar heat washed through her.

"Thank you. Would you like some coffee?" She would rather drag him into the bedroom. It'd been so long, and her dream last night had been too brief. Thinking of John dampened her desire with a cold shot of guilt.

"Eric?" Christine asked. "Where do you go when you die?"

The question surprised Susan as she poured coffee into a mug. Setting the mug before him, she watched as Eric turned the question over in his mind. He glanced at her, and Susan shrugged.

Susan had discussed this with Christine before, after John's death. She was sure they'd come to an understanding. Daddy was in heaven where he could watch over them and protect them from the mean people in the world.

"You go to heaven." Eric answered, his gaze going from Christine to Susan.

"Nu–uh," Christine said shaking her head, "not everybody. If you're a bad little boy or girl, you go to the dark place."

Susan almost dropped her mug, splashing coffee on her shirt as a tremble ran the length of her arm. *How?* She wondered. *How could she know?*

A memory from her childhood filled her with cold dread. The closet under the stairs in the house she'd grown up in was small and cramped, designed to hold coats, or serve as storage. After their father left, their mother found another use for it. It became the punishment closet for her and Robert, her older brother. To them it was the dark place. No light penetrated the darkness when the door was closed. Not even a sliver of illumination appeared around the door frame.

The dark place was fathomless to a child, expanding beyond the physical borders of the known world, filled with nightmare creatures that slithered through ebony solitude. When Robert was with her she felt safe. When she was alone, which happened often, her moans of terror countered the silence as she cowered from the creatures of the night her mind assured her were gathered all around.

When their mother became too drunk to deal with them, she would send them to the closet. If they asked her a question she couldn't answer, she sent them to the closet. If they failed a test at school, if they didn't straighten their room, if they didn't listen, she sent them to the closet.

"Why do you say that?" Eric's question pulled Susan from her thoughts.

"My new friend told me that all bad little boys and girls go to the dark place."

"One of your friends at school or at Brenda's?" Susan asked. Brenda ran a daycare from her home and took Christine in when they moved to the area. Watching her when Susan had to work late, or on days when there was no school.

Christine shook her head. "No, it was my new friend, Lizzy."

"Where did you meet Lizzy?" Susan asked.

Christine stared at Susan as if looking right through her. A cold chill wound its way down her spine, and she was filled with a grim certainty that if she turned around right now, Lizzy would be standing behind her.

"Last night," Christine said. "She said she had a secret she wanted to show me."

"Where is this dark place?" Eric asked.

Christine shrugged, her gaze never leaving Susan's.

How did she know? Susan looked from Christine to Eric and back again. A knock came from the front door, shattering the stillness settling around them.

Eric got to his feet and lowered Christine to the floor. "I'll get it," he said.

Susan didn't know what to say. John's death had been hard on both of them. Because there was so little time for Christine to get to know her father, Susan assumed she wouldn't miss him as much. Maybe she was wrong. Maybe Christine missed him more than she thought.

"Are you all right?"

Christine nodded as she returned to her seat and focused on trapping the last few pieces of cereal floating in the milk. "Can I have more cereal, Mommy?"

"Sure, but you're going to have to get ready soon." Susan glanced at the clock on the wall above the stove. "Brenda will be here to pick you up for school."

"Do I have to go today?"

"Yes, you do. We don't miss school without a good reason."

"But I'm not feeling good," Christine said, rubbing her forehead with her hand.

"Let me see." Susan placed her hand on Christine's forehead. The flesh felt cool. "You don't have a fever."

"It's my tummy."

"Then you better eat up," Susan turned to the counter, and as she did she caught a flash of movement from the corner of her eye. A shadowy form in the hallway. She turned around, expecting to find Christine gone, but she was still sitting at the table playing with her spoon.

Susan's gaze turned to the hallway. *Was it a trick of the light?* No, there'd been a shadow there, and the chill returned. Had something escaped the dark place? Following her to this time and place? Drawn by her memories. Don't be ridiculous, she chided herself.

"Susan," Eric called from the front door, "there's someone to see you."

"I'll be right there," she said.

She'd seen something in the hallway. She was sure it had been someone's shadow. Maybe it was John watching over them. She pushed the thought away, refusing to follow it to its logical conclusion.

Ghosts did not exist in her ordered world. They were the product of overactive imaginations, hackneyed fiction writers, and reality television shows that used shaking cameras and fast pans to lead viewers into believing they were seeing the real thing. No, there was a logical explanation for what she'd seen, or thought she'd seen.

Susan passed the hallway and glanced down its length. *Nothing there,* and she exhaled in relief.

6

"Here she is now," Eric said as Susan entered the foyer. At the door stood an older woman holding a covered platter. She wore slacks and a button-down shirt with the sleeves rolled halfway up her slender arms. Not a strand of the gray hair on her head was out of place, and she watched Susan with bright blue eyes that conveyed honesty and warmth.

Susan felt immediately at ease in her presence.

"I'm sorry to drop by so early," the woman said. "My name's Mildred Raines. I have the farm next door. I just wanted to welcome you to the neighborhood." She extended the platter to Eric, who took it. She then extended her hand to Susan.

"Thank you so much," Susan said as she shook Mildred's hand, surprised at the strength in her grip.

Mildred peered into the house's gloomy interior. "I'm so glad somebody bought the old Jenkins place and fixed it up. It's such a shame it sat empty for so long."

"Would you like to come in and see what we've done?"

"Of course," Mildred answered and stepped across the threshold, "and I brought you a little housewarming gift."

Eric peeked under the foil, and a smile spread across his face.

Mildred said, "There's snicker doodles, chocolate chip, peanut butter, and oatmeal raisin cookies, with a hot batch of cinnamon buns I whipped up this morning."

"They smell delicious," Eric said.

"Thank you," Mildred said as Susan led her through the foyer into the kitchen. "I do most of my baking for my friends at bingo and church nowadays. I've no family at home, so it was a pleasure to make this for my new neighbors."

As they came into the kitchen Christine jumped down from her seat and slipped behind Susan.

"It's okay, sweetie. It's just Mrs. Raines from next door." Susan placed her hand on Christine's head.

"That's Miss Raines. But please call me Mildred."

Christine's eyes were wide with fright as she hid behind Susan's leg.

"I don't know what's gotten into her," Susan said. "Come on, Christine. Come out and say hello to Miss Raines."

Christine shook her head, her bottom lip quivering with fear. Susan knelt and placed her hands on her shoulders that trembled beneath her robe.

"What's wrong?" she asked.

Christine's voice was so soft Susan couldn't hear her.

"What was that?"

"It's the witch, Mommy, the one from my dream, the one who said she was coming to get me."

"Who? Miss Raines?"

Christine nodded with her gaze focused on Mildred.

"Is anything wrong?" Mildred asked.

"We had a nightmare last night," Susan said. "Someone's been listening to too many rumors and scary stories. She dreamed a witch was coming to get her."

"It wasn't a dream, Mommy, it was real. She was outside my window and said she was going to get me."

"That's two stories up. How did she get outside your window?" Susan asked.

"She's a witch. She used magic," Christine answered as if she were speaking to someone who couldn't understand all the strange things that can happen when you're a child.

"I used to have nightmares when I was your age too. They'd scare the Bejesus out of me," Mildred said.

Christine looked around her mother, up at Mildred. "What's a Bejesus?"

Mildred considered the question. "You know, no one ever told me what a Bejesus was. My mom used to say it, and my grandmother too, so I just started saying it."

"Did you dream about witches?" Christine asked.

"Heavens, no. I'd dream about something much scarier than some old witch."

"What could be scarier than a witch?"

Mildred crossed her arms over she chest and shivered. "I'd dream about clowns."

"Clowns," Christine said. "Clowns aren't scary, they're funny."

"Aren't you afraid of clowns?" Mildred asked.

"What so scary about a clown?"

"What so scary about some old witch?" Mildred asked.

Christine nodded after a moment. "You're right, what's so scary about some old witch?"

"Do you like cookies?" Mildred asked.

"Do you have oatmeal raisin?"

"Of course, they're my favorite." Mildred took an oatmeal raisin cookie from the platter and handed it to Christine.

Mildred turned to Susan. "I must admit one of the reasons I stopped by was to see if you and Christine have found a church you like yet, and if not, I'd like to invite you to stop by my church, Saint Ann's in Grantsville. That is if you practice the Catholic faith. Father Brentfield is such a blessing to us all." Mildred stopped. "I don't mean to intrude. I'm just an old busy-body nobody should pay any attention to."

"It's okay," Susan said, reaching out to take Mildred's hand in her own. "I was once Catholic when I was younger, before my dad left. Afterward we drifted away from the church."

"If you ever feel the need to reconnect I'd be happy to introduce you."

"That's so kind of you to offer,

"You know," Mildred said as she turned to Christine, "you look just like the little girl who once lived here. Her name was Abigail."

"My name's Christine," she replied and then bit into the cookie.

"Abigail and my niece were inseparable. Best friends forever, they used to say."

"Does she still live around here?" Susan asked.

"Who?"

"Your niece."

Mildred shook her head as a deep sadness settled about her. "No. She went missing when she was seven. It was the same year several other children vanished."

"Oh my," Susan said as her gaze went to Christine, who was munching on the cookie. "Honey, maybe you should get ready, Brenda will be here any minute."

"But I'm not feeling well," Christine said, one hand on her tummy, the half-eaten cookie in the other.

"If you're well enough to eat a cookie, you're well enough to go to school," Susan said.

Christine looked from Susan to the half-eaten cookie in her hand, then back again. Without another word she retrieved Puddles and vanished down the hall to get ready for school.

Susan watcher her go, then turned to Mildred." I'm sorry, I didn't want Christine listening to this conversation, we already have enough trouble with the stories she been carrying home from school."

"I understand, dear, she's such a sweet child."

"Did they ever find out who took them? Or what happened to them?" Eric asked.

Mildred shook her head. "They had their suspicions, but they could never prove anything."

"Is it...," Susan was unsure how to proceed.

Mildred reassured Susan. "That was over thirty years ago. Nothing has happened since, and it likely won't happen again."

"How can you be so sure?" Susan asked.

"No one can ever be sure of anything, I suppose. But I wouldn't worry too much. Like I said, that was thirty years ago."

"Would you like some coffee?" Susan asked Mildred.

"I'd love a cup," Mildred said.

"Pull up a seat. I'd like to find out all I can about the neighborhood." Susan crossed to the counter and took down another mug. For the first time she was worried that maybe it had been a mistake to move to Porter Mines.

Christine stomped down the hall. She was trying to be loud, to let her displeasure be known, but the carpet muffled her footsteps. As she passed the stairway to the laundry room, the sound of a child crying came from the darkness below.

She stopped and looked down the short flight of steps into the murky depths. Glancing back, she saw her mom and Miss Raines—Mildred, she corrected herself, talking over their coffee.

Maybe he needs help. She stood at the top of the steps, undecided. She needed to get ready for Brenda who would be here soon. But the little boy needed help and Daddy wasn't here to help him. She had to do something. She almost called for her mother but changed her mind.

They wouldn't understand. They couldn't see what she'd seen. They were grownups who had forgotten what it was like to be afraid. Pushing away old beliefs about things that went bump in the night. Now they justified every strange noise, every strange thing they saw. Coming up with a plausible reason for its existence.

That was why the creatures of the night only fed on children. Their imaginations were fertile grounds for the seeds of nightmares.

Sniffling came from the shadows below. Since daddy wasn't here, it was up to her and before she could change her mind, she took the steps down into the laundry room.

With each step the temperature dropped a few degrees. At the bottom, with the emptiness gathered around her, her breath formed small clouds as she reached up to turn on the light. She detected movement to her left as something shifted within that impenetrable gloom filled with monstrous possibilities.

Her other arm tightened around Puddles as she crushed him to her chest, and she took a deep breath before flipping the light switch. She was expecting something to grab her hand and drag her kicking and screaming into that black abyss.

"She takes all the bad little boys and girls," Marjorie whispered in her mind, the sing-song chant of girls skipping rope lending credence to her words.

One, two, the Witch is due.

They chanted in their collective voices, the tempo rising and falling in a disjointed manner, lending the words an eerie rhythm.

Three, four, she's at the door.

Five, six, who will she pick?

Seven, eight, at night she waits.

Nine, ten, don't let her in.

With the last, the gathered voices scattered with laughter and screams of terrified delight, like a murder of crows taking flight. Soft yellow light filled the room, pushing back the shadows to reveal a typical laundry room.

Yet the cold was anything but normal. She stepped down from the last step into the room, her breath pluming before her, small clouds of terror dissipating into the chilled air as she crossed to the far wall.

The washer and dryer stood against the wall to her left, a utility sink to the right, with an empty section to the left. In time a set of shelves would stand there, their surface covered with assorted laundry detergents, cleaning supplies, and other sundries necessary to keep a house clean. For now, it was a blank wall, serving no purpose save to keep the chill of the ground at bay, a job at which it appeared to be failing.

From behind the featureless façade, came the snuffling again and she crossed to the wall. Reaching out she touched its cold surface with her fingertips. She felt him then, on a deep emotional level, a little boy lost.

She leaned in closer. "It's okay, Puddles will protect us." She brought her stuffed bunny close to the wall, relinquishing the warmth it had produced by hugging it.

The smell of smoke came to her then, coming from the wall, as that snuffling became a wail of terror that sliced through her. She backed across the room as faint tendrils of black smoke, the ebony essence of the night, came from the top and bottom of the wall, reaching for her like clawed hands that reminded her of the witch she confronted the night before.

For a moment she saw the witch with her mind's eye, the blistered face covered in a network of fine cracks that pulsed and glowed with hellfire churning beneath the surface. Her black eyes alight with the yellow glow of vengeance as she clawed at Christine's window with twisted hands.

She put some distance between herself and the ribbons that threatened to envelop her. One brushed the hem of her pajama bottoms, singeing the fabric as panic clawed its way up her throat. She tried, without success, to take a backwards step up the stairs and away from it. She almost lost her balance as those smoky strands assembled in the center of the laundry room, forming a person who reached for her with impossibly long arms.

She tried to back away but was locked in place, her feet taking root in the carpet as her heart thundered in her chest. The wispy tendrils of night closed around her and she felt something against her chest where she held Puddles in a one-armed hug. A faint beat that came from within the stuffed bunny's poly-filled interior.

"Daddy?" A soft heartbeat accompanied the warm sensation of being wrapped in her father's loving embrace.

"Stay out of this!" A voice shrieked in her mind and she fell back onto the step as the light in the ceiling grew bright, filling the room with a white brilliance before winking out with an audible pop.

Then it was gone, and she realized she stood alone against this creature. No, not entirely, and she glanced down at Puddles. He had daddy's heart, and his love, she only hoped it would be enough. She turned and fled up the steps, glancing to her right to find the adults still sitting at the kitchen table, unaware of her plight. A part of her wanted to run to them, tell them what was happening right under their noses, but she knew they wouldn't believe her.

After getting dressed, she was halfway down the steps when the sound of Brenda's horn came from outside.

"Brenda's here," her mom yelled.

Christine glanced into the laundry room as she passed. The smell of smoke had dissipated as if it had never been there. But she knew it had, and she knew why. The Witch was coming, and the only thing that stood between her and the Witch's fiery grasp, was Puddles.

$$8$$

Susan washed the breakfast dishes while Eric dried. It felt to him like they were a real family doing a few dishes before they retired to the living room to spend a lazy morning reading the paper, or just talking. As a child, he and his family would get together after a big Sunday breakfast to lounge around the living room. He and his sister Jessica would spread the funny pages on the floor while their father read the financial section and their mother expressed her opinion of the op-ed page.

That had been before, and here he stopped, unwilling to follow the memory to its conclusion. Some things were better left in the past.

He turned his attention to Susan. Watching her filled him with a sensation he hadn't known for years. He hoped she felt the same way about him, and he had to laugh at himself. Here he was, a well-respected builder with a business worth more than a million dollars, almost forty years old, yet he felt like a teenager with a crush.

She had that effect on him. He'd been in several relationships before, so he was no stranger to such emotions. A couple had proven serious enough for him to consider a trip to the jeweler's, but none of the girls he'd dated made him feel the way Susan did. It was like the first time all over again, as if he'd stepped back to the moment in high school when the hottest girl in class first said hello.

"What do you think?" she said.

"About what?"

"Mildred."

Eric shrugged. He was familiar with her history.

"She's a sweet old lady who seems a bit lonely. Maybe Christine and I will pay her a visit, let her adopt us."

"I wouldn't get too cozy with her."

"Why?"

"Remember what she said about those missing kids? What she didn't tell you was her sister was involved." Eric stopped short of revealing what happened to his own sister. He had been six when she vanished, and he had no real memory of her, aside from several pictures in an old photo album. All he could recall of the incident was the sense of despair that followed him for a few years after.

"She never mentioned having a sister. How was she involved?"

"Why would she? Her family swept everything that happened that summer under the rug."

"Where's her sister now?"

"Last I heard she was in a mental hospital in Ohio. If you go online and check the archives for the local paper, you can get all the details."

"That's so sad."

"Don't tell me you feel sorry for her."

"Why not?" Susan said. "Did she do anything wrong?"

"Not that they could prove."

"So according to the authorities she was innocent."

"I guess. What are you driving at?"

"Have you ever heard of guilt by association?" she asked.

"What does that have to do with anything?"

"Everything. Are you that close-minded?"

"What?" Eric stepped back surprised. Susan dried her hands before dropping the towel on the counter.

"Do you honestly believe she was involved in what happened?" she said.

"She had to have been."

"Why?"

"She lived in the same house with Mildred."

"You're saying since she lived in the same house, she was involved and is now laughing at everyone because she's gotten away with it for years."

"Exactly."

Susan shook her head. "Have there been any more disappearances since her sister went away?"

"Well, no."

"So, once the sister was sent away, Mildred lost all interest in what she'd been doing?"

"Something like that," Eric said, aware his own beliefs were being called into question. Susan was smart as hell, and not one to follow the well-trodden path.

Though he believed Margaret was involved, he felt the public dealt Mildred a bad hand. She'd been a schoolteacher and lost her position when it was revealed her sister was responsible for what happened. But that happened years after the children vanished, after Margaret was sent away.

Susan bent to clean up a few crumbs as Eric watched, once again overcome by a growing need. She had a wholesomeness about her that appealed to him both physically and emotionally. The look of a cheerleader without the snarkiness you would expect. An innocence that brought out his chivalrous nature.

Straightening, she turned to face him, and he realized she'd caught him staring at her. He felt his cheeks burning as a flash of color splashed across Susan's cheeks below hazel eyes that threatened to swallow him whole. They stared at one another across the dustpan in her hand as something unseen passed between them, an acknowledgment they were each thinking the same thing.

"One wall in my laundry room feels cold," she said. "Could you take a look at it?"

"Sure," he managed to say as she crossed to the garbage, where she emptied the contents of the dustpan. His eyes never left her as she walked across the room. Though she was wearing sloppy sweats and a tee shirt that was several sizes too large for her, they only served to heighten her sexuality. He was aware the house was empty, and they had the whole day to themselves, but instead of turning back to him, she went down the hall, waving for him to follow.

Business first, he thought, not a little disappointed.

As soon as they entered the downstairs laundry room, he felt the difference in temperature. It was at least ten degrees cooler than the rest of the house, which didn't seem right. If anything, it should have been warmer as it was below ground level, and the rest of the house was cool as a result of the changing season. Spring was in the air, but the nights were still cold, and the sun wasn't as warm as it would get.

Eric flipped on the light switch and nothing happened.

"Bulb's burned out," he said as he removed the flashlight from the leather holster on his hip. In less than a minute he replaced the bulb and flipped the switch to fill the room with light. He crossed to the outer wall and placed his hand against it.

"That's strange," Eric said. "Have you heard any sounds coming from behind the wall?"

"What?" Susan seemed startled by the question.

"You know, like running water."

"No, I haven't heard any sounds," she answered, a quiver in her voice.

She grasped the handrail with both hands, a sick expression on her face, her eyes large and frightened. What he'd said disturbed her, and he wasn't sure how to proceed or even if he should. Maybe this was one of those times he needed to keep his mouth shut and do his job.

9

Memories she'd fought for so long to keep at bay washed through her, and Susan reached out to steady herself.

Eric knew. Susan was sure of it. He knew everything he needed to know about her. It was her fault. It was always her fault. No matter how hard she tried to do the right thing, it always came out wrong. She was the reason her father left. She was the reason her older brother committed suicide. She was the reason her mother acted like she did. It was all her fault.

"Are you all right?" Eric asked, crossing the room to help her.

She nodded, not quite aware of where she was, or what she was doing. All she knew for sure was it was all her fault. Her knees were weak, and she let Eric guide her to the bottom step.

Eric knelt in front of her. "What's wrong?"

She shook her head as she struggled against her emotions and letting them have their way with her. It would be so much easier to sit back and let everyone else take control of everything. Just lie in bed all day and let them handle the heavy lifting.

No! She couldn't allow it. She'd fought too hard for too long to let her emotions get the upper hand again. After John's death, she'd allowed them to have free rein over her life, compliments of the base doctor who prescribed a little something to help her sleep. It did more than help her sleep.

It turned her into a zombie, and had it not been for her neighbors in those first few weeks, Christine would have starved.

No!

She felt Eric's hand on her shoulder. She glanced at the scar running across the back, below the base of his thumb. Compliments of a utility knife that slipped. The thought of all that blood made her sick to her stomach, and she lurched across the room to the utility sink where she threw up her breakfast.

"Do you want me to call a doctor?" Eric asked.

She shook her head, rinsed her mouth, and straightened up. "I'll be all right. Just some things from my past sneaking up on me. Can you fix the wall?" She tried to smile and failed. She didn't feel like smiling right now.

Eric looked at the wall and nodded.

"I'll need to pull the drywall, get a look behind. There should be insulation unless my sub cut a few corners. If he did, I'll fix it, and this will be the last job he gets from me."

"Thank you. I have to go into town later. If you'd like, I'll get what we need for dinner tonight."

"Can't pass up an offer like that."

"I'm sorry," she said.

"For what?"

"For the way I acted a moment ago."

"We all have our crosses to bear."

"It's odd you should say that."

"Why?"

Susan sighed. "Someday I'll tell you about crosses to bear."

"When you're ready."

Susan turned and vanished up the steps.

10

Eric watched her go, his gaze fixed on her hips as he imagined what he'd like to do if he ever got the chance.

"Oh well," he said to the empty room, "the party's just getting started," and he turned his attention to the offending wall.

In no time he'd removed the drywall, exposing the pink insulation packed between the studs. With the drywall removed, the chill was even deeper, and Eric detected the movement of air through a few narrow gaps between the insulation and the studs.

"Sorry, Dave," he whispered to himself. After removing the plastic vapor barrier, he pulled out the bats of insulation to expose the stone wall behind it. Here the foundation was made of field stone instead of concrete block, dating back to the late eighteen hundreds.

The house began life as a one room miner's shack like most of the other older houses in the area. In most of them you could chart the owner's progress through their working life by the materials they used to expand their homes.

As he removed the last bat of insulation, he exposed a small black hole, about eye level, in the foundation wall. During construction it appeared they had knocked a stone loose. From the opening cold dank air came through in a steady breeze.

He aimed the beam of his flashlight through the opening, revealing a narrow passageway that vanished into a deeper gloom. He was struck by the unmistakable sensation that he'd just opened a grave. Goose bumps danced across his arms and down his back as the short hairs on his neck stirred.

He'd found several of these tunnels before. Most times they led to a dead end. In one he found an old musket the homeowner was able to sell for several thousand dollars. But this tunnel was different. It led somewhere, as was evident by the steady breeze.

He was about to turn away when he heard a child's voice, faint, crying out for help. A chill danced down his spine as something dark and oily uncoiled in the pit of his stomach. He leaned forward to peer into the thick gloom crowded at the end of his flashlight beam. He was going to need his halogen work light for this.

Should I tell her? He stepped back from the small opening. *Wouldn't it be simpler to cover the hole and repair the wall, keep this little bit of information to myself?*

Would it be fair? After all, she was paying him to do this work for her. Even though there appeared to be more to their relationship than either of them was letting on at the moment, he was still under contract, and you did not break the terms of a contract, not if you wanted to be successful.

Besides, if he kept this to himself and she later learned about it, it would destroy any trust he had built between them.

He was on his way back from his truck with his work light in hand when Susan pulled in. He stopped and waited for her as she grabbed a bag of groceries. She'd changed into a pair of snug fitting jeans and a flannel shirt that accentuated her curves.

"How do pork chops and baked potatoes sound?" Susan asked.

"Sounds like I'll be eating good tonight."

"Did you find out what the problem was?"

"Yeah."

"What is it?"

"Come on, I'll show you."

Eric led her to the laundry room and pointed at the small opening. "The stone probably fell out when we put the wall up."

"What's back there?"

"A tunnel." Eric hooked up his light and carried it to the opening. "A lot of the buildings in this area started out as single-room shacks. Over time the owners expanded them, adding rooms as they got the money, each generation building on what had been done before. Many of these tunnels later became pantries."

The beam from the halogen light filled the tunnel to a depth of at least thirty feet before fading into black emptiness.

Susan peered into the narrow passageway. "How far does it go?"

"It's anybody's guess, but it leads somewhere."

"How do you know?" Susan asked.

"You can feel a steady breeze, so air has to be getting in from another opening."

On the floor, twenty feet in, lay a pile of bottles that looked as if they had once been carefully arranged in a box. Time and moisture had removed all traces of the box that once held them, but the bottles remained, some leaning haphazardly against their neighbor.

"Wonder what's in them?"

"Bootleg liquor. I'd be willing to bet those bottles are nearly a hundred years old. No doubt they've been here since Prohibition."

"Do you think?"

Eric shrugged as he searched the dark depths, looking for an explanation for the voice he heard. Or thought he heard.

He hadn't brought it up and probably wouldn't, considering Susan's reaction earlier. He saw no need to alarm her. Besides, he was beginning to believe that what he heard was nothing more than his imagination brought on by the discomfort he'd felt when he discovered the opening.

"What do you think I should do?" Susan asked.

"If it was me, I'd cover it up and forget about it."

Susan considered this for a moment. "I think it's cool having a hidden cave in my basement. Wonder what they were hiding besides liquor?"

"Why do you say that?" Eric asked.

"Don't know. I just have the feeling there's more to this tunnel than what we can see."

"Do you want me to cover it up?"

"Not yet. I'm gonna see what I can find out about it. Until then, open it enough for someone to get in."

Or out, Eric thought with a shudder. "Are you sure you want to do that?"

"Absolutely. There's nothing in there that can hurt me, right?"

"Don't see how there could be," Eric said, his gaze drawn once more to the narrow opening. As he stared into those shadowy depths, an image of his sister at his bedroom window filled his mind.

"If you think it's safe." Susan said, bringing Eric back to the present.

He didn't believe it was safe to leave it open. But how could he explain his feelings to Susan in a way she would understand?

"I guess." Eric answered while silently vowing to keep a close eye on things around here, to make sure nothing bad happened.

"You mean you're not sure?"

He shrugged. "You know how I feel about you. I just worry, that's all."

"No, I don't know how you feel about me."

"I look at you and I see a beautiful young woman, but at the same time I see a widow who's still grieving the loss of her husband."

"Is it that obvious?"

Eric placed his arm around her shoulder. "Very."

"I didn't realize."

"Well it is, and it's the reason I've held off on talking to you about what we might have together. I was waiting for you to finish mourning."

"Do we have something together?" she asked.

"I believe we do. Do you?"

"I hope so."

He'd never felt this way about anyone before. A hot flash of need washed through him. Something much deeper than a sexual need, something that went beyond physical attraction.

11

It was the quiet stretch between breakfast and lunch when Sheriff Paul Odenton, and Deputy Reynolds entered Little Sandy's Diner. Reynolds had been with Paul the longest, and in addition to his becoming a trusted aide, they had, over the years, developed a relationship akin to that of an old married couple.

The lake area was a gold mine with investors and realtors referring to it as the Lake Tahoe of the East Coast. Business was booming, property values were skyrocketing as money, both old and new, flowed into the area. Construction was at its peak, and several local contractors had become millionaires.

A group of tables stood to the right of the door. Around one was your typical cookie-cutter tourist family with the professional husband trying to play the role of interested dad across from a vapid wife who seemed more suited to beauty parlors and fine dining establishments than a roadside diner perched at the edge of the wilderness.

The kids became quiet as Paul and Reynolds made their way through the maze of tables to a booth along the side wall. Paul smiled at the boy, who looked away and whispered to his sister, who refused to look away.

After they settled into their seats, Marla, the waitress, approached from the back.

"Have you passed the bar yet?" Paul asked.

"I still have another year of school, then an internship before I'm ready," she said.

"How's your mom and dad?"

"They're doing well. Daddy said to tell you the next time I saw you that he figured out the problem with the fence. So, what are we having today?"

"We'll start with coffee," Reynolds said as he studied the menu.

Paul nodded in agreement, and Marla left to retrieve their drinks.

"Get in touch with Pete," Paul said. "See if his dogs can find a scent to follow. Have the crime scene unit check the room for blood."

Reynolds wrote in the small notebook he'd opened on the table. "Do you think she did it?"

It was Paul's first thought when he entered the trailer. Something was off about the way Beth acted. Like she had something to hide, yet he sensed genuine concern as she answered their questions. The kitchen, as well as the trailed was spotless, with everything in its place. Giving the appearance of a well-ordered household. Yet the refrigerator was empty save a thirty pack of Milwaukee's Best, half empty, and a quart of milk that expired a few days before.

He felt no real comfort in the home. It lacked the nurturing environment a child needed to flourish. Bobby's older sister, Twila, had shown more emotion over his disappearance than his mother.

Marla returned with their coffee and placed ceramic mugs before them. "Have you boys figured out what you want?"

They gave their orders, and once Marla was out of range, Paul answered the question. It was something he'd given a good deal of thought to. He knew Beth, had seen first-hand the way she acted with certain male patrons at the bar where she worked.

She was also related to him in a roundabout way. Of course, most of the locals in the area were related to each other in one way or another. Some families could trace their lineage all the way back to shortly after the Revolutionary War, when everything was untouched wilderness. The Porter family was the oldest, and like a parasite their blood had seeped into everyone's over the years.

"I don't think she'd hurt the child," Paul said, "but you can never be sure. It's better to be safe than sorry. I've notified the state police and the FBI."

"What about the rest of us?"

"Have Burton and Fields canvass the trailer park, get the others back out on patrol. The tourists have started arriving." He nodded at the family in the dining area. "You know what that means. What else do we have for the day?"

Reynolds flipped through his notebook. Usually they held this meeting at the Sheriff's office, but today was no normal day. A child had gone missing in the night and though he never voiced his concerns, Paul's thoughts rarely strayed far from the seven slender folders in his desk drawer at home.

"You have a two o'clock with councilman Hartrick to go over next year's budget."

"Probably wants to cut it again."

"You also have a meeting with Cub Scout pack 89 at seven this evening."

"Finally, something to look forward to."

"Oh, and Barnes put in another request for transfer to days."

"How long has he been on nights?"

"A few weeks."

"Leave him on nights for another month, remind me next month, and I'll decide then if I want him in the rotation."

The mention of Deputy Barnes caused that sour spot in Paul's stomach to flare up. The amount of coffee he'd drank since last night did little to ease the pain. He'd been at it for almost thirty hours, and with a full day ahead of him, he doubted he'd get any sleep until that night, if then.

Marla brought their plates, piled high with bacon, eggs, and toast, and the rest of their meal passed in silence as they focused on eating. The reputation of Sandy's diner was evident in their meal and they ate like ravenous wolves.

Paul's cell phone buzzed, and he glanced at the number before answering it. He listened for a moment, said thanks, and closed his cell phone and placed it on the table beside him.

"What's up?" Reynolds said and then shoveled a forkful of eggs into his mouth.

"They found Andy Watkins hanging in his bedroom." The pain in his belly intensified.

"Suicide?" Reynolds asked around his mouthful of eggs, killing Paul's appetite.

"Don't know for sure. Guess we'll find out." Paul gazed across the empty dining room. The family had left.

His mama always said when it rained it poured. It was pouring, all right. Movement drew his eye to the parking lot.

Frederick Summers was pulling his vehicle into a spot. A reporter for the local paper, Summers had been hounding Paul about the rumor he'd been using county employees to investigate the disappearance of the seven children who vanished thirty years ago.

"Keep him away from me," Paul said.

Reynolds looked up, spotting Summers as he entered the diner. Reynolds pushed himself from his seat, intercepted the reporter, and steered him toward the counter.

12

Andy Watkins' body had already been removed when Paul and Reynolds arrived. All that remained was the frayed end of the rope where the coroner cut down the corpse, and a damp stain on the floor beneath. Andy pissed himself as he strangled to death, and the smell of urine was strong in the room.

Still angry from his near confrontation at Sandy's Diner, Paul popped several antacids to settle the burning in his stomach as he stared at the frayed end of the rope. Something else was going on here, he was sure of it. He knew Andy well enough to know he wasn't the type to take his own life.

Unless.

"Check to see if he's had any recent doctor's appointments," Paul said.

"Do you think he got some bad news?" Reynolds asked.

"It would have to be pretty bad that slow strangulation was preferable. I want to cover all the bases."

"If they'll tell us anything—doctor patient privilege and all that."

"Since he's dead, there are no more secrets to hide. But if they refuse, we may get something from the autopsy."

That wasn't all. Something tickled the back of his mind, something familiar. He looked around the room, trying to jog the memory.

At the dresser he surveyed the assorted perfume bottles standing before their twins reflected in the mirror behind. It was a variety of women's perfume, no men's cologne. Andy lost his wife several years before and was sleeping in the living room, leaving the bedroom as it had been on her last day.

Why would he hang himself in her bedroom? What's the connection? The questions tumbled through his mind as he surveyed the pictures taped to the mirror, forming a frame of memories.

Andy and his wife Wilma had raised three boys and a girl. They lost two of the boys. One to the war in Vietnam. Several years after that, Jacob, their youngest, vanished without a trace. His missing person's report lay in one of the folders that occupied Paul's desk drawer. A case that, to Paul's way of thinking, was still open, though the rest of the world considered it closed.

Paul was confident they were dealing with a serial pedophile who, for reasons yet to be determined, emerged once every thirty-plus years. On the surface that explanation was as crazy as its alternative. That the legend of the Witch of Porter Mines, an old wives' tale, contained more truth than fiction.

But what else did he have to go on? Nothing, unless each parent was involved, which was even more far-fetched than the witch. Besides, he'd lived here his entire life, and had seen nothing to lead him to believe the parents were responsible.

Some parents were abusive, and Bobby's mother was a prime example. But nothing in the trailer, aside from a lack of caring, indicated she had anything to do with Bobby's disappearance.

While Andy had been an upstanding citizen, he was also a slave to the demons that haunted his dreams. He served with the Marines in World War II in the Pacific theatre. He never talked about what he'd done, preferring to keep it bottled up where it gnawed away at his last shred of humanity.

Every so often he'd get into the drink and become violent. It was on one such call, as a rookie deputy, that Paul first met Andy. His partner at the time, an old hand at dealing with these random outbursts, walked up to Andy, who was waving his pistol around as his neighbors cowered behind their curtains. Having been on the force for only three months, it was the first time Paul was confronted with an armed suspect, and he was honestly terrified.

Buck, his partner, approached Andy with the calm demeanor of someone who has done this before, and took the pistol out of Andy's hand. Andy settled down and let Buck cuff him. Paul remained on the other side of the cruiser the whole time, wanting something between himself and any slugs that might come his way as Buck led an apologetic Andy to the cruiser.

"See, nothing to worry about," Buck said as he opened the back door and guided Andy into the back seat.

"I'm sorry I scared everybody," Andy said while Buck dropped the magazine from the handle of the pistol and pulled back the slide, ejecting a shell into his hand.

"What if he shot you?" Paul said.

Buck shrugged. "This ain't the first time Andy's gone off the deep end, most likely won't be the last."

"And they let the crazy drunk get away with it?" Paul was incredulous at the idea of leaving an armed man, with obvious mental problems, on the street.

Buck turned and pinned Paul with a hard stare. "That crazy drunk, as you call him, waded ashore on Iwo when he was nineteen years old, under heavy enemy fire, over the dying bodies of his friends. What did you do when you were nineteen? As far as I'm concerned, he's entitled to a little more consideration than you're willing to give him."

It was at that moment everything he'd been led to believe was brushed aside by one simple fact. They were people, not suspects. Good or bad, drunk, or sober, under it all they were no different than he. Some had grown up in a sheltered environment, masked from the brutality of an uncaring world. Others had been thrust into life and death situations that would scar them both physically and emotionally.

It was one of the lessons that contributed to the leader he'd become. One of the many meetings that tempered his own brutality toward those who would harm the men, women, and children he was sworn to protect.

For every action there is a defining moment that shapes us to respond. For Paul that moment came when he graduated from rookie to someone who might know what he was doing. Several children vanished over a period of two weeks, and old man Potts, the sheriff at the time, was hesitant to call in the State Police to help. He believed he could handle things himself.

A possible witness was brought in to shed some light on what was going on. Adam Tasker, a self-employed electrician, was known by everyone in the area. He'd worked on every house around at one time or another. He was also the last person to have seen several of the children alive.

He wasn't even a suspect.

That didn't stop them. Word spread as it will in a small town, and before long a crowd gathered outside the substation. Inside they were talking to Adam, who'd brought his son Donnie along for the ride and a chance to see the inside of a police station.

Soon the crowd grew unruly, calling for the deputies inside the station to let them question their suspect. The most vocal among them being Andy, who lost his son Jacob the week before.

With no response from the sheriff or any of the deputies, the crowd grew restless. Sheriff Potts tried to calm them but by then it was too late.

Andy, his neighbor Charlie, and Duane Bowers, who lost his daughter a few weeks earlier, forced their way into the station and took Adam onto the street. For a moment Paul stood at the door blocking them, his revolver aimed at Andy's gut.

"You gonna squeeze that trigger, boy?" Andy said, his eyes alight with something that stirred an old terror deep in Paul's soul. He didn't care if Paul shot him or not. Paul found he was unable to, and the mob swept him aside as it flowed into the station to claim its prize.

The memory receded into the depths of the past and he sniffed the air again, detecting a faint odor beneath the overpowering scent of urine and a room full of memories that had been locked away for too long.

He stepped into the hallway with Reynolds on his heels.

"What are you looking for?"

Paul held up his hand as he moved down the hall to the bathroom at the end. Opening the medicine cabinet, he scanned its contents before closing the door.

"Somebody else was here."

"How do you know?"

"I smell their aftershave."

"I can't smell anything but piss, and shit."

"It's there." Paul returned to the bedroom and took a deep breath. He spotted the shotgun leaning in the corner.

"Have that checked for prints." He stepped to the center of the room. "I think we'll only find Andy's, but it's best to be thorough." He turned to cross the room, then stopped. "Call the local hotels about any new check-ins during the last week."

"Who are we looking for?"

"Donnie Tasker." Paul stared at the frayed end of the rope as he remembered something his grandfather used to say. He'd been a preacher with a small church over in Friendsville. *Let the punishment fit the crime,* that gruff old voice whispered inside. Paul knew it as well as he knew the back of his hand. Donnie was back, and he was coming for revenge.

13

The playground was a babble of excited voices as the children, wearing a variety of colorful coats and hats, burned off their pent-up energy from a boring morning in class. Most of the activity was centered around the swings and the monkey bars.

Several older boys were playing a pick-up game of basketball, racing back and forth as they chased the ball, taunting one another as was natural for pre-pubescent boys. Calling into question one another's birth status and questioning if their parents had any children that lived.

Near the fence, at the edge of the blacktop where the older boys were playing, Christine and three of her friends hovered outside a group of older girls gathered around Marjorie. They huddled together against the biting wind that still carried the memory of winter's recent passing.

Marjorie carried herself with the attitude of someone who felt everyone else in the world was there to serve her. The fact she had a cell phone at the age of ten sealed her position as the leader of this small group, at least until the others were permitted to own such a device. It wasn't any run of the mill cell phone, either. It was the latest Motorola razr2 that came standard with a whopping 420 megabytes of storage. But that wasn't good enough for Marjorie. She insisted, and been given, the upgraded model that contained 2 gigs of available memory.

"I downloaded 'Irreplaceable' last night after my mom went to bed."

"How much did it cost?" Becky asked in a hushed voice, her eyes wide.

If they tried something like that they would have been grounded for weeks. Marjorie shrugged as she answered in a bored manner, "Who knows. Mom won't even notice it on her credit card statement."

They were agog at Marjorie's obvious disdain for anything as mundane as worrying about how much something cost. All but Christine, who found her gaze drawn to the woods beyond the chain link fence bordering the playground.

"I have a secret." The soft whisper of the girl's voice from the night before entered her mind.

She slipped her hand into her pocket and fingered the small piece of plastic she carried. It had once been the pupil of Puddles's eye. She missed Puddles, but she couldn't let herself be seen carrying him. She was growing up and would soon replace those things from her childhood with more mature objects, a fact that saddened her. By joining Marjorie's group, she'd found a place among the popular kids at school, and she dare not do anything to jeopardize that.

Her attention was drawn back to the others when Beyonce's tinny voice came from Marjorie's phone. They all circled around, singing along as they pointed to their left.

"Daddy had to leave late last night," Shelly said after the song ended. She shook her head and pushed back several strands of brown hair. "The sheriff called him out. I heard mom talking to him this morning about a little boy who was missing."

"Who is it?" Marjorie asked and returned her phone to the small purse she carried.

"I don't know." Shelly shrugged.

"Do you think the Witch got him?" Becky said.

"Of course, the Witch got him." Marjorie reasserted her place as the leader of the group.

Becky turned her attention to the busy playground. "Who's not here today?"

"Anybody seen Tweedle Dee?" It was Marjorie's pet name for Twila, a girl her own age who lived at the distant edge of the universe in which she traveled. She was not one of the popular kids and never would be. The daughter of a single mother living in a mobile home on the edge of town did not move in the same circles as Marjorie, whose parents owned several businesses around the lake.

Christine didn't like the way Marjorie treated those beneath her, but she knew better than to say anything.

"I haven't seen her," Becky said.

"Me either," Shelly chimed in.

"Anybody seen her snot-nosed little brother?" Marjorie said.

The others shook their heads.

"I guess the Witch has taken her due." Marjorie snickered.

"I saw her last night," Christine blurted out. She didn't know why she did. She wasn't planning to share this with her friends. After all, it had been no more than a nightmare like her mommy said. But if that was true, then Lizzy's visit had been a dream as well. But it couldn't have been. She was so real. She told her about the dark place where all bad little boys and girls were taken.

"You saw *who*?" Marjorie said as her eyes narrowed.

"I saw the Witch. She was at my window."

Becky and Shelly stepped back, shocked by her revelation.

Marjorie stepped closer. "Then why are you still here?" She didn't like being upstaged.

"Cause I wouldn't open my window."

The bell rang, signaling the end of recess. In Marjorie's eyes she saw a begrudging respect tinged with a hint of jealousy. She stood up to the Witch. No one else had ever done that before, at least no one they knew. When the Witch came, she got what she wanted.

"C'mon ladies, let's go," Mrs. Draven called from the school door. The girls scattered as they returned, leaving Marjorie and Christine alone at the fence. Marjorie turned on her heel, her nose in the air, as she marched back to the building. From the forest behind her came the soft sound of movement, and Christine turned to look into the gloomy depths as something glided into view. It was a young girl dressed all in white, watching her from the shadowy forest.

"I know where your daddy is," that voice whispered in her mind, and Christine turned away as something dark crawled through her belly.

The voice was lying. Her daddy was in heaven. She raced back to school and slipped her hand into her pocket to fondle Puddles's pupil. It brought her a small measure of comfort, but she still wished she had Puddles with her as she passed through the door under Mrs. Draven's arm. He would protect her.

"I don't know what's gotten into you girls, but you need to pay more attention."

"Yes ma'am," Christine answered as she entered the school.

14

While Eric worked in the unfinished half of the basement, Susan focused on the laundry. Only two of them lived in the house but judging by the amount of dirty clothes you would think there was three times that many. Most belonged to Christine, worn once, then dropped to the floor where they lay until Susan got on her to clean her room. Some were barely worn, but they touched her skin, and that was all that mattered.

John had been the same way. Even if he tried on a shirt to see if it matched his pants, it went into the hamper as soon as he took it off. One of those minor annoyances that pop up in any marriage. In most cases, they remained no more than that, insignificant irritations that were passed over as quickly as they arose.

She glanced at the tunnel as she dropped the basket to the floor. A chilled breeze came from the opening, carrying with it the smell of old places closed up for far too long. She gazed into the dark depths beyond the opening as an odd sensation crawled through her belly, and a slight tremor danced along the flesh of her arms.

Her excitement at the discovery had faded, and she was considering having Eric close the hole for good. Christine's explanation that all bad little girls went to the dark place had kept her on edge all morning, and she eyed the tunnel with trepidation.

While her early childhood had been typical, after her father left it became a living nightmare. When she was eight, her mother started following one of those televangelists with his own channel, always begging for money, quietly insinuating that the size of the donation would be the determining factor in one's ability to enter heaven.

Her mother gobbled it up, hook, line, and sinker. Sending every penny, she could beg borrow or steal to the personable preacher whose only goal was to ensure Charlene Porter would sit on the right hand of God after her death.

They'd been planning a cross-country trip for several years and their father decided this would be the year they went. Unfortunately, Charlene found the money and sent it to Reverend Hale to help his ongoing battle against godlessness.

Susan and her older brother, Robert, remained in her bedroom as their mother and father argued over losing the vacation money. They'd argued before, as was typical when individuals worked at being a couple, but nothing like this. Screams and shouts drifted up to Susan and Robert, who tried his best to distract her from what was happening downstairs. Finally, he gave up and they sat together on her bed, his arm draped over her shoulder, as the battle raged into the night. The front door slammed, shaking her bedroom windows. As an eerie silence filled the house.

They held their breath, waiting for what came next.

From downstairs came the sound of boxes being shuffled about, punctuated by grunts. Robert went to the door and opened it, peering into the hallway before motioning for Susan to wait. Instead, she followed him, and together they approached the stairs.

They found their mother on her knees next to the small closet under the steps, pulling out the boxes stored there. Boxes filled with Christmas decorations and school papers from their journey through the public education system. As she worked, she muttered to herself about respect, honoring the Lord, and how children were supposed to mind their parents.

It appeared their dad left, leaving them alone with a woman teetering on the edge of madness as she followed Reverend Hale's teachings.

The first tenet she embraced was "spare the rod and spoil the child," although she didn't use a rod. Sometimes, as the day stretched into night while confined to the closet under the stairs, Susan wished her mother would beat her. Sure, it would be painful, but it would be over with quick. Which was preferable to the long hours of kneeling with their hands clasped before their chest.

The closet under the steps became the dark place to Susan and Robert. With the door closed there was nothing to see. No light could penetrate the darkness that ruled, and in those shadowed depths their imaginations were unleashed. For a young child, in the dark, the normal sounds of a house settling upon its foundation were amplified. Coupled with their imagination every creak and groan grew from a sinister source. There was only the darkness and the unyielding surface of the hardwood floor under their knees.

Robert tried sneaking a flashlight into the closet once, something to ease the terror they felt in that lonely place. Their mother found it and tripled his punishment time. She kept the door open that day, watching Robert the entire time, and every time he slouched, she shouted at him. In the end she had to give up. Robert became too exhausted to remain on his knees and fell to the floor as his mother berated him.

Later, her mother carried Robert to his bed where she tucked him in with a gentle kiss on the forehead. It was so out of character that it threw Susan off. Maybe it was over, Susan remembered wondering as her mother smoothed the covers over him.

However, when her mother turned around and spotted Susan spying on her, she learned it was only the beginning. That act of kindness was the final glimmer of humanity she would ever see in her mother's eyes.

As the pressure eased on Robert, Susan became her mother's favorite target. Nothing she did was good enough. The A+ she brought home on her geography exam was only possible because Susan was a liar and a cheat and needed to be punished.

Spare the rod and spoil the child.

Although the pressure was eased on Robert, he still faced the closet many evenings as Susan and her mother sat silently at the kitchen table. No talking was permitted at the mealtime table, in sharp contrast to the happiness that once surrounded it when her father lived with them.

They did nothing at the table but eat. When they finished, the dishes were washed, dried, and put away. If homework needed to be done, you did it. If not, you could sit and watch the good reverend, or you went to your room and studied the Bible, unless punishment was in order, and it was always in order.

In their home happiness fled, in its wake all that remained was the dark place under the stairs and the monotonous routine of leading a double life. In public they carried on the charade that everything was all right. They were alone, abandoned by their father, forced to face the monster that wore their mother's face.

After two years Robert took his own life, unable to withstand the relentless punishment any longer. He was only thirteen. While everyone slept, he hanged himself in the basement. Susan found him the following morning when she went down to retrieve eggs, turning from the refrigerator to be confronted by Robert's contorted features.

Her mother had no choice but to call the police and Susan was liberated from the home. However, her stint in foster care was short-lived. Her mother hired an attorney and a judge decided, against the advice of Child Services, that it would be best for the child to not break up the family during such a difficult time.

Robert's suicide did accomplish one thing. After she returned, she was no longer required to spend time in the closet. It remained empty, yet an ever-present threat that things could return to the way they had been in an instant.

Punishment was reduced to simple confinement in her bedroom. As it was, life continued. While her friends were having parties and going to the mall, Susan remained at home, confined to her room.

15

Childhood memories parade through Susan's mind while she sorted the laundry. As she did she realized Christine was starting to grow up. Her taste in clothes were changing. She preferred pants, jeans when possible, to the dresses she used to wear. It saddened her to realize her little girl was growing up. Before long she'd be going out on dates and would eventually find a man to build her own family with. The thought of losing her little girl saddened her while dredging up more of her own past.

In her junior year at high school she fell for the age-old line about proving her love for a young man. Terry Blankenship, whose father owned the Cadillac dealership on Route 36 between Cumberland and Frostburg, he had wavy blond hair that hung in his eyes. This irritated his father no end but caused palpitations in the hearts of the young girls in her class, herself included.

Susan proved an easy target for Terry's predatory nature. As they fumbled in the backseat of his father's demo during lunch, she fell for his promise of marriage, imagining life as Mrs. Terry Blankenship as he slipped off her panties.

The following day she got her first real lesson in humiliation. What she endured at her mother's hands was minor compared to her emotions after Terry rejected her. She approached him, expecting him to honor his promise, only to be laughed at and told he would never marry her. She fled his degradation with tears streaming down her face, running home in search of comfort that no longer existed.

A month later, she missed her period, and a cold dread settled into the pit of her belly where a new life was forming. Two weeks later she confirmed her suspicions with a pregnancy test she bought with lunch money she saved by missing several meals. She confronted Terry in the hallway with the test strip that bore the truth of their union. He brushed her off, his next conquest riding his arm.

Later that same day, he cornered her in the hall, demanding that she keep quiet about what they'd done. He promised he would help her end the pregnancy so they could each move on with their own lives.

The memory receded as she filled the washer with dirty clothes. The short hairs on her neck rose in response to the feeling that she was being watched.

"Eric?" She spun around only to confront the empty laundry room behind her.

Then she heard it. A whimper coming from the narrow tunnel next to the dryer as the old memories responded.

Terry managed to get the money for the procedure from his father. He even took her to the clinic and waited with her in the waiting room, sitting next to her as some inane talk show droned on from the television on the opposite wall. She remembered everything with startling clarity, as if it happened the day before instead of twenty years earlier. He didn't hold her hand or offer any comfort to ease her terror. She knew she was doing wrong, but what choice did she have? Her mother would go off the deep end if she found out Susan was pregnant.

She had not begun to show, yet she changed her attire from jeans and sloppy shirts, to dresses that would provide ample room to hide her belly. Still she was afraid her mother could tell what happened by looking at her. Her mother took it as a sign that she was getting through to her and Susan was embracing the path she'd been nudging her towards.

Had her mother known the truth, her brand of justice would have been swift and sure, and Susan was confident the room under the stairs would become her cell.

Unable to tell the one person who could have offered some guidance, had her mother not been so wrapped up in her beliefs, she was forced to rely on strangers, and a young boy who professed his love only to get into her pants. He only offered to help to keep his name from being dragged through the mud.

After it was over, all she could think about was how she disappointed everyone. Her mother, but she was always disappointing her mother in one way or another. And God.

God said, "Thou shalt not kill," and he had killed one of his children.

She imagined the ghost of the child haunting her. Often awaking at night to the cries of a hungry child. She had no one to tell her what she was experiencing was a normal reaction to her act. No one counseled her about the emotional side effects a woman faced after an abortion. With no one to turn to, she bore the guilt alone, retreating even more from the world around her, until one day she realized, like Robert, she had only one option open to her.

After drawing a warm bath, she climbed into the tub, still wearing her pajamas. She didn't want strangers seeing her naked. Using the razor blade, she found in the medicine cabinet she slit her wrists. It hurt at first, but the pain mellowed as she lowered her bleeding arms into the warm water and settled back to drift off as exhaustion overwhelmed her.

She did not cut deep enough to do any real damage, and when her mother found her, she was sleeping peacefully. She couldn't remember what happened. But her mother did call an ambulance, which surprised her.

She awoke in the hospital where a therapist tried to guide her through the minefield of her past. To help her cope and heal from the abuse she'd suffered, and her guilt over what she'd done. Her mother interfering at every turn.

After she came home her punishment grew. The closet under the stairs became her cell as Reverend Hale extolled the virtues of life under the guidance of a vengeful god.

The sorrow of Susan's past overwhelmed her, cracking her normally stoic façade as tears traced wet lines down her cheeks. She crossed the laundry room and sat down on the carpeted step as that faint crying came from the emptiness of the tunnel.

Was it the child she aborted? Robert sniffling behind that dreaded door. Her own remorse over the loss of innocence she'd suffered at the hands of a woman teetering on the edge of madness. Like bitter bile, the agony of her past welled up within her.

Above it all came the numbing sorrow of loss as John's face swam into view, his impish grin and that devil-may-care attitude that sent him halfway around the world to a desert land where he would meet his end when a roadside bomb took out the vehicle he occupied. Many believed death was the first step on a new journey. For her, John's death had been the final blow in a life filled with bitter disappointment.

She was still sitting slumped over on the steps when Eric found her. When he placed a hand on her shoulder, she jumped to her feet and wrapped her arms around him.

"Are you all right?" he said.

"No," she cried, as fresh tears spilled down her cheeks. "Don't ever leave me."

Eric wrapped his arms around her.

16

A faceless crowd surrounded him, screaming their hate with one voice as the coarse rope tightened around his neck, making it difficult to breathe. He was lifted from his feet as the noose tightened, and he clawed at the rope with his fingers, digging his nails into the flesh around his neck, tearing at the soft tissue as the need to breath became the only thing that mattered. The faces around him blurred as his vision dimmed, their angry voices swallowed by a growing roar that overwhelmed everything as he was lifted higher into the air.

Donnie sat up with a startled cry, covered in sweat, as the memory of his nightmare and the helplessness it provoked, faded. He looked around the small motel room, at the dilapidated dresser across from him, the ancient television sitting on top. In the mirror above the dresser he saw himself, a bearded wild man with shoulder-length hair sticking out in every direction.

From beside him came a muffled snort, and he glanced at the woman lying there as he recalled what he'd done two nights before.

Andy knew what he wanted. He knew Donnie would return and had been waiting for him. He was willing enough at first, but that willingness gave way to reluctance when Donnie slipped the noose over his head.

Afterwards he'd gone to a local dive and knocked back one shot after another, stumbling back to his hotel room drunk. The following night he returned to the same bar. There he met the hooker who occupied his bed. He couldn't remember who picked up whom.

He slapped her ass. "Come on, get up," he said. She stirred in response and pulled the sheet over her head. He got out of bed, crossed to the bathroom, and emptied his bladder before stepping into the shower.

The water was hot and helped wash away his distaste over the night's activities. He still had so much to do. So much hate to get rid of, so much revenge to dish out. In his mind he carried a list, and Andy, who'd been one of the ring leaders the day his father died, occupied the top spot. The next spot belonged to Duane Bowers. Donnie learned that Duane died of a heart attack several years earlier.

Two down, three to go.

One of his targets now occupied a local nursing home. But his daughter worked at a nearby diner. Was she prepared to pay for the sins of her father?

"Want some company?" The hooker pushed back the shower curtain and stepped into the tub with him. She was a full foot shorter than he, with short blonde hair and small perky tits. She reached down, caressing him with experienced hands, and once he was hard, she knelt before him. He closed his eyes as her soft, warm mouth enveloped him.

After their shower she stood at the mirror, brushing out her short hair as Donnie watched from the bathroom.

"You know you owe me for last night, and this morning."

"So," was his only response.

She turned and fixed him with a hard stare that carried a hint of fear.

"You don't pay up, I'll tell Ray. He'll kick your ass clean out of town."

"Will he?"

"You better believe he will."

Donnie crossed the space between them in three quick steps and wrapped his hand around her throat. He yanked up, nearly lifting her from her feet as she raked his bicep with her nails.

"What if I don't let you tell him?"

Her eyes bulged, and Donnie struggled against the desire to snap her neck like a matchstick. Her fear fed a dark and twisted side of him that had been cultivated in the California penal system, where he'd spent most of his adult life. His last stint was a six-year turn in Chino for aggravated assault. He was a two-time loser with a sealed juvenile record longer than most of the rap sheets of the prisoners he'd known.

His darker half had always been there, shrouded by the shadows of his soul, birthed when he was six and witnessed firsthand the power of the mob and its ability to turn ordinary law-abiding citizens into screaming maniacs seeking revenge. He watched from the sheriff's office as his father was dragged from their protection into the street where he was tried, found guilty, and executed all within the space of fifteen minutes.

His father was innocent, and had he lived, Donnie's life might have turned out different. Sent to live with his mother in southern California, he became a typical problem child as he rebelled against every form of authority from the schoolteacher to the beat cop. He spent more time in state custody than anywhere else, and as such had learned one important lesson. If you were going to survive in the jungle, you had to be the baddest motherfucker there.

He released his grip, and the hooker dropped to the thin carpet, choking and gagging. Donnie threw a hundred bucks on the floor next to her.

"If your boy Ray wants to find me, I'll be having breakfast." He threw her clothes at her. "Now get dressed and get your ass out of here."

He stepped back into the bathroom as she quickly dressed and vanished out the door.

17

The Green Lantern Diner was no different than many of the others Donnie had been in before. A counter ran the length of the room, opposite a row of booths along the windows that looked out on the parking lot. Everything was covered with a layer of grease from years of cooking on the ancient grill behind the counter.

Donnie sat in the end booth, his back against the wall, watching the front door like a predator waiting for its prey. Two booths down, four old men argued among themselves over a card game that had taken place the night before, or years ago. Donnie wasn't sure. He caught only one side of the argument from a guy who was nearly deaf and apparently believed everyone else was too.

The waitress behind the counter glanced his way. Donnie checked her out when he first came in, noting the makeup that did little to hide her age. She had to be in her late thirties, trying too hard to look twenty. Probably had a couple of kids, was divorced or had been abandoned by the kids' father. Or maybe she was trapped in a dead-end marriage to a guy who came home every day to get drunk in front of the television.

She approached his booth with the coffee pot. The name badge pinned to her shirt read Marie. Bingo, she was the one.

"Would you like some coffee, hon?" she asked.

Donnie nodded. She leaned over his table as she poured, the top button of her shirt undone to afford him a better view.

Might as well have some fun first. She couldn't be any worse than the hooker he had the night before. Safer too, unless she was married, and her old man roused himself from his drunken stupor long enough to notice she hadn't come home.

"What time do you get off?" he asked as a muscular man entered the diner.

"I finish my shift after lunch."

"What are you doing after that?"

The muscular man scanned the diner. His gaze settling on Donnie, who smiled and nodded.

"Don't know yet. You're not from around here, are you?"

The man approached, grabbed Marie's arm, and pulled her away from the table. "Get out of the way, Marie, I've got business to take care of with this asshole."

Donnie remained seated.

"Dammit, Ray, I've told you before to keep your filthy hands off me."

The group at the other table stopped their argument and turned to watch the drama unfold.

"Shut up." Ray turned to Donnie. Resting his fists on the table, he leaned down close. "You choked one of my girls?"

Donnie remained silent, refusing to acknowledge Ray's presence. He knew the type—all bluster and no balls.

"Dammit, you better pay attention to me, boy." Ray reached for Donnie's shirt. His hand never made it.

Donnie lashed out, driving his heel against Ray's knee, bending the leg backwards to the tune of popping ligaments.

With his left hand he intercepted Ray's as he drove up with a right cross. Ray fell to the floor, clutching his injured knee as Donnie slid out of his seat and knelt beside him.

"Don't fuck with me, boy," he said before pushing himself to his feet. He tossed a few bucks on the table and made his way to the front door as the old men watched.

Marie caught up with him as he crossed the parking lot.

"Ray's gonna be hunting you after that."

Donnie shrugged. "Why do you care?"

"I don't. Only thought I'd let you know."

"I thought you had to work through lunch."

"Wouldn't be the first time I left early."

"You might get fired."

"Why do you care?"

"I don't."

Donnie swung his leg over the seat of his Harley.

"Where are you staying?" Marie asked.

"Route Forty motel."

"What room?" The need in her voice was clear. Like a million other waitresses stuck in dead-end jobs in dead-end towns, looking for a way out.

"Seven."

She smiled as the Harley roared to life.

Easing off the clutch, Donnie roared out of the parking lot, watching her in his mirror. Looking into her eyes he realized they shared something on a deep, primitive, level. Something painful. And that worried him. He couldn't let himself become attached if he wanted to accomplish what he'd set out to do.

18

Donnie was sitting on the bed watching television when the knock came shortly after lunch.

"It's open," he shouted, believing it was Marie.

The door swung open and before he could react, the room was full of police officers. One trained his pistol on Donnie who raised his open hands. "I'm not resisting."

"Good idea," came a voice from the door. Sheriff Paul Odenton pulled around the room's only chair and settled into it.

"Want us to cuff him?" a deputy asked.

Paul shook his head. "I don't believe that will be necessary. Do you, Donnie?"

Donnie shook his head as he remembered where he'd seen the Sheriff. He'd been one of the deputies the day his father was hanged. The only one, in fact, who at first refused to surrender his father to the crowd.

"What do you want?" Donnie asked.

Paul looked at the deputies. "Wait outside for me."

"But Sheriff..."

Paul held up his hand. "If I need you, I'll call for you. I'd like a private word with our visitor."

"You heard the man, let's go."

The deputies filed out. Reynolds was the last to leave, and he hesitated at the door.

"Close the door behind you, please."

"What if he tries something."

"I don't believe Donnie's that stupid. After all, where would he go with six armed deputies waiting for him?"

"I still..."

Paul raised his hand and Reynolds pulled the door shut behind him.

"So, how have you been, Donnie?" Sheriff Odenton said.

"Can I put my hands down now?"

"Of course, relax, I want to talk to you. Just came from Andy Watkins place. Old guy living alone like that. Everyone he cares about is either dead or doesn't want anything to do with him anymore. Couldn't blame him if he started thinking about ending it."

"Are you trying to tell me something?"

Paul shook his head. "Wanted to welcome you home, let you know we're watching out for you."

"Like you did my dad?"

"That was a long time ago. Things have changed since then."

"What do you want?"

"That's what I like. Let's quit beating around the bush." Paul's eyes narrowed as he leaned forward. "I know you were responsible for what happened to Andy."

Donnie denied the accusation and the Sheriff held up his hand to stop him. "If I had any real evidence to back up my feelings, we wouldn't be having this conversation. In fact, you'd be sitting in one of my cells. As it stands, I can't prove, yet, that you did anything. If and when I can, you'll be the first to know."

"So, what do you want?"

"I want you out of my town. Today. Right now, in fact."

"It's a free country."

"For ninety-nine percent of the hardworking population, that may be true. You're not a member of that group. You're an outsider, a biker at that. No one is gonna give a shit if I lock your ass up."

"You can't do that."

"Son, when it comes to protecting what we have here, I can do anything I damn well please, and if you fuck with me, I'll put you in a hole." Paul stood. "What happened to your dad was a real shame but coming back to get revenge will get you killed. Put it behind you, move on with your life." He turned and rested his hand on the doorknob. "I'm sorry it's come to this." Then he slipped through the door.

Deputy Reynolds stepped into the room as Paul left.

"What do you want?" Donnie asked.

"Sheriff wants me to make sure you get on your way okay. Personally, I'd prefer it if you resisted."

19

Curiosity was a powerful motivator, and it was her curiosity that brought Susan to Oakland. It was amazing how one day could put things into better perspective and this morning the tunnel had not been as sinister as the day before. After Christine left with Brenda, she retrieved one of the bottles from the tunnel hoping it might shed some light on the past. The online archives for the Garret Tribune were a bust, forcing her to come into town to satisfy that itch.

The buildings along Main street were from another time. Some were nearly three hundred years old. Their brick facades and ornate window ledges looking down on the busy street with a stately elegance. Here and there modern block structures added a more modern touch.

Affixed to the heavy oak door was a brass plaque thanking the Porter Family for the donation of the building to house the library. As soon as she walked in, she was struck by the smell of books—not any books, but old books that spoke of knowledge waiting to be discovered.

The smell reminded her of the times she and her dad would visit the library down the street from where they lived. The memory brought a tear to her eye and she wondered briefly what might have become of him. It was a part of her life she was missing, a part of her past she would never be able to reclaim.

Though small, the library filled three floors of the building, each furnished with hand-crafted wooden shelves surrounded by ornate woodwork that spoke of a day when craftsmen proudly displayed their expertise in everything they built. Scattered among the bookshelves were sitting areas with overstuffed chairs and tables that created cozy reading nooks. Behind the front desk the librarian, an elderly woman, worked through a pile of returned books. She looked up when Susan walked through the door.

Susan crossed to the kiosk. "Excuse me."

"Yes, may I help you?"

"Do you have the archives for the Garret *Tribune*? I called the paper this morning, and they said I needed to come here."

"Of course. Do you have a library card?"

"Umm, no."

"That's not a problem. It'll only take a minute to fix you up. May I see your driver's license please?"

Susan dug through the contents of her purse. Finding her wallet, she removed the laminated card, and passed it to the woman.

"Are you a tourist?" the librarian asked.

"I'm, sorry, what? No, I live on Fiddlers Pond Road."

The librarian slid Susan's license across the counter, and she realized she'd handed over her California license.

"I'm sorry." Susan pulled her Maryland license from her wallet and gave it to the woman. "We moved to the area a year ago. Don't know why I hang onto this," she said holding up the out-of-state license.

"That's all right." The librarian took Susan's license and entered information into the computer.

"Are you from this area originally?" the librarian asked.

"I'm from Cumberland, actually."

"Really, what part? I grew up in North End."

"We lived in South End, Pennsylvania Avenue. Did you go to Allegany?"

"Absolutely, I was an Arrowette and everything, you?"

"Fort Hill, of course," Susan said.

The librarian nodded politely.

"I was never involved in extracurricular activities. More focused on my studies." Susan suppressed the memory of her mother and the closet.

The librarian smiled as she entered Susan's information. "You mentioned Fiddler's Pond Road. Is this your current address?" The librarian held up her license.

"No. We recently moved to 11870 Fiddler's Pond Road. I haven't had time to update my license."

"That's in Porter Mines?"

"Yes."

"I thought the address sounded familiar. You bought the old Jenkins place, didn't you?"

"I did, we're almost done fixing it up."

"Such a shame what happened there." The librarian returned her attention to the computer.

"What happened?"

"No one told you?" The librarian looked up.

Susan shook her head.

"A young boy killed himself. It's why the family abandoned the house."

The revelation stunned Susan. No one she'd spoken to about the house before she bought it said anything about a suicide. "I didn't know anything about that."

"They should have told you. I think it's a law or something. They have to share things like that, don't they? Maybe I'm wrong."

Aware the conversation was about to veer into dangerous territory, Susan brought it back on track. "About my library card?"

"I'm sorry," the librarian said as she resumed work on her computer. After a few keystrokes, the older woman glanced at her. "Have you seen anything?" she asked.

"I'm sorry, what? What do you mean?"

"Forgive me," the librarian said. "My hobby is paranormal investigation and when you told me you lived in the old Jenkins house, I got excited. We've wanted to get into the house to check it for years, but no one would let us."

"We?"

"Me and my friends. We visit places where tragedy has struck in search of the spirits of the dead. I shouldn't have been so forward. please forgive me, it was improper. I'm sorry."

"That's all right, I guess." Susan was a little shaken by the librarian's approach and unsure how to proceed.

"Let me finish this for you." The librarian returned her attention to the monitor. After a few seconds she said, "There you go." She slid a yellow plastic card, and Susan's license, across the counter to her.

"Now that you're an official card-carrying member of the Garret County Library, what dates from the *Tribune* can I help you find today?"

"Prohibition era and nineteen seventy-three to the early eighties."

"You're looking into the house's past, aren't you?"

Susan nodded with a strained smile as she opened the small folder and removed a sheet of paper. On it she'd written the name from the bottle. "Does this sound familiar to you?"

The librarian took the sheet of paper and studied it for several moments. "No, but I haven't lived in this area for long. The person you need to see is Harriet Phillips. She was a dispatcher for the Sheriff's office and knows practically everything there is to know about the area."

"Where would I find her?"

"Last I heard they moved her to the Golden Living Center in Cumberland. It's a nursing home. I believe she's pushing ninety."

"Thank you. Now about those files?"

"Of course. They're on microfilm. This way."

Susan followed the librarian to the back of the library where the reference materials were located. Behind them, a young couple with two unruly children stepped into the library.

"I'll set it up for you and show you how to use it. It's pretty easy once it's loaded. And if you have any questions, I'll be at my desk."

Behind a row of free-standing bookshelves, three machines sat on a low table with a chair before each. Susan watched as the librarian removed the proper spool and loaded the machine. "Use this handle to advance the spool and the platen to magnify what you want to see." She moved the handle, and the image of the newspaper appeared on the screen. "When you're ready for the next roll, let me know and I'll load it for you."

"Thank you." Susan sat down, and the librarian returned to her station.

After a few tries, she figured out how the film responded to the handle and platen and was soon cruising through the pages of the *Tribune* from the early 1920s. Occasionally she would stop to gawk at the ads. Paul Jones cigarettes, twenty for ten cents. Miss Brasso to help metal shine as brightly as the sun. Stop thumb sucking with the Baby Alice thumb guard.

She smiled at the simplicity of the ads. There were no sales, no final clearances, no last in a lifetime buyouts. You have a problem? We have an answer.

Moving on, she came to the photo of a familiar house and stopped. The house she now owned stood tall and brooding, backlit by the sun, giving it a foreboding appearance. Whoever took the shot purposely put it in a bad light to add to the drama of the headline above it.

Two Men Shot Dead in Booze-fueled Argument

The story below detailed the falling out of the Schroeder brothers when an argument erupted over the profits from an illegal still on the property. The story was continued on page three, and she quickly turned to it to find a full-page spread, complete with photos of the basement where the still was located.

The same room that was now her laundry.

One photo featured the still. Behind it the wall of field stone ended at a black corner. Clinging to the corner a small figure gazed into the camera. It was hardly noticeable in the grainy black and white photo, but she picked it out immediately. The faint image of a child peered around the corner of the tunnel, and as her focus zeroed in on the image, a soft stirring along her spine raised the short hairs on her neck.

She flipped through the pages, trying to put the image out of her mind, but it was no use. Those troubled eyes continued to haunt her. She was on the verge of uncovering a truth that'd been staring at her all along, a truth she had little desire to reveal.

"Jimmy, get back here," a woman shouted on her right, and Susan turned to see a young boy watching her from the end of the aisle. The woman she'd seen coming in came up him.

"I'm sorry he was disturbing you," she said as she placed her hand on the boy's shoulder.

"It's all right. He was no bother, really," Susan said.

"Didn't I tell you to stay with us?" The young woman pulled the child back down the aisle. "Honestly, if you and your brother don't learn to listen to me, the Witch is going to take you away. Do you want that to happen? Do you want to lose your mommy and daddy because you wouldn't listen?"

The child cried in response and Susan's heart went out to him. What the young woman was doing was no better than emotional abuse. An abuse she once endured at the hands of a mother walking along the fine edge of insanity. Though angered, Susan understood that it was not her place to correct the woman. It was another of the little facets of living in Porter Mines she would have to get used to.

Susan called for the librarian and watched as the woman efficiently changed out the rolls. She wondered if the librarian ever looked at those same images during her paranormal research. If so, did she see that faint impression of a child, or was it simply a figment of her own imagination? She wanted to go back, to look again, to confirm she really saw it. Instead she waited quietly for the librarian to finish. It was better to doubt what she'd seen than confirm its existence. It was easier to rationalize something when you had no concrete evidence it was real.

She scrolled through the pages, pausing at any picture that might be connected to her house, and every obituary section searching for a single name. Then she came across a photo of a young boy with a wide smile.

> Peter Andrew Jenkins, age 13, passed into the loving arms of his Savior Jesus Christ surrounded by his family. Surviving are his mother and father, and one sister, Abigail.

Nothing in the obituary led her to believe he'd taken his own life. Why would somebody that young, with so much to look forward to, take his own life? It made no sense.

She struggled to put the notion out of her mind as she scrolled through the pages. She was trying to get to the bottom of a mystery that wasn't a mystery at all. A headline caught her eye and she stopped.

Suspect Dies in Custody.
Porter Mines, MD (AP). — Adam Tasker, a local electrician, was found hanging in his cell at the Porter Mines satellite Sheriff's office where he was being held

for questioning. Authorities have not confirmed or denied his involvement with the recent string of child disappearances. Other sources that have asked to remain anonymous have linked the electrician with several of the missing children.

Susan stopped reading, sensing that something else was going on behind the story of Adam Tasker. She spun the dial slowly, moving through the following pages, searching for any mention of Adam. Nothing. It was as if he and the story dropped off the edge of the world. Or been swept under the rug.

A photo caught her attention and a tingle caressed the base of her skull. A little girl wearing a summer dress gazed at the camera with an innocent smile, her hands hidden behind her back. Next to the image of the child was a photo of Fiddlers Pond. The headline exclaimed in bold type:

Police Dredge Fiddlers Pond in Search for Missing Child

A shiver rode down her spine as she read the story.

Friendsville, Md. (AP). – Police today expanded their search for seven-year-old Lindsay Railey, who's been missing since last Tuesday, to include Fiddlers Pond. She is the seventh child to be abducted since five-year-old Robbie Wilson was taken in the early days of spring.

Robbie, Bobby, Robert... Was there a connection? Bobbies were dying left and right in Porter Mines.

The Sheriff's office has refused to request state and federal assistance to help find the missing children, and those responsible for the abductions. They are asking anyone with knowledge of their whereabouts to please step forward. A hotline has been established to handle your tips. 301-555-1555.

Dredging at Fiddlers Pond began yesterday morning and immediately resulted in several gruesome discoveries. From the murky depths a 1955 Chevrolet Bel-Air was recovered. Sources who have asked to remain anonymous said the vehicle is believed to belong to Raymond Salts, who was reported missing in 1958 when he was nineteen years old.

Also recovered was the body of Henry Fields, who was last seen working at the Railey farm over seven years ago. His remains were carefully wrapped in a canvas tarp weighted down with stones.

Police have remained silent as the investigation continues.

Susan stopped reading and rubbed her eyes. She was wasting her time here and knew it. She had too much other work to take care of before she went back to work. Though she felt like she was on a fool's errand, her curiosity drew her back to the screen. Headlines whizzed by as she cranked the handle. Coming to a stop, she scanned the page and focused on one of the images. It was of a younger version of Mildred being escorted by several Sheriff's deputies. Beneath the image was the story with the lead in.

Local Woman Arrested for Murder

Friendsville, MD (AP) — Residents were stunned today when Margaret Raines was formally charged with murder in the beating death of Henry Fields, whose remains were discovered during the dredging of Fiddlers Pond in the search for Margaret's missing seven-year-old daughter Lindsay.

The indictment was handed down after authorities revealed her bloody fingerprints were found on the murder weapon wrapped in the same tarp that contained Field's remains. The Raines family lawyer has issued no statements at this time and attempts by the paper to contact them have been met with silence.

Susan stopped reading as a cold chill spread through her body.

What have I gotten myself into?

20

Dodging an old woman in a wheelchair, Susan made her way through the obstacle course of the nursing home's hallway. Nurses, visitors, and elderly people in wheelchairs were scattered along its length.

With a spring in her step she was feeling better than she had in months. The trip from Porter Mines was like a breath of fresh air. Coming down off the mountain, she mentally felt the distance between herself and all her problem lengthen. The further she got from home, the more her worry about vengeful witches, ghosts, and missing children drained away.

For the first time in a long time, it was like she could think clearly and reasonably about what was happening and realized it was nothing more than rumor and conjecture. Old wives' tales elevated to legend, stories to be shared around a campfire in an attempt to scare someone.

That someone was her, and she saw it clearly now that she was no longer right there.

Harriet Phillips was a bust. A full-blown case of Alzheimer's left her unaware of where she was, much less able to remember something that happened over thirty years ago. As Susan moved down the hall, a familiar name on the door for one of the rooms stopped her. Abigail Jenkins, the handwritten sign read, and she stepped to the closed door.

Is she Peter's sister? Only one way to find out.

After composing herself, she knocked before pushing into the room, and was immediately brought up short by the sight that greeted her. The room was bright, filled with assorted lamps strategically placed to prevent even the slightest shadow.

In the center of the room Abigail sat in her bed, watching television. Slowly she turned her head to look at Susan.

"Hi." Susan waved as she gently closed the door behind her.

"Who are you?" Abigail scowled. "What do you want?"

"I'm Susan. I recently bought your old house. Do you mind if I ask a couple of questions?"

"You can ask anything you want. Doesn't mean I've gotta answer."

"That's fine." Susan stepped around the end of Abigail's bed and sat in one of the two chairs against the wall. Again, she looked at all the lights, and held out her hand as if to ask, why?

"They hide in the dark," Abigail said, "in the shadows gathered in the corners."

Goose bumps washed across Susan's arms. "What hides in the dark?"

Abigail refused to answer, returning her attention to the television where a game show was on.

"What happened to your brother?"

Abigail's gaze remained fixed on the television.

"I know he shot himself."

Abigail's gaze wavered and she lowered her eyes. "How do you know that?"

"I read about it in an old newspaper."

A single tear traced a wet line down Abigail's cheek. "It wasn't his fault," she said.

"What wasn't his fault?"

"They wouldn't leave him alone."

"Who?"

Abigail looked away. "The children," she said. She spun her head back around and fixed Susan with a piercing stare. "She's real, you know."

"Who?"

"The Witch. My momma used to threaten us with her. Said if we didn't listen the Witch would come take us away."

"Was it the Witch that took your brother?"

Abigail shook her head, struggling, it seemed, with memories only she could recall. "Lindsay took Peter," she said with a sob.

Susan was confused by her response. In everything she'd read during her research, Lindsay was an innocent victim.

"Why?" It was the only response she could think of.

Abigail shook her head.

"She was your best friend."

"Who told you that?"

"Her aunt Mildred," Susan said. "She's my neighbor."

"You bought my house?"

Susan took a deep a breath. She was close to the truth, yet it lay just beyond her grasp. She nodded, trying to maintain her patience. "Yes, I bought your old house."

"Do you have any children?"

"My daughter, Christine." Susan took out a photo of Christine and showed it to Abigail, who nodded as if answering a question only she could hear.

"Get her away from there. Porter Mines is no place to raise a child. For her sake, and your own, as her mother, take her far away from there. She's grown restless, and none of them are safe."

"Who? The Witch?"

Abigail shook her head as she looked absently into her lap, "Lindsay," she said quietly.

"What happened to Lindsay, Abigail?"

"She died." Tears sparkled in Abigail eyes, "She said she had a secret. Don't you like secrets? Everyone likes secrets. But they're not really secrets, are they? Not after you share them. The only real secrets are those we keep to ourselves."

Susan leaned closer. "What's your secret?"

"I'm not telling." Abigail returned her attention to the television.

"Good morning, Abby." A nurse entered the room, stopping when she spotted Susan, who was rising from her seat.

"I'm sorry, I don't recognize you," the nurse said. "Are you a member of Abby's family?"

"I'm an old family friend."

"Really, and what's your name?"

"Susan."

The nurse's eyes narrowed. "I don't recall any Susan's on Abby's authorized visitors list."

"She wanted me to tell her my secret," Abigail said.

"You're going to have to leave," the nurse said. "Abigail is only allowed visits by those on her list. Are you a reporter?"

"No. Like I said, I'm a family friend."

"If that's true, then you need to have your name added to the list."

"I'm done anyway." Susan slipped past the nurse and turned down the hallway.

21

Instead of returning to the freeway, Susan followed Marion Street to its dead end at Oldtown Road. The narrow two-lane road meandered through a residential area. It was a homecoming of sorts, as she hadn't been this way since she moved out of her mother's place.

You'll never amount to anything. Her mother's words followed her out the door.

She was surprised to find Oscar's Restaurant still standing at the corner of Oldtown and Massachusetts Avenue. A little farther down the street was the convenience store where she used to buy an occasional soda on her way home from school. It was strange to see these familiar places with the eyes of a visitor.

The convenience store behind her, she passed through the flashing yellow light at Wempe Drive, and up a slight hill with Saint Mary's Catholic Church towering over her on the right. A silent reminder of her mother's obsession, and the pain it caused her as a child. While her friends attended Sunday services, her mother kept them home so she could read to them from the Bible. It was why she never connected with the church, and she resented her mother for taking away that part of her life.

Pennsylvania Avenue came up on the left, and before she realized what she was doing, she turned down the street. Here, memories assailed her as she drove past the familiar homes of childhood friends.

She'd visited many of these houses when she was young, hanging out with her friends as they shared the misery of homework and their dreams of the future. For most of them, herself included, it was a future that didn't reach far beyond becoming a mother and wife.

A couple of her friends had bigger dreams. Emily wanted to be an artist and had filled the walls of her room with her own drawings. The progression of her talent was clear to anyone willing to look. Progressing from simple crayon drawings to detailed pencil drawings that many found amazing.

"Whatever happened to Emily?"

She picked out the gabled end of the roof as it emerged from behind the edge of another, and though the exterior color was different from when she was a kid, this was the house she'd grown up in. She pulled to the curb in front and climbed out of her car.

The front door stood open. No curtains hung from the windows that gazed onto the street with an empty stare. The yard was a jungle of overgrown weeds, dwarfing a low chain link fence that was not there when she was a child. The whole neighborhood had the run-down look of a place that has forgotten what it's like to smile. A door slammed somewhere up the street, followed by a shout that was punctuated by a dog's bark. Other than those brief disturbances, the neighborhood lay as silent as any tomb in Rosehill Cemetery.

The house across the street was boarded up, but at the corner of one window the boards had been removed to permit access. The house to the left appeared to be as empty as the one she grew up in, while from the house on the right came the faint sound of music.

A car slowed as it neared, and when it passed, she saw it was full of children. A small blonde girl waved at her. Her face drawn into a mask of disappointment. As if she knew what Susan intended to do and disapproved of her plan.

Let sleeping dogs lie. She'd heard the expression somewhere but couldn't recall where. It was a fitting epitaph, a warning not to go forward, that it would be best to keep going without stopping.

She hadn't planned to go into the house, but as she watched the taillights of the car dwindle into the distance, she came to a decision and stepped around the front of her car.

The sidewalk was cracked from neglect so prevalent in this part of town. At one time the people cared about things of that nature, but that concern appeared to have dried up.

The gate squealed in protest when she swung it open, and she was overcome by the sensation of someone watching her. She turned in a full circle, checking the windows of the neighboring houses.

What would she say if anyone asked what she was doing? What would she tell the police if they came? This was where she grew up, and she was curious, was a weak argument for trespassing.

There are no signs, she reassured herself, seeking permission for what she was about to do.

Finding no one watching her, she turned back to the house and gazed at its shadowy façade. The sun had moved to the west, casting the front of the structure in shadows that deepened its menace.

Nothing good ever came from dwelling on the past. Linda, from *Love's Way*, was always saying that. Susan took the first of three steps to the porch. She almost turned around and left right then.

Curiosity might be a powerful motivator, but it was more than curiosity that compelled her to climb the remaining steps to the porch proper. Before she could stop herself, she crossed to the storm door sagging in its frame. Beyond the fly-specked glass, the front door stood open. It was anything but inviting. Within those shadowed rooms old memories lay in wait.

She knocked, hesitantly at first, the sound of her timid rapping rattling the door. After waiting an appropriate amount of time, she knocked again, louder this time, the sound of her persistence echoing through the empty structure.

"Nobody's lived there in years," a voice came from her right.

She turned towards it, startled to find an old man leaning against the wall of the house next door. He stood in the shadows of his front porch, and Susan wondered how long he'd been watching her.

"They come every so often to cut the grass, but not enough. usually only after it's gotten knee high."

"Have you lived in the neighborhood long?"

"All my life." He pushed himself away from the wall of his house. "Used to be a crazy lady that lived there," he said, nodding towards Susan. "Ran off her husband, drove her kids to kill themselves. They say the boy hung himself in the basement, the girl cut her wrists. You don't want to go in there alone, young lady, there's bad things in that house." He turned and shuffled across the porch towards his own front door. "They need to tear the place down and start over. It's the only way to make the dead move on." Then he vanished into the interior of his own house.

Susan tried to recall who lived next door when she was growing up, but her memory of the time was fuzzy, dominated by the terror she and her brother experienced at the hands of the woman who was supposed to love and nurture them.

She opened the storm door, the hinges grating with a dry sound. The inside door opened to the right, and its current position blocked her view of the staircase she knew was there. A condemnation notice was taped to the door. The letters washed out against a faded yellow background.

Pushing the door open the rest of the way, she revealed the stairs, and as she took a hesitant step into the house, she saw the door to the room under the steps stood open. Memories flooded her at the sight of it. Long hours spent kneeling in the dark as the secret sounds of the house settled around her.

Most of the time Robert was with her, and they would lean against one another, seeking and sharing the emotional support they needed to make it through another day.

Sadness welled up at the thought of her brother. He tried so hard to protect her from their mother, many times taking the brunt of her punishment upon himself, but who'd been there to protect him?

No one!

Sometimes their mother kept the closet door open to watch them, and they had to remain rigid and upright, hands clasped before them, every movement drawing another fifteen minutes added to their punishment. The grain of the hardwood floor had left its impression in the flesh of their knees.

Susan moved deeper into the house, and the sensation that she didn't belong washed over her. She had relinquished any rights to this place long ago. Floorboards squeaked beneath her feet as she took several steps, her eyes never leaving the gaping maw of the closet.

Deep shadows gathered there, pregnant with the despair that once filled the cramped space. There are those who believe a place will carry the emotional imprint of its past occupants. It's the reason many people believed old mental institutions were haunted, along with prisons and abandoned hospitals. From the closet came the terror she and Robert felt when confined within its dark heart.

From the back of the closet came a rustling, and Susan's hand went to her mouth as a whimper escaped her lips. She expected to see Robert emerge from the closet depths. Something moved in the shadows close to the floor, and she was about to turn and flee when a mouse appeared. It raced along the wall, vanishing into the kitchen, and she followed.

Discarded blankets lay along one wall of the kitchen. Empty beer cans and wine bottles were scattered across the floor along with other discarded objects. In the center was a blackened spot, the vinyl cracked and blistered. Someone had built a fire right on the floor. It was a wonder they hadn't burned the house down. The window above the sink was gone and a breeze blew into the house, disturbing the papers scattered across the floor.

She returned to the stairs, looking up at the second floor, undecided, not sure why she came in. She didn't know what she was searching for but felt compelled to climb the steps. Upstairs the hallway was gloomy, the doors to the rooms on either side open as soft bands of sunlight streamed into the hall.

At the end was the bathroom they had always fought over. The first door on her right led to Robert's room, and she peered inside. Faggott. The epithet was spray-painted in tall red letters on the wall above where his bed used to stand.

Anger blossomed in the pit of her stomach as she turned away from the slur. *Who gave these people the right to come in here?* The next room was her own, the walls covered in senseless scribbles of black spray paint.

She crossed to what was once her parents' bedroom. The room had an abandoned feel to it. While the walls had escaped the touch of vandals, they were devoid of love, hate, or any emotion at all. A blank canvas waiting to be filled.

She crossed to the closet door that stood open. Sunlight streaming through the window illuminated the narrow depths. Several empty coat hangers hung from a wooden rod. She was about to turn away when an object caught her eye. It was a folded newspaper sticking out past the shelf above the rod.

She pulled the paper down from the shelf and spread it open to read the headline.

Concern Grows Over Stock Market.

It was dated for October third, nineteen eighty-seven, and she shrugged. Flipping the paper over, she was scanning the page when she spotted a familiar name in the death notices.

Porter, Robert E.

Her breath caught in her lungs as she turned to page five-A. There it was, a photo of her dad, gazing into the camera with a smile that said he was ready for anything the world threw at him. The story attached was anything but happy. It was an obituary. She read it with disbelief, then read it again. They wondered what happened after he left, assuming he wanted nothing to do with them.

Now she knew, and the knowledge was like a physical blow that staggered her. All these years she'd felt a deep bitterness towards him, unaware that he'd died right after leaving them.

But how?

The obituary contained little more than a brief summary of his life, she and her brother received mentions as his children, their mother as his estranged wife. Following was a list of brothers and sisters, uncles and aunts, and his parents who had preceded him in death, and nothing more. Nothing to celebrate the short life he had led, nothing to set him apart from every other person who had died, to explain the hurt he'd known at the loss of his family. Nothing save that interment would be in the Holy Park Cemetery in Grantsville, her next stop.

22

Overwhelmed with sorrow, Susan ran from her parents' bedroom and fled down the steps, the newspaper clutched in one hand. Reaching the first floor, she heard voices on the porch. The screen door squealed as it was pulled open. There was no time to run back upstairs, nowhere else to hide, unless— Her gaze fell on the open closet door under the stairs.

It was far more cramped than it had been when she was a child. She managed to squeeze into the narrow space and sat on the floor with one hand holding the door closed, as rough voices came from the other side.

"I told you if you ratted us out, you'd pay," a young male said. There came a scuffle of feet, a muffled shout, and a window rattled in response to someone being thrown against the wall.

Susan tried to shrink into the back of the closet, praying to a god she no longer believed in that they didn't open the door. From outside came the smack of flesh against flesh, a whine of pain, followed by another strike.

"I didn't say nothing to nobody."

"You lying sack of shit, we saw you talking to five oh." Another hit punctuated by a cry.

"They was busting my ass over jaywalking."

"Yeah, and an hour later Sparky was hauled in."

"I didn't have anything to do with that."

A smack followed this. Another voice joined the first two, an older man by the sound of it, an adult. Susan almost called out then, believing the adult had come to save the one being beaten.

"Has he talked?" the adult asked.

"Not yet, but he will." The comment was followed by a flurry of punches and grunts.

"He ain't gonna talk that way. Here, let me show you how it's done," the adult said. "Is there anybody else in the house?"

"No."

"Did you check?"

"Didn't need to…"

The sound of a slap stopped the boy.

"What did I tell you?" The adult's voice was full of menace. "Didn't I always tell you to check, to never assume."

"Assuming makes an ass out of you and me," the boy responded with a sullen tone.

"Exactly. Now make sure the house is empty, and I'll show you how to make this bastard talk."

The adult's comment was followed by the sound of footsteps pounding up the stairs over her head. Susan ducked as she looked up. From her right came a soft sigh of movement, the shadows stirring as a chilled breath of air washed across her face. She almost cried out as icy fingers slipped into her hand, interlacing themselves about her own fingers that she closed into a loose fist.

The presence of the hand comforted her more that it frightened her, reminding her of the many times she and

Robert sought comfort from one another. *A little boy lost.* Sadness embraced her.

Heavy footsteps stomped down the steps over her head, shattering the moment, reminding Susan that she was a door's thickness away from being beaten or worse.

"Like I said, there's nobody up there."

His comment was followed by a slap.

"Whadidja do that for?"

"Don't back-talk me, boy."

There came a high-pitched cry of pain, followed by the sound of slapping. Susan squeezed her eyes shut and clamped her hands over her ears as the beating continued.

After about twenty minutes she lowered her hands and listened.

"Do you think he gave us everything?"

"Everything we wanted," the man said. Something clicked with a metallic sound, and the man spoke again. "I catch you talking to the police again, and I'm going to kill you. Do you understand?"

Silence answered him and Susan's thighs cramped from staying in one position for so long. A tingling pain passed through them as she struggled to remain silent and she rubbed her thighs with her hands, trying to get the circulation going again.

"Now let's get you cleaned up," the man said. "You should really be more careful around the steps in these old buildings." The man's words were marked by the screech of the storm door opening and closing as their footsteps faded into the distance.

There are bad things in that house, the old man repeated in her mind, and she had to agree.

Though her legs screamed with the need to move, she waited until she was sure they were gone She emerged from the closet under the stairs, struggling to stand as pins and needles danced across the flesh of her thighs. She straightened up and walked around in circles as the blood began to flow and she was able to walk without limping.

She reached the front door when a thunk came from the basement below. She stopped and glanced at the basement door. The thump came again, and the image of Robert's face swam into view.

The slack jaw, the protruding tongue, his open eyes bugging out as if they would explode.

With the image filling her mind she fled from the house, crossing the porch as the old man cackled on the porch next door. She raced down the walk to her car and slipped behind the wheel. She struggled briefly to get her key into the ignition. After several attempts the key slipped in and she twisted it. The car roared to life, and she slammed the shifter into drive, pulling onto the road with a bark of rubber on pavement.

She drove to the end of the street, fleeing the memories stirred up by her curiosity, trying to escape a past she could never outrun.

23

Susan parked along the narrow gravel lane, next to a plot of newly turned earth marking the point where the groundskeeper told her to stop. Her eyes were drawn to that fresh grave as a chill slithered through her. The polished marble headstone was yet to be finished.

The Porter family plot was located in the southwest corner and until this moment she had not made the connection between her maiden name, and the name of the town she settled in. It was not a conscious decision on her part to move to Porter Mines. Through her contacts in the real estate office where she worked, she learned of the availability of the Jenkins homestead by accident.

That connection with the oldest family in the area brought to mind a number of questions with no easy answers. If he had family here why did her dad move to Cumberland? Were they related to the Porters that first came to the area, and carved civilization from the wilderness as they sought to establish trade with the local tribes? What broke them apart? What caused the split? And of course, following on the heels of this was another that sent a chill down her spine.

Was the ghost of the Witch after them?

Nonsense. She pushed the notion away as she crossed the cemetery. She knew the moment she entered the corner dominated by the Porter family. Not only was the name displayed on the headstones gathered there, but the style of each gravestone spoke of old money. Marble angels adorned many of the markers in this section.

Near one edge of the cemetery stood a mausoleum with the Porter name carved above the doorway. On top of the pentagon-shaped marble structure, winged serpents sat at each point, their heads hanging between their wings as they watched the ground with granite gazes.

She went from one tombstone to the next, reading names that sparked old memories from her childhood.

Helen Ann Ressenger Porter. *Nana.* Robert used to call her Na Na. She was a big woman, jovial, always wrapping them in her loving warmth when they came for a visit. Which wasn't often enough. Her voice called out across the years, and Susan responded with tears.

What happened to tear them apart?

Near the edge closest to the forest, to the right of the mausoleum, she came upon a large slab of polished granite that dominated the head of a family plot. Smaller granite stones, each with a P carved into the top, marked the corners, establishing its boundary.

Robert Erwin Porter, the first name read, and beneath that was the date August 16, 1953. August 16 was her dad's birthday. She opened the paper she carried and read the obituary again. Robert E. Porter died September 23, 1987. The dates matched. This was her father's grave.

She saw his face, what she could recall of it, and her sadness deepened. He'd left when she was so young, and they never saw him again. At the time they didn't know he died in a car accident. But their mother knew, and it was information she chose to keep from them.

Charlene Marie Siemmer Porter was next to her father's name. Born December 12, 1956, died August 4, 2005. Her mother was dead, she wasn't even fifty when she passed, and Susan was disturbed by the notion that her father's family would lay his estranged wife to rest next to him.

A third name occupied the next space, and her breath caught in her throat as the memory of finding him in the basement surfaced.

Robert E. Porter, Jr. 1974 to 1987. He had been much too young to carry that weight.

The fourth spot was unmarked, an empty grave waiting its occupant, and with a shudder she realized it was reserved for her. After all, she was a Porter by birth, and deserved everything that legacy entailed.

Everything.

She turned and fled from the cemetery, nearly tripping as she wound her way through the tombstones. She slipped behind the wheel of her car as she struggled to reign in her fear.

Why? Why had she moved here? On the surface, the reason had been so innocent. To be closer to John's parents. Was there a darker reason for her return? Had the past reached out to draw her this way? Of all the places they could have moved to, she had chosen the one guaranteed to put her daughter in danger.

How much truth was in those old stories about a witch? After all, it was just an old wives' tale used to keep unruly children in check.

Or was it?

24

Careful, so as not to burn herself, Twila placed the buttered side of the bread into the hot pan. Next to it she placed another. Onto these she laid the last two slices of cheese in the fridge, covered them with another slice of bread, the buttered side up.

The milk was starting to turn, but she poured herself a glass anyway. It didn't taste that great, but it was better than the alternative, asking her mother to pick up a fresh carton.

The social worker from the county, who was working to help Bethany through her sorrow, left an hour earlier. After the woman was gone Bethany retrieved a bottle of whisky from the cupboard, seeking her own solace, and was well on her way to reaching oblivion.

The drinking brought out the mean side in her mother. A sharp tongue backed up with a hand ready to strike at a moment's notice if she wasn't afforded the respect she felt she deserved.

"Why does this stuff always happen to me? I could have been an actress, living the good life, but no I had to have kids." Bethany said, the half-empty whiskey bottle on the table before her. Her hair hung around her face in sweaty strands, her eyes red and puffy from crying the last few days. She wore an oversized tee-shirt with dried food staining the front, and a pair of sweats a size too small.

As Twila watched the grilled cheese sandwiches fry, her thoughts turned to Bobby, and a tremendous sadness welled up within her. She struggled against the tears that threatened to flow. She glanced at her mom who reached for the bottle and poured another shot that she downed in one gulp. Bethany herself launched from her chair with lightning speed.

"You think I'm responsible, don't you?" Bethany staggered around the table towards Twila, who shrank from her approach.

"I'm sorry, Mommy." Twila kept her eyes down as she tried to vanish into the corner where the stove and wall met.

"You're like all the rest, looking down on me because I don't have a regular job, because I drink and smoke."

Twila remained silent, watching her feet as the grilled cheese sandwiches continued to cook.

Bethany glanced from Twila to the stove and back again, her hand starting towards the skillet, stopping halfway as Twila steeled herself for what was coming.

"Always thinking you're better than me, you and all your little friends. Laughing behind my back while I work my fingers to the bone to give you and Bobby a nice home." Bobby's name elicited a primal scream that came from somewhere deep in her mother's soul.

It was the same old song and dance, the imagined slights her mother endured at the hands of Twila's friends. The sad part was Twila was as much an outcast as her mother. She had no real friends at school or the trailer court where they lived. In fact, she was the butt of everyone's jokes.

The grilled cheese sandwiches were about to burn, Twila could smell it, but she knew better than to make a move to flip them. Movement was tantamount to talking back and doing so guaranteed a physical response. It was safer to lower her eyes and endure the verbal abuse her mother meted out.

It was a lesson Twila learned early in life. You did not argue with Mother, not if you wanted to be able to sit in the immediate future. As her mother's drinking grew worse, so too did the punishments. Spanking graduated to slapping, and that had evolved into punching and kicking.

Bethany stood over her, her hands opening and closing as Twila prepared herself for the coming onslaught. But it didn't come.

Bethany turned and settled into her seat before pouring herself another shot. "You better flip them."

Twila looked up, blinking in surprise. *Is this mom?* she wondered as she flipped the sandwiches. They were a dark brown, but not burned. Had she waited another half minute, they would have started smoking, and that would have fueled her mother's rage.

With the sandwiches done, Twila placed them on two plates and set one on the table before her mother.

"Thank you, sweetie," Bethany said.

Twila returned to her own seat. She was confused. Her mother had never thanked her before, and she wasn't sure how to respond. Twila drank her near-sour milk, her stomach churning in response as it mingled with the almost burned grilled cheese sandwich. Later, after her mother passed out, she would have to dump out what remained, letting her mother believe Twila drank it all.

They ate in a silence interrupted only when Bethany told Twila how good her sandwich was. Twila was so surprised by her mother's comment she failed to respond and missed the one clue that could have saved her.

The look in her mother's eyes.

It was almost as if they were a real family sitting down to dinner as the day gave way to night. She was lost in the fantasy of having a normal family when reality intruded and her mother slapped her across the face. Stars exploded behind her eyes as Twila tumbled from her seat and curled into a ball on the floor.

Bethany knelt beside her as she cradled her head in her hands.

"When someone compliments you, it is customary to thank them!"

Twila was stunned by the sudden turn of events. "I'm sorry, Mommy."

"Too late now." Bethany retreated to the living room, the half-empty bottle in one hand. "Now clean up your mess and go to bed."

Twila lay for a moment as the ringing in her ear subsided. She pushed herself to her feet and gathered up what remained of her sandwich.

25

Puddles sat across from Christine at her Little Princess table, his chin resting on its surface, watching her with a one-eyed stare.

The tip of Christine's tongue poked from the corner of her mouth, and her forehead scrunched as she struggled to make sense of the numbers on the page.

Why is it so hard?

She missed the easy work she had the year before. Looking up into Puddles's silent gaze, she recalled the day her father won him. It was an old memory for a child so young, and she gave herself over to its comforting embrace.

The smell of funnel cakes, cotton candy, and candy apples swirled around her in a mouth-watering cloud as she and her father walked hand-in-hand through the busy midway. His hand swallowed her smaller one, holding it comfortably as they strolled through the midway, reassuring her that as long as he held her hand, nothing bad could happen to her.

To their right, carnies called out for the gullible to try games of chance that required more luck than skill. From the left came the screams of riders on the amusement park rides, controlled by short men in grease-stained tee-shirts who chain-smoked non-filtered cigarettes as they took money from riders who were searching for a thrill.

From time to time Christine glanced up to reassure herself that her father was still there. His shadowy form towered over her with a clear blue sky stretched out above his head.

One booth in particular stood out as they moved through the crowds of people. Hanging from one of the uprights of the Milk Bottle booth, was a stuffed bunny nearly as long as she was tall. It was one of the prizes for anyone strong enough to knock all three milk bottles to the floor.

Three throws for a buck, the sign proclaimed. She was confident her Daddy was strong enough to knock over a few paltry milk bottles.

"Now there comes a strong lad with his young lass. What say, ya young man. Three throws for a buck. Knock em all clear off the table and take your pick of a dandy prize for the young lady."

She looked up as the carnie's words flowed over tobacco-stained teeth. His skin was the color of tanned leather, a smoldering cigarette squeezed between two stubby fingers missing above the first knuckle.

Her father held up his hand and shook his head. "Not today, old timer."

"Before you leave her, give her something to remember you by."

Her father had been about the turn away, but the man's words stopped him.

"How do you know I'm leaving?"

The carnie shrugged. "You work this as much as I have, you learn to see things. Twenty-Nine Palms is down the road a piece, and judging by your haircut, I'd say that's home for you. I know a unit is shipping out in the next day or so, and I put two and two together."

"Can't afford to throw my money away on some game."

"Daddy, please." She squeezed his hand as she gazed up at him with imploring eyes. There was nothing special about the bunny, but Christine was overwhelmed by a sudden need to own the brightly colored creature.

"Tell ya what, seeing as you're soon to ship out, I'll cut you a break, half off. That's fifty cents for three chances to knock over the bottles."

"I don't know. I've heard these games are rigged."

"I know many of my brothers and sisters who run these booths tend to pad the game in their favor. But you have my word I'd never do that. It's a game of skill."

"Daddy, please, I want him." She pointed at the sappy-faced grin of a blue and white bunny.

"But honey." He knelt to look her in the eye. "You remember what Mommy said. We'll have to watch our money while I'm gone."

"I don't want you to go."

"Now we talked about this. You know it's what Daddy does. I have to help them people."

"It isn't fair. Why can't someone else help…"

Her father placed his finger on her lips.

"Give her something to remember you by," the carnie said, and her father nodded as he stood, and turned to the booth.

"It would be cheaper to buy her a stuffed bunny from Walmart," her father said.

"It wouldn't work," the fellow said with a wink that spoke volumes. "It has to be earned."

It had to be earned. Nothing was ever free in this world. There was a give and a take for every transaction, payments made in forms beyond regular currency, deposits credited to accounts that existed far from the established order of the local bank.

For his part, her father put forth a valiant effort, drawing back and firing the ball at the three steel milk bottles stacked atop a narrow table. His first throw bounced off the table, causing the bottles to teeter briefly before they settled back into place. His second throw knocked the first bottle clear off the table, leaving the other two standing. His third throw knocked over both bottles, sending them rolling to the edge of the table. One fell off while the other teetered on the edge for a moment before coming to rest.

"You still have another round coming from the buck you gave me." The carnie slid three more balls across the counter.

Her father nodded as he took the first of the three balls, his face set in a mask of determination as he wound up for his next throw. Again, after three throws one bottle remained. Without hesitation he dug into his pocket and pulled out another crumpled bill that he passed to the man, who nodded with a knowing smile.

Two more rounds down, another buck gone, vanished into the grimy apron around the carnie's waist as he lit a new cigarette off the old one.

Her father was possessed by a determination to defeat the game and leave something of himself, something he had earned, for his daughter to always remember him by.

With another buck down he pulled his wallet from his back pocket and dug into the compartments. Hidden behind his military ID was a ten spot he'd been holding onto. This he passed to the carnie, holding up his hand when the carnie attempted to make change. He was gonna win it. Come hell or high water, he would emerge victorious.

The day passed in a blur as her father wound up for the pitch and fired the ball at the three milk cartons now teasing him with their refusal to fall off the table. He grunted as he threw the ball faster and faster. Sweat stained the armpits of his shirt and beaded along his brow as he focused all of his energy on one target.

He'd reached the end of his money. A small crowd had gathered, drawn by his determination, clapping when he knocked over the bottle, sighing in disappointment when he missed. On the first of his last three throws, the ball hit the table in front of the bottles, bouncing up into them, hitting them square in the middle where all three touched. The top bottle was thrown to the side as the bottom two were flung back, one bottle remained, spinning from the force of the blow as it crept closer to the edge of the table. It teetered for a moment as the crowd drew an expectant breath, and then it too dropped over the edge.

Payment had been made.

The Carnie knelt beside Christine. "Which one would you like, sweetie?"

She pointed at the blue-and-white one and watched as the Carnie removed him from the upright, their eyes locking as he passed the plush animal to her. "As long as you have this bunny by your side, your daddy will always be with you, no matter what. He earned that right today," the man said, and she sensed the truth behind his eyes.

She took the bunny into her arms, squeezing it close, and knew that she would name him Puddles. The why didn't matter. The name fit, and that was reason enough.

While lost in that happy memory the room around her had become chilled. Her breath hanging in small clouds in the air before her as she shivered.

"I have a secret," a child whispered behind her.

Christine spun around. "Lizzy?" Her gaze tracked across the room as she searched for her new friend.

"I know where your daddy is," Lizzy said.

It sounded like it came from the closet, and Christine's gaze settled on the closed door. She whimpered deep in her throat, where fear lived.

"I can show you," Lizzy said, drawing Christine to her feet.

Christine placed one foot in front of the other as she approached the closet door and reached for the knob glowing in the late-afternoon sun. Her fingers closed around the cool metal, tightened as she turned the knob. A grating sound came from the bolt. Then the door popped open, Christine stumbled back, expecting the witch from her dream to emerge from the dark depths of the closet.

Nothing.

Turning back to her Little Princess table, Christine passed the window and caught a glimpse of something outside. She turned and looked out at the dense forest behind the house. Lizzy stood next to an old oak tree, watching her.

Christine waved.

Lizzy waved back.

"I know where your daddy is," Lizzy said, then turned and vanished into the trees, motioning for Christine to follow.

26

Reaching the staircase, Christine took the steps one at a time, her head on a swivel as she maneuvered down the stairs. At the hall on the first floor, she stopped as voices came from the basement. Peeking around the corner, she saw her mom and Eric talking at the basement door.

She tiptoed across the opening, watching Eric for any sign that he was about to look up. If they asked, she would tell them she was sneaking down for another cookie, she decided, as she reached the other side of the open doorway.

At the front door, she slipped on her jacket and opened the door before stepping into the late afternoon sunlight. Evening was fast approaching, the air growing chilly as a purple band of night spread across the horizon to the east. She raced around the corner of the house into the backyard and came to a stop. Lizzy stood inside the tree line.

"I know where your Daddy is," Lizzy repeated in Christine's mind, motioning for her to follow as she turned and vanished into the forest.

"Wait for me." Christine raced across recently cut grass to the dense brush separating the woods from her backyard. Pushing through the holly, she scanned the forest for any sign of Lizzy. Tree trunks marched away in ordered rows that vanished into a growing gloom.

Lizzy emerged from behind a tree less than thirty yards away, and for the first time Christine got a good look at her. She was tall and thin, with long black hair that framed a slender, expressionless face. She wore a white dress that seemed so out of place.

Old was the word that came to mind.

Lizzy exuded an ethereal quality that awakened a primitive fear in the pit of Christine's stomach. She recalled how the girl at her window had changed into that terrifying creature the other night and was about to turn around when Lizzy stopped her with a question.

"Do you want to see your Daddy?"

She turned back to face Lizzy, her grip tightening on Puddles as she nodded. She knew her father was in heaven, but she'd never figured out where heaven was.

There was some who said heaven lived in your heart. A few of her friends suggested that heaven could be reached with a bus ticket. Without the teachings of the church to guide her, she could only assume that heaven lay right around the next bend. Maybe it was on the other side of the forest or even at the pond her friends always talked about.

Lizzy turned and walked deeper into the forest, and Christine followed.

Around her the shadows deepened as the ground became rocky beneath a thick layer of foliage. Small piles of tumbled stone stood around her, each with a dark opening that led to secret places beneath the earth.

She became aware of the silence. No birds twittered from the branches of the trees forming a latticework of interlaced fingers above her. Nothing moved through the thick layer of leaves blanketing the forest floor. Not even a breeze disturbed the preternatural calm that held the woods in its grasp. She was terrified, yet at the same time drawn by the promise of seeing her Daddy again.

"Lizzy?" The stillness consumed her voice.

Something slapped against her leg, and she jumped. Spinning around to see what touched her. Puddles slipped from her arms and a hand grabbed his dangling leg, pulling him toward the ground.

She screamed, an unintelligible cry of terror and anger. Holding onto Puddles's leg was a hand at the end of a slender arm protruding from one of those shadowy openings.

"He's down here, waiting to see you." Lizzy's voice came from the opening, and Christine leaned over to see Lizzy's face framed by the black depths of emptiness around her.

"Your Daddy's waiting for you." Lizzy pulled at Puddles's leg. Stitches tore as the fabric was stretched to its limit.

"Let go." Christine pulled back, leaning into the task, bringing all of her weight to bear on the weakened joint.

"Give him to me and I'll let you see your Daddy."

"You're lying, my Daddy's in heaven."

"He's down here waiting for you." Lizzy's features shifted, her flesh roiling across the bones of her face like the surface of water at full boil. Her father's voice came from Lizzy's mouth.

"Give them Puddles."

"No." She sensed the lie. He couldn't be down there, in the dark place. He was in heaven. The dark place was for bad little boys and girls who didn't listen.

Like she refused to listen when she snuck out of the house.

"Give him to me." Lizzy's voice was deeper, grating, with a rumble like two ancient boulders rubbing against one another in the depths of the earth.

More stitches popped, and Christine realized Puddle's leg was about to be torn off. She couldn't let that happen to him. *What good is a bunny missing a leg?*

She was faced with a choice most adults would fall into a quivering heap over. Let go and preserve Puddles in his entirety, or let Lizzy tear his leg off.

She looked into his sappy grin and realized she couldn't hurt him any more than he'd already been. She loosened her grip as a tremendous sadness overwhelmed her. She dropped to her knees at the opening as Puddles vanished into those shadowy depths.

"Please give him back?" She cried.

Silence answered her.

27

After learning it would be a few more weeks before the basement was ready, Susan returned to the pile of dishes in the kitchen. She didn't tell Eric about her trip to Cumberland, or what she found at the cemetery. Time and distance had taken the edge off her fear, and she was confident she had nothing to worry about. One thing she did know for sure, it was time to roll up her sleeves and get serious about finishing the work that needed done.

Empty boxes stood stacked against the wall. Their contents crowded on the counter beside the sink. Her plan was to wash everything before putting it away. Most of it had been in storage since she left the west coast. Some things had been tucked away since her wedding and opening them was like tearing the scab off the healing wound of her sorrow.

The front door closed.

"Eric," she said, thinking he'd stepped out to his truck. Turning away from the sink, she caught sight of the paper on the table.

Still No Leads in Child Abduction!

She sat down and read the story next to the photo of a small boy. No more than a rehash of the earlier story about his abduction. A straight up piece of reporting that awakened more questions than it answered. Unlike the previous story, neither the curse nor speculation about the motive for the boy's disappearance, was explored. Nor did they call into question the Sheriff's ability to do his job, though the headline would lead a reader to expect it.

Susan's mind was in a turmoil as she read. She wanted a safe place to raise Christine, a quiet place that moved at a more leisurely pace. Where crime was no more dangerous than a news story from the larger metropolitan areas. It was too late to change now. Everything she had was invested in this house. She had no choice but to stay and face whatever might come their way.

From outside came a faint shout, and Susan crossed to the window to catch a glimpse of Christine vanishing into the woods. That was why she heard the front door close.

"I told her to stay inside." She turned and vanished down the hallway, stopping at the top of the steps leading to the basement.

"Eric, could you help me?"

"Sure, what's wrong?"

"It's Christine, I told her to stay inside, but I saw her going into the woods behind the house. You know your way around better than I do. Would you help me find her?"

"We better get going. Don't want her to reach Fiddlers Pond."

"What's Fiddlers Pond?"

"You don't know about the pond?"

"I remember somebody mentioning a pond when I bought the place, but I didn't pay much attention to what they said."

"It's not really on your property, but there's a small pond on the other side of the woods behind the house."

"Is there a fence around it?"

"Used to be, but the kids in the area kept tearing it down. The pond was a popular swimming hole until Frank's girlfriend drowned during a party."

"Oh my."

"I'm sorry. She should be okay. The pond's a good ways off, and it's hard to get to."

"We need to go, then."

Eric climbed the stairs and followed her down the hall.

***

"Christine," Susan shouted and then stopped to listen to the forest. Growing among the trees that towered above her was a thick jungle of holly that kept her from following a straight path. As she struggled through the dense growth, she regretted her decision to wear a jacket. Though it had been cool when she started, she found herself sweating as she worked her way through the thick growth.

"We're almost to the other side."

"The other side of what?"

"The holly. Once we get through, it'll clear up and we'll be able to make good time."

"I hope so." The idea of Christine falling into Fiddlers Pond urged her onward. Pushing aside a branch, she saw what Eric meant. On the other side of the band of holly was the forest proper. Here the straight trunks of the trees marched away into the distance in rows that looked as if they had been planted by someone.

"This is all second growth." Eric answered Susan's unvoiced suspicions. "There used to be a sawmill near the pond. When it was in full operation everything around it had been stripped bare to provide for the mill."

"Who planted the trees?"

"The government came in over fifty years ago and reclaimed the land." Eric looked around. "I haven't been up here in ages. I didn't know it looked this good."

Susan tilted her head back and cupped her hands around her mouth and shouted. "Christine!"

The silence of the forest answered her.

She started in one direction and Eric stopped her. He pointed at the shallow dip in the ground ahead of her.

"Go around," he said.

"What is it?"

"Mine sink. This whole area is honeycombed with natural caves, tunnels, and abandoned mines. Some are miles long while others are only a few feet. If you're not careful, you could fall into one."

"What is this place? I was looking for a safe place to raise Christine and get on with my life. We've got the ghost of a witch, a dangerous pond, and now mine sinks. What's next?"

All Eric could do was shrug before turning and walking deeper into the forest.

With every step, her sense of urgency grew as she imagined Christine alone in the pond. Christine didn't know how to swim, and Susan's imagination ran away from her, picturing her little girl panicking as she fell into the water. The image, coupled with her worry, awakened an old memory from her own childhood, one she'd forgotten, from a time when she nearly drowned. The suffocating sense of drowning left her gasping for breath and she leaned against a tree.

"Are you all right?" Eric asked.

As the memory faded, Susan became aware of everything around her. The coarse bark of the tree limb she'd grabbed to keep from falling over. The air about her was full of the odor of past decay from the layers of dead leaves covering the forest floor. But for the briefest of moments it carried the sweet taste she'd remembered when she was a child breaking the surface of the pond after almost drowning.

It reminded her that no matter how bad it got, she was still alive. All of the sorrow and fear and worry had drained away in an instant, and for the first time in a long while, she felt what it must be like to be alive. The sensation was overwhelmed by the mountain of worry that had become her life, and she regretted that she wasn't able to continue feeling that way.

"I'm okay," she replied.

"Are you sure? You look like you've seen a ghost."

Susan attempted to smile. "I'll be all right."

Eric studied her for a moment before turning his attention back to the forest.

"Where's Christine?"

"There she is." Eric pointed at Christine who stood among the trees, gazing at her feet.

"Christine!" Susan shouted.

Christine looked up in her direction. "Mommy?"

Christine remained rooted in place as they approached. She looked from her mother back to the narrow opening at her feet.

"What is wrong with you, young lady?" Susan's voice was harsh with barely restrained panic. "Didn't I tell you to stay inside?"

Christine looked up with a terrified expression, and Susan gathered her up in her arms.

She hugged Christine tight. "I'm sorry, but you scared Mommy." From the corner of her eye she spotted the black opening of a narrow cave and shuddered, overcome by the sensation that someone, or something, was watching them from those dark depths.

"Are you all right?" Susan said.

Christine sobbed as her tears flowed. "I lost Puddles."

"Where is he?"

She pointed at the narrow opening and Susan approached it. "I don't see him."

"He's down there, all alone. We have to get him out!"

Eric glanced into the black depths. "There's no room for anyone to go down. I'm afraid we won't be able to get him out."

"No, we can't leave him. He'll be all alone!"

"It's okay, sweetie, he's just an old stuffed bunny. We can get you another one."

"No," Christine wailed, and a blue jay took flight with a raucous cry.

Susan tried to comfort her. "We can't reach him."

"Eric can dig him out." She looked at Eric with a hopeful expression. "He has a bulldozer."

"I wouldn't be able to get back here with it."

"Mommy, please, we can't leave him."

"I'm sorry. I don't know what else we can do."

Christine dropped her head as tears fell from her eyes and her shoulders shook with deep, shuddering sobs. Susan glanced at Eric, who squatted to peer into the shadowy recess. He pointed the flashlight he carried into the small hole.

"There he is." He dropped to his stomach and reached into the hole.

"I'll have to come back with something to reach him. I've got some rope in my truck, maybe I can fashion a loop to snag him."

"Can you?" Christine looked up with renewed hope.

"I can try." Eric brushed away the tears on her cheeks.

"We better get back," Susan said, glancing at the darkening sky as the realization she didn't want to be in the forest at night filled her with a desire to flee. She became aware of the ordered rows of rocky mounds that marched away from her in every direction. Like the headstones in the cemetery she recently visited.

Eric returned to the forest with a broom handle. At the end he'd attached a length of rope that formed a loose hoop. Using his flashlight, he knelt down, and spotted Puddles sitting at the bottom of the narrow opening. While it might have been nothing more than a stuffed animal to him and Susan, he understood that to Christine, Puddles was a reminder of her dad. Susan told him the story about how John won Puddles for Christine before he shipped out to Iraq, and the knowledge strengthened his resolve to recover the stuffed bunny.

As he worked, he became aware of the unnatural stillness of the forest around him. Stopping several times to look around, he felt like someone, or something, was watching him. The sun had already gone down, and the shadows had grown deeper, filled with menace. He tried to ignore the sensation and concentrate on what he was doing, but the unnatural stillness was getting under his skin.

There should have been birds singing in the trees. Small animals moving through the blanket of leaves covering the forest floor. The rustle of leaves, the soft creaking of tree limbs stirred by a breeze. Nothing disturbed the steady stillness that awakened a primitive fear in his soul.

He had intruded upon a place he did not belong.

From behind him came a soft sighing sound and he spun around to look into the forest depths. Nothing moved, not even an errant breeze. It was then, as he returned his attention to the task at hand, that he became aware of the other outcroppings of stone around him.

One was six feet to his right, another the same distance to his left. Beyond them the mounds created curving lines. Aware of their presence, he picked them out all over the place. To his front and rear. Left and right. The stones formed small piles that marched away into the forest all around him. Lined up in ordered rows, like the tombstones in a graveyard. He shuddered at the comparison. They looked like ancient burial mounds whose occupants had escaped, leaving a jumbled pile of stones in their wake.

He pushed that last away and returned his attention to the task at hand. Kneeling, he gazed into the shadowy depths, the flashlight beam illuminating the well-worn rabbit gazing up him with its one eye. He guided the hoop down the hole and was pleased to see it come to rest atop the stuffed animal's body. Pulling the free end of the rope, he closed the loop around Puddles and pulled him toward the surface.

A low growl came from the depths of the hole. The rope went tight in Eric's hand as the broom handle snapped in half. He tightened his grip as the rope became taut and leaned back to keep control. The rope slid through his hand, burning the flesh of his palm.

He dropped the rope with a frustrated shout. Before the last of it vanished, he grabbed the end and wrapped it around his hand. The rope was pulled tight, his arm yanked straight out ahead of him, and he was dragged off his knees.

The air was driven from his lungs as he slammed into the ground, and he struggled to catch his breath while he fought to maintain his grip on the rope. Panic washed through him as his hand vanished into the opening and he wedged his free hand against the outcropping to stop himself.

From the black depths came a menacing growl before the rope went slack. He lay gasping like a fish out of water as fear squeezed his throat. Getting himself under control, he pushed himself to his knees, brushed off his shirt, and peered into the opening.

One two, the Witch is due. The old nursery rhyme echoed in his mind, adapted by the children of Porter Mines to reflect the threat all of them lived under.

Three four, she's at the door. A nursery rhyme created by the grandparents of his grandparents who as small children faced the same threat that every child living in Porter Mines faced.

Five six, who will she pick. A secret code shared on schoolyards to warn the uninitiated of their impending doom.

Seven eight, at night she waits. A nursery rhyme every parent knew and understood.

Nine ten, don't let her in. About an old wives' tale that was more fact than fiction.

Eric looked around the forest. Birds twittered in the trees around him. Leaves rustled as a squirrel darted about on his left. Whatever had passed this way was now gone. He glanced into the hole, and in the shadowy depths he detected movement. A darker shape that detached itself from the deeper shadows, and he backed away, afraid of what might emerge.

From the deepening gloom of the forest came a shriek that sent ice water through his veins. Turning, he hurried away from the opening, not wanting to admit how he felt, his stomach cramped with unease. He was sorry he hadn't been able to retrieve Puddles and would try to make it up to Christine.

Another shriek echoed from the shadows, adding urgency to his step. He shuddered at the memory of reaching into the opening to retrieve the bunny. What would they have done if something grabbed him and pulled him into those shadowy depths?

What would he have done?

29

Susan finished the dishes while Christine sat at the table eating a peanut butter and jelly sandwich. From time to time Susan glanced at her, noting the worry that knitted her brow. She wore the strained expression of someone under a tremendous amount of pressure.

"Everything will be all right." Susan tried to reassure herself as much as her daughter.

Christine nodded without looking up, focused on her food.

The front door opened, and Christine was off her seat and halfway across the kitchen before Susan could follow.

"Did you get him?" Christine asked, and Susan knew it was Eric.

"He couldn't get Puddles," Christine moaned. "He's down there all by himself."

"He'll be okay. Remember what you said. He's got Daddy's heart, and Daddy was strong."

"I know but..." Christine turned and vanished down the short hall. After she was gone, Susan turned to Eric.

Eric shrugged. "I'm sorry. I tried everything I could think of."

"I know." Susan glanced down the hallway. "I'll be back."

Susan found Christine sitting at her Little Princess table. Two other stuffed animals occupied the chairs in the set, the one across from Christine vacant. A place reserved for Puddles.

Christine looked up as Susan knelt next to her.

"I'm so sorry, sweetie. I don't know what I can do to make it better for you."

"She took him."

"Who took him?"

"Lizzy. She's not my best friend anymore. She said she knew where daddy was a secret, then she took Puddles."

"But you dropped Puddles in the hole." Susan was bewildered by the turn their conversation had taken.

Christine shook her head. "Lizzy took her."

"Where is Lizzy?" Susan didn't want an answer, afraid of what it might be.

"She lives in the woods, in the dark place, and she took Puddles with her."

Goosebumps danced across Susan's arms, and she peered out the window. The forest stood silent and gloomy as the evening gave way to night. A forbidding place full of mystery. "We can get you another rabbit like Puddles."

"No, you can't. Daddy gave me Puddles, and he had to earn him. The man at the carnival said so."

She recalled the argument they had over John spending nearly fifteen dollars to win the rabbit. How that night they went to bed angry at one another, and she woke up the next morning while it was still dark to find John's side of the bed empty and cold. She found him in Christine's room, watching over his daughter as she slept, her arms wrapped around Puddles.

In three days, he would leave for Iraq, and it was like he was trying to cram every good memory he could into his head before he left. With a twinge of guilt, she realized she denied him a degree of happiness with her worries over money. They would survive as they always had, and not only had John been given good memories to carry him through the task that lay ahead, in return he provided something concrete for Christine to hold onto after he left. He'd given her a reminder of his love that transcended words.

Susan struggled to control her emotions. "I'm so sorry."

Christine wrapped her arms around Susan's neck and held her tight, burying her face in Susan's shoulder.

"I miss Daddy," she said.

"So do I."

30

While his mother hung clothes, Nathan sat in the sand box playing with his tractor. Using the scoop, he'd build a pile of sand and then crash through it with the red tractor. He liked the red tractor. His father got it for him during their last trip to town, and he loved it so much he took it to bed with him, though his mother complained about the sand in his sheets.

She hummed as she worked, and Nathan looked up at her. A tall silhouette against the clear blue sky. It was chilly and a steady breeze ruffled the clothes hanging on the line.

"Mommy has to get some more clothes, Nathan. Don't go anywhere. I'll be right back." Jessica vanished inside.

He ignored what she said, his attention focused on building another pile as he added sound effects to the tractor's movement.

The sky darkened as black clouds raced across the face of the sun, driven by an ever-present breeze that stirred the branches of the trees around him.

I have a secret, a young girl whispered in his mind, and he looked up. Movement in the gloomy depths of the forest bordering the back yard drew his eye as something white glided between the trees. She stood in the tree line where the yard stopped, and the wilderness began. A young girl with long black hair watching him with a haunted expression.

I have a secret, that inner voice repeated while the girl beckoned for him to follow.

Getting to his feet, he brushed himself off, and with the red tractor held close to his chest, followed her into the forest.

Among the trees, thick shadows filled with unseen things watched him from the emptiness. He was reminded of the monsters hiding under the bed, and those in the closet. They only came out at night and though he had never seen them, he knew they existed as only a child could. A knowledge that lived on a deep, primal level, where our fears hid from the light of day.

He walked deeper into the forest, drawn by the promise of a secret revealed, the tractor against his chest. His thumb strayed to his mouth as he followed the faint white smudge into the crowding gloom.

They came to Fiddlers Pond and Nathan stopped, afraid. The black waters below lapped gently against the sheer stone wall, disturbed by an unknown thing that recently passed. Along the rocky shore, on the opposite side, he spotted the young girl as she motioned for him to follow.

He should not have followed her. He should have stayed right where his mother left him, playing with his favorite tractor, where it was safe, and his mother was nearby. Tears rolled down his cheeks as he carefully picked his way through the underbrush along the edge of the pond.

He looked down at the red tractor, remembering how his father held him as he picked the one he wanted from the store display. He felt safe in his father's arms. Secure in the knowledge that nothing could hurt him. He wished his father were with him now, but he was away working and wouldn't be back for several days.

Mustering his courage, he skirted the edge of the pond. Several times he looked back the way he'd come, confused by the unfamiliarity of the forest around him. He was lost and knew the only way out was to follow the young girl wherever she led. After all, she had a secret to share, and as Nathan had learned, it was best to keep some secrets to yourself.

Reaching the rocky shore, he picked his way along the water until he was close to the girl. She smiled, and he took a small measure of comfort from her friendly expression.

Without a word, she turned and ducked into a small tunnel. Nathan stood for a moment alone, undecided. He looked into the tunnel depths where the young girl waited in the deeper shadows. She beckoned for him to follow, and he crouched as he entered the tunnel.

Solitude wrapped the pond in its embrace. From the black depths of the tunnel came a gentle sobbing that faded to nothing as silence reasserted its hold.

***

Jessica dropped the basket of wet clothes when she realized Nathan was not where she left him.

"Nathan," she shouted as she scanned the backyard. A giggle came from the playhouse and she darted across the yard to fling open the door.

Empty.

"Nathan, where are you?" He'd never run off before, and Jessica was filled with a cold dread as she raced back and forth, checking every conceivable hiding place, and even a few he could never manage to get into.

Coming up empty, she stopped. Her gaze was drawn to the forest bordering the backyard. She had asked her husband several times to put up a fence, but he always refused, claiming the expense was unwarranted.

It was warranted now, dammit. But now might be too late. Turning, she ran into the house to call the police.

31

They've always said when it rains, it pours. After a few hours of fitful sleep, feeling as grumpy as an old bear, Paul arrived at his office. He was not surprised to find Frederick Summers, the reporter for the Garrett *Tribune*, waiting for him. The squad room was a muted bustle of activity as the search for Bobby continued.

Doug's dogs turned up nothing, the trail going cold less than a hundred yards from the trailer. Speculation was growing among the searchers that Bobby's mother was responsible for what happened to the boy, or one of her male visitors had done something to him. Either way, they felt she was aware of what happened.

Paul wasn't going to move the investigation in that direction, not yet, not until they finished their background checks on Bethany and her latest boyfriend. He always moved quietly in matters like that, he didn't want to tip his hand too soon.

After three days with no results the search was now focused on a body, instead of a child. From experience they knew the first twenty-four hours were crucial, and in most cases once the search extended beyond that time frame, the child's chances of survival dwindled with the passing of each hour. The twenty-four-hour deadline was now forty-eight hours in the past.

When Frederick spotted Paul, he made a beeline for him, his smug expression all Paul needed to know this would not be a friendly visit. Of course, with Frederick it rarely was.

"Sheriff, if I could have a moment of your time. What steps have you taken to secure the return of the missing child?"

"The child's name is Bobby, if you care." The sour ball that had taken up residence in the pit of Paul's stomach blossomed. "The state police have been notified, an Amber alert with the child's description has been issued, and I've got a team of volunteers and deputies searching the area around the home for any sign."

"Do you feel the mother's involved?" Frederick asked, and Paul was overwhelmed with the desire to slap the smirk off his face. He wasn't looking for news, he wanted something sensational to push more small-town papers and promote himself as a serious reporter.

"It's too early to tell. Now if you'll excuse me, I have a search to coordinate." Paul pushed past Frederick and started across the squad room.

"Sheriff, do you believe Bobby was abducted by the Witch of Porter Mines?"

Paul stopped in his tracks and slowly turned to face Frederick who took a deep breath and continued his line of questioning. "Isn't it true you've been conducting an investigation into that possibility, using your own deputies to follow up on leads, and wasting the taxpayers' money that could be better spent on expanded road patrols?"

Paul crossed to the smaller man in three quick steps, towering over the reporter, looking down at him as he shrank beneath his gaze.

"What are you talking about?"

"The Witch of Porter Mines. There are rumors you have been investigating the abductions that took place in the seventies, and the forties."

"As the cases are still considered open, it's within my authority to do so. Who told you about that?"

"I can't reveal my sources."

Paul held his gaze for a moment, then smiled as he relaxed. "I wouldn't put too much stock in anything Deputy Franke, or his father-in-law, has to say about me. It's politics as usual."

"Sheriff, you have a call on line three," his secretary said. "It's councilman Hayes."

Paul smiled at the cowed Frederick, winked, then spun around and crossed into his office, slamming the door behind him.

Damn him. That son of a bitch was doing everything he could to force him out of office before the election. Sure, he'd used a couple of his more trusted deputies to help him out, but that had been on their time, not county time. He'd have to pull back now. Let things blow over.

With a frustrated sigh born of years of dealing with out-of-touch politicians who promised all for nothing, he sat down at his desk and lifted the receiver.

"Sheriff Odenton."

"How ya doing, Paul?" Councilman Hayes' voice was friendly yet distant, telling the Sheriff all he needed to know.

"No sense complaining," he replied, following the unscripted, yet customary, exchange.

"Who'd listen anyway," the councilman answered.

"Exactly."

"What happened, Paul? We faxed our request for clarification of your proposal last week but never received a response."

"Hang on a minute." Paul put the councilman on hold. "Sherry," he shouted.

Sherry opened the door and stuck her head in. "Yes?"

"Did we receive a fax from the county council last week?"

Sherry shook her head. "I haven't seen one."

"Damn fax machine. Hold on a minute. I'll be right back," he said.

The only fax machine they could afford was located in the dispatch area. Dropping to his knees, he looked under the stand the machine sat on and fished out several pages of faxes from the shadowy area beneath it.

"One of these days." He looked through the dusty pages. A couple of menus from local restaurants was mixed in with two wanted bulletins, and the request for clarification of expenditures from the county commissioner.

"See to it that these get distributed." He handed the wanted bulletins to Sherry as he dropped the menus into the garbage. Returning to his office, he picked up the phone, prepared to plead his case, only to discover that the councilman had used the opportunity to hang up before he had to face the sheriff.

It was a hell of a way to run an office. Their technology was so outdated they still relied on faxes from other law enforcement offices to keep abreast of major developments.

With the money that poured into the county's coffers during the tourist season, you'd think the powers that be would be interested in keeping up with the changes in technology that would make everyone's job easier.

If he had known in the beginning his job would be less about enforcing the law and more about meeting an unrealistic county budget, he would have gone into another line of work. He could have opened his own pizza joint or something. He would have been busy either way, but at least he could hire help when needed instead of trying to predict during the slow months what his manpower needs would be for the coming budget deadline.

Deputy Reynolds stuck his head in the door. "Doug's finished at the mobile home park." The sheriff waved him in. "Neither of his dogs could find any sign beyond the trailer." Reynolds settled into a seat across from Paul.

"Do you think she did it?" Paul asked.

"I've known Beth the better part of thirty years. She's not what I would call mother-of-the-year material, but in her own way she loves those kids."

"I don't think she would hurt either of them, not purposely. What do we know about her boyfriends?"

Deputy Reynolds shrugged. "Not much yet, we're still digging."

"Keep going. Let's keep this under the radar for now. I don't want to go off half-cocked."

"Do you believe it's the old legend?"

Paul smiled at that. "Now don't you start on me. I get enough of it from the council. Which reminds me, were they able to fix the computer?"

Reynolds shook his head. "They said it needed an update. Apparently, the state upgraded their systems and now we need to upgrade so we can communicate with them. When I asked how much it would cost, they laughed. Said if I had to ask, I couldn't afford it."

"Nice." Paul shook his head. "Not only do we have to beg for funds from the council, we gotta deal with their relatives ripping us off every chance they get."

"Sheriff," Sherry said at the door. Her face was pasty, the corners of her mouth, turned down.

"What is it?"

"Nathan Fraley was taken from his backyard. His mom stepped inside for a moment, and when she came back out, he was gone."

"Call Doug. Have him bring two of his best dogs." Paul pushed himself to his feet. He needed a nap. But it didn't look like he'd be getting one anytime soon.

He was getting too damned old for the job. Maybe it was time to retire and let the youngsters have it. The thought of Deputy Franke becoming Sheriff Franke, even though it would only be until the next election, was too chilling to contemplate.

32

Paul surveyed the Fraleys' manicured back yard. A sand box sat next to the swing set with a playhouse beyond that. The main house was relatively new, having been built three years earlier. Jessica's husband worked at a manufacturing plant out of town and was currently on his way home.

The scene was in sharp contrast to what they found at the Carr house. Here it looked like the child was well cared for by his parents. The number of toys scattered across the backyard mute testimony to their love. Proving once again that perceptions really mattered. While Bobby's mom was the first to come under suspicion when they arrived at her house, Nathan's mom wasn't even on the radar as a possible suspect.

Jessica sat in a lawn chair, staring at the forest behind the house as one of Paul's deputies knelt beside her. "I told him to put a fence up. He said there's nothing to be afraid of in the forest, and now my baby's gone."

The walkie-talkie in Paul's hand crackled as Deputy Reynolds's voice came through the static. "The dogs have found another trail. You need to look at this, over."

"On my way, over." Paul entered the forest, and after working his way through the band of holly that formed a barrier inside the tree line, he followed the barking dogs. He'd only had a few hours of sleep here and there over the past three days and the strain was wearing through his resolve.

Around him tree trunks marched away into the distance in ordered rows like soldiers in formation marching into battle. It was easy going, and with every step the barking of the dogs grew louder. When he reached the location where the search team waited, Deputy Reynolds met him.

"We've only let Doug and his dogs through the area. He says they found another scent that leads in a different direction, and what appears to be a disturbed area where a possible struggle took place." Deputy Reynolds pointed at an outcropping of stone.

As Paul focused on the spot, he became aware of other outcroppings scattered among the trees. His gaze drifted from one to the next as something stirred in his subconscious. They looked like ancient burial mounds that someone, or something, had dug into to disturb what lay within. As he picked out more of them, he realized it was not something digging into the mound, but something had pushed its way out. He shuddered as he approached the area cordoned off with yellow tape that twisted back and forth in a steady breeze.

The first thing he noticed was the way the brush was flattened near one of the outcroppings. Getting closer, he spotted the tumbled pile of stones surrounding a narrow opening in the ground. Glancing to his left, he saw another opening six feet away. To the right was another surrounded by a pile of moss-covered stone.

Returning his attention to the area around the first hole, he noticed the moss on one of the stones was torn loose. Motioning for Deputy Reynolds to approach, he pointed at the area around the hole.

"See if you can spot anything down there."

Deputy Reynolds removed the flashlight from his belt and got down on his knees. As Reynolds explored the hole, Paul turned to Doug and Peter, who waited nearby with their bloodhounds. "What have you found?"

"I picked up two trails," Doug said. "One leads east, the other goes south."

"Which one is the boy's?"

"The east trail. I'll follow that and have Peter follow the one that goes south," Doug replied.

Paul nodded and turned back to Reynolds, who was shining his light into the hole.

"Can you see anything?"

"Not a damned thing." Reynolds jockeyed into a new position. "Wait a minute." He lowered himself onto his belly and reached into the hole with one hand.

"What is it?"

"Hold on." Reynolds backed away from the hole with a piece of rope in his hand. Pushing himself to his knees, he pulled the rope from the hole.

"Doesn't feel like there's anything on it."

The frayed end came into view. Paul picked it up and studied it, noting the way the fibers were shredded.

"This wasn't cut. Too frayed for that." Paul ran the nylon rope through his fingers. It was regular clothesline rope used by many of the people in the county. Available at any hardware store, or the Walmart Super Center on 219 north of Oakland, nothing to distinguish it from any other piece of rope.

Paul stared at the opening as a cold chill danced along his spine. "I don't want anybody in or out of this area. We need to get the state boys down here with their equipment," he said.

"What are you thinking?" Deputy Reynolds asked.

"I'm thinking we might have found our culprit's dumping ground."

Deputy Reynolds removed his hat and brushed back his hair. "Who could it be?"

"Who lives close enough to this area to know it well enough to move about at night?"

"There's six or seven families whose homes border this part of the forest."

"Have Williams get a list of everyone who lives next to this area. I want only Williams working on this, quietly. Do not approach any of the families. Let's take a look at them first, figure out the best way to do this. I don't want to scare them off. For now, let's get back to the Fraleys. Until I can get the state out here, don't say anything to anyone about what we've found."

"Got it."

With that, Paul took a final look around, his gaze drawn to the piles of stone that dotted the ground. They were getting close to the truth, he felt it in his bones. Somewhere among these strange outcropping was the answer that had plagued generations. He suspected it might point in a direction none of them was prepared to look.

Not yet at least.

33

After reacquiring the scent of the missing boy, Doug followed Tyrese, a bloodhound he'd named after his most recent ex-girlfriend. He named his dogs after the women he'd known. To him it fit because most of them, with the exception of his mother, were bitches. With her nose on the ground, Tyrese pulled him through the forest with a pace that told him she was hot on the trail.

Passing close to several of the stone cairns that stood everywhere, he became aware of the shadowy holes hidden within each. It was as if something had pushed its way out of the earth, moving aside stone and dirt as it ascended to the forest floor.

A chill danced down his spine and he became aware of the stillness of the forest around him. They were getting close to Fiddlers Pond. Ahead the trees thinned. Dense brush gathered around their trunks, a tangled mass of overgrown weeds and briar bushes filled with prickly pears and enough thorns to shred the flesh of anyone stupid enough to fight their way through.

Beyond the barrier lay Fiddler's Pond, its smooth black surface holding the secrets of the past. Many rumors surrounded those brackish waters, the legend of the Witch being the most prominent. It was said on a moonlit night she could be seen rising from the unplumbed depths to seek the descendants of those who murdered her.

Pulling Tyrese up short, Doug stopped and surveyed his surroundings as she sniffed at everything around her. She looked at him with a questioning expression and he reached down to pat her side, to reassure her, and himself.

The silence was deafening. There should have been squirrels running through the treetops, birds flitting back and forth, singing in their incessant voices. Not even a soft breeze blew through the trees, and he had the unmistakable feeling that someone, or something, was watching him.

Tyrese barked and he jumped, letting out an involuntary cry of alarm. "Don't do that, dammit."

She looked up with an impatient expression that told him she wanted to get back on the trail.

"Let's go then," he said, and she turned back to the trail, nose on the ground, as she led him to the edge of Fiddlers Pond.

They came out on the southeastern corner, where sheer walls of stone towered over the pond. Across from him was a sloping hillside, covered with tumbled boulders, that led to the water's edge. To his left lay an open area at the ledge and beyond that a path wide enough to drive a car. The path led back to Fiddlers Road and the town of Porter Mines.

From his vantage point he looked down into the water. Beneath the surface lay a massive black form. At its edge, the bottom dropped off to a depth no one had been able to calculate.

Several years before, a college professor, and several of his students attempted to find the bottom of the pond. They tried with a hundred-foot spool of rope. Reaching the end without touching bottom, they switched to a thousand-foot roll. Once five hundred feet had been played out, still without finding the bottom, they reeled it back in and gave up. Rumor had it they gave up when the rope was pulled from its spool by something beneath the surface. They managed to recover six hundred feet of rope and the end came up frayed and torn as if something gnawed through it.

Doug didn't put much credit in the tale, yet as he stood looking down into those shadowy depths, he understood how one's imagination could run wild in such a situation. Then he saw it, near the bank, a bright spot of color on the surface of the black water. Something red bobbing on the surface.

After tying Tyrese's lead to a tree, he worked his way down the slope, jumping from one boulder to the next, careful not to fall between them. At the water's edge he retrieved the red object. A toy tractor.

34

As Doug retrieved the toy tractor from Fiddlers Pond, Peter was running to keep up with Viola. With her nose to the ground, she followed the new trail they'd stumbled across at the opening.

Coming to a thick bramble of brush, Viola lifted her head and bayed, then dropped her nose to the ground as she sought to reacquire the scent. Finding it, she pulled Peter around the edge of the thick brush and out onto a dirt road, one of many that crisscrossed the ridgeline.

Here the trail ended, and in the mud along the side of the road Peter found the imprint of a tire along with several boot prints.

After calling in his find on the walkie-talkie, he lit a cigarette and watched the road for the Sheriff's arrival. Viola lay down at his feet, lowered her head to her paws and fell asleep, her part of the day's adventure done.

He lit another cigarette off the butt of the first, then field-stripped the first, letting the pieces drift away on a soft breeze blowing in from the south. The wind carried the scent of freshly turned fields full of the promise of the approaching spring, and a new beginning. Though the air still carried the faint chill of the winter's recent passing, the sun was warm on his back, and kept the chill at bay.

As he was lighting his third cigarette, he became aware of a change in the atmosphere. The sun was no longer warm, and the wind had died down. Viola lifted her head and looked at him with a questioning expression. She whined.

"What's wrong, girl?"

Viola lowered her head and watched the road with him.

How much longer is he gonna be?

In the forest, the sound of all movement stopped, replaced by a silence filled with unnatural things. The hair on his neck stirred in response to a chill that wound its way up his spine. He had the sensation that somebody was watching him, and he spun around to gaze into the forest depths. Leafless branches created a lattice work of dark lines. Narrow tree trunks marched away into the distance, and the rock outcroppings that dotted the forest floor around Fiddlers Pond covered the forest floor here.

He recalled the story his grandmother used to tell about the lady in white who wandered the forest searching for her child. Anyone who heard the child crying was doomed to die within three days. It was one of the many tales and legends that flourished in this part of the country. The story contained a grain of truth at its core, embellished over the years to become a ghost story good for scaring little kids.

He spotted movement and stepped off the edge of the road for a better look. His cigarette forgotten, he peered into the shadowed depths of the forest. He saw it again, a small patch of white gliding through the gloom. A young girl stepped into view from between two trees. Her head down, she glided through the forest, her long black hair hanging about her face in wet strands.

Peter was so startled by her appearance he was struck speechless. Then he found his voice and called after her. She continued through the forest, moving away from him, without looking up to acknowledge his call.

"Hey," Peter shouted, his hands cupped around his mouth. She continued away from him. Viola whined behind him and he glanced back at her. She was lying on the ground, her ears back, as she watched the forest depths.

"You stay," he said to Viola, and entered the forest. After working his way through the band of thick brush that bordered the road, he struck out through the trees, never taking his eyes off the young girl, who continued to ignore his calls.

He should have been watching where he was going. The ground was dotted with small holes hidden beneath the thick carpet of dead leaves.

The girl vanished behind a holly bush and Peter hurried to keep her in sight. The ground gave out beneath his foot, and he knew he was screwed. His foot broke through into a small opening, the toes pointed down, and his leg became lodged in the hole as his momentum carried him forward. With his arms pin-wheeling, he struggled to regain his balance before it was too late. His knee bent the wrong way, ligaments snapped, and Doug forgot about the girl as intense pain exploded in his knee.

He tried to pull himself free, but his leg was wedged in the rock-lined hole, and every time he tried to lift it out, agony flared from his knee. A shadow fell across him, and he looked up into the pale face of the young girl he'd been chasing.

"Help me," he said as he reached for her, and her gaze went from his face to his hand, and back again. When their eyes met, he became aware of the preternatural stillness that filled her black eyes. That and the fact that she had no pupils served to awaken a cold ball of fear in the pit of his stomach.

"Stay away," she said, and her words gave birth to primitive images of ancient things dancing around raging fires lost in the emptiness of the unknown. In the soft firelight he caught glimpses of taloned hands, the razor-sharp claws glowing with a dull light. Flat, dead, eyes that watched him with a ravenous hunger for the life he contained as they danced with wild abandon and he struggled to cling to his sanity.

Like others who lived around Porter Mines, he'd grown up under the threat of the Witch. And like most adults, until this moment, he'd paid little mind to the warnings.

Now he knew better.

35

It took Paul the best part of an hour to find the location Peter called. Leading a convoy of patrol cars, they raced down the dirt road known as Fiddlers Road. Reaching Peter's last known location. They found Viola sitting along the side of the road watching their approach with a sad, hound-dog expression.

Doug arrived as Paul exited his vehicle, and he called for Viola, who ran toward him with her tail wagging. Paul walked to the edge of the road and looked into the forest.

"Peter," he shouted, "where the hell are you?"

"Over here," came the reply and Paul, followed by several deputies, worked his way through the thick band of brush that bordered the forest.

Once in the forest proper, the group located Peter and called an ambulance. As they waited, two of the deputies worked to free Peter's leg from the hole he was trapped in.

"What did you find?" Paul noted the pasty expression on Peter's face. He was going into shock and Paul knew he'd better get what information he could while he still had the chance.

"Tire tracks, footprints," Peter said through clenched teeth. He looked around then. "Did you find the girl?"

"What girl are you talking about?"

"She was here a minute ago." Peter looked around the forest.

"Have you been drinking again?"

"No sir, I swore off the bottle permanent, like I promised."

"There's no girl here."

"There was."

"Well, she's not here now." Paul stood up to gaze into the forest depths around them. He didn't know if Peter had been drinking or not. It didn't matter now. The woods had a strange effect on anyone who ventured into them alone. The whole ridge around Fiddlers Pond was the setting for many a wild tale and local legend. The Witch being one of a number of different stories that were shared among those who lived near enough to bear witness to these strange occurrences.

As his deputies finished extracting Peter's leg, his constant bitching about his pain provided a running commentary on their progress, Paul retuned to the side of the road.

Peter marked his find with a bright orange flag like the ones used by construction crews to grade the land. It fluttered in a soft breeze as Paul approached, and he knelt to look at the fresh tire track that stood out in sharp bas relief in the mud. The pattern was familiar to anyone who drove a pickup truck. And as such the area around them contained thousands of tires like the one that made the track.

He was close, closer than he'd ever been before. Why someone would do such a thing was unimportant. All he was worried about was putting an end to it. Let the doctors and psychologists figure out the why. He wanted the children to be safe.

One thing he'd learned in his years as first a deputy, then the sheriff, someone always saw something, no matter how alone they might think they were. Someone was watching, and that one person could lead to a break. It was a matter of locating that witness, and he remembered the house they passed on the way in. A car was parked in the driveway when they went by.

Paul pushed himself to his feet. "Reynolds."

"Yes, sir." Deputy Reynolds approached the Sheriff.

"Contact the state police once you get back to the office, turn over what we have so far, and see what they can shake out. I've got a little stop to make on the way back. You're in charge while I'm gone."

Returning to his cruiser, he left the other deputies to take care of Peter as he retraced their path. Reaching the driveway to the old Jenkins farmhouse, he stopped to check the tracks in the dirt.

Most of the sets he noted went in one direction, toward Whispering Hollow Road a couple of hundred yards away. One pair of tracks led in the opposite direction. Back the way he had come. Tracks that matched the print Peter had found.

We're getting close.

A dusty Ford wagon sat in the driveway and Paul confirmed that the tread pattern did not match the tracks they'd found. The other set of tracks confirmed another vehicle was regularly parked there.

As he was returning to his cruiser the ambulance drove by. Deputy Reynolds followed the ambulance and stopped next to Paul.

"What did you find?"

"Don't know yet, might be nothing. I'm going in and talk to these people, see if they've seen anything." Paul indicated the house.

"It's the old Jenkins place," Reynolds said, "looks like someone's fixing it up."

"Maybe they saw something or know something. A vehicle with the same tread pattern we found on the road has been parked here in the past."

"Do you want me to stay with you?"

"I'll be all right. What I want you to do is get with the state police, have them bring in their dogs. I don't think we're gonna get much more help from Doug and Pete."

"Why do you say that?"

"Did you see the look on Pete's face? He's scared to death. Something in the woods spooked him. Besides, the state has more resources than we do."

"Do you think he was drinking?"

"Might have been, but whatever scared him sobered him up."

"You sure you don't want me to come in with you?"

"I'm sure. I might be old, but I ain't dead yet."

"And I want to keep it that way."

"Go on, get out of here. I'll be all right."

"I'll be a call away." Reynolds dropped the shift lever into drive and pulled away.

Paul watched him until he turned onto Whispering Hollow Road, then he looked up at the house.

He remembered the Jenkins who once lived there. He and William had been friends until they moved away after Robert killed himself. The boy had been nine years old, and many a night after it happened Paul would lay awake wondering what could be so terrible in a nine-year-old's life that made suicide a solution.

This was of course followed by a simple question.

Did we miss something?

That was always possible. No one else was around to ask, at least no one that could answer in a coherent manner. Abigail, William and Betty's daughter, Robert's older sister, was the only one left alive, and she was whiling away her days as a resident of the Golden Living Rehab Center, watched over twenty-four hours a day by the nurses that worked there.

They called it a rehab center. On the surface it was a nursing home for the elderly. Some of the occupants were there for reasons that didn't involve growing old.

With a sigh, the weight of the world resting upon his shoulders, he approached the front door.

36

Susan was at her wit's end. Ever since Eric failed to retrieve Puddles, Christine had been in a funk. Refusing to leave the house, worried that if she did the witch would get her because she no longer had Puddles to protect her.

Though Christine was underfoot, Susan still managed to make progress. It wasn't the real issue, the fact that she missed two days of school worried her. She couldn't allow it to continue. The time was coming for her to put her foot down and play the responsible parent.

To further complicate matters, she had not spoken to Eric since the day he failed to retrieve puddles. It was as if he'd fallen off the edge of the earth or was purposely avoiding her. Was it something she did?

The basement still needed to be finished, which he said he would do. Then there were the feelings she had for him. She imagined they had something. Now she wasn't so sure.

Retrieving her phone, she dialed his number again, letting it ring until his voicemail answered. Though recorded his voice stoked the fires of her need and deepened her concern that she did something to ruin what they had.

But what?

As she ended her call, a knock came from the door and Susan crossed into the formal dining room. Through the window, she spotted a police cruiser sitting at the end of the driveway.

If they're here because Christine missed a couple of days of school... the thought gathered steam, then died as she made her way to the front door.

Susan opened the door and for a moment her heart climbed into her throat. The officer on her front stoop was an imposing figure, his hat adding more than three inches to his already towering height. The hat's brim kept his eyes in shadows with only the lower portion of his face illuminated. It revealed an angular jaw set in a hard line. With the way the house faced, the front door was in a deep gloom that added to the menacing nature of her visitor.

"I'm sorry, ma'am, I didn't mean to startle you." Paul removed his hat, revealing a thick head of gray hair, and lively blue eyes that carried a strong degree of intelligence tempered by a touch of humility.

"That's all right, for a moment I thought..."

"Thought what?" Paul glanced into the house, his eyes darting back and forth as he took in everything.

She wasn't sure what she was thinking. "Nothing, everything's fine."

"I'm glad to see someone is finally fixing up the old place."

"It's been a job. Would you like to come in? I have coffee on." Susan stepped back.

"I'd love a cup." Paul stepped across the threshold into the foyer. His uniform was impeccably pressed. His shoes, though dusty, carried a hard shine. Around his waist was a utility belt that included a holster. The black butt of a pistol stuck out of the back. Guns made Susan nervous, and she felt a twinge of panic at the idea of one entering her home.

But he's a police officer.

As a military wife she was familiar with weapons and had even visited the range with John several times to shoot. But they still made her uncomfortable when they were brought inside.

In the kitchen Susan poured a cup for her visitor. "Have a seat."

Paul settled into a chair and reached for the offered mug. "I must say you've done some amazing work here."

"I haven't done it all myself. I've had help."

"I'm sorry, where are my manners? I'm Sheriff Paul Odenton, please call me Paul." He extended his hand.

Susan found it warm and confident, and she sat down across from him. "Would you like cream or sugar?"

"I'm good." He took a sip. "That's good coffee, not like the swill we make."

"Thank you. Is there something I can help you with? I know she's missed a couple of days, before that she had perfect attendance." The look of confusion that crossed Paul's face stopped her. "You're not here about my daughter missing school, are you?"

"No. I saw somebody was fixing up the place, and I wanted to see how things were going. Call me nosy."

From the hallway came the sound of footsteps and Christine entered the kitchen.

"Hey sweetie, look who's come for a visit." Susan held out her arms.

Christine frowned. "I thought Eric was back with Puddles." She climbed into her mother's lap. "You're a policeman. You can get Puddles back for me, can't you?"

"Puddles? A family pet?" Paul ventured, confused.

"A stuffed bunny that went missing a couple of days ago when someone went where they weren't supposed to."

"She took him, Mommy, Lizzy took Puddles, and now daddy won't be able to protect me anymore."

"I'm sorry, I'm not quite following what's going on here."

"Sometimes that's every day for me," Susan said with a smile. "My husband, Christine's father won Puddles at a carnival before he left for Iraq with the marines..."

"It had to be earned," Christine interrupted.

"We've talked about this," Susan said, "I was talking, and we don't interrupt."

"That's what the man at the carnival said, it had to be earned for it to work."

"What man at the carnival?" Paul leaned forward, resting his arms on the table, a smile teasing the corners of his lips.

"You know the one, three throws for a buck, knock over the bottles and win a prize. Daddy won Puddles for me before he went away."

"When will he be coming home?" Paul asked.

Christine's frown deepened as she lowered her eyes, "He's in heaven now, where he can watch over us. Can I be excused, Mommy?"

Paul straightened in his seat, his smile fading. "I'm sorry, I didn't..."

"It's all right." Susan brushed a tear from the corner of her eye. "It's okay, sweetie, you go back to your room. I'll be up in a bit."

Christine slid down from Susan's lap and waved to Paul as she crossed to the hallway.

When she was gone, Paul reached across the table and placed his hand over Susan's. "I am so sorry, I didn't know. I didn't mean to stir up bad memories for either of you."

Susan struggled to control her emotions, sniffling as she wiped her eyes. "It's okay. It's been two years since she last saw her father."

"Such a shame. Again, I'm sorry if I've caused you any pain."

His hand over hers was comforting. A strong hand, much like John's, and its presence made her feel secure.

"So how long have you been sheriff?" Susan said, changing the subject.

He sat back, dropping his hands into his lap. "Longer than I care to remember. I was a deputy from seventy-three to ninety-four when I became the sheriff."

"Maybe you can help me with something, then."

"I can try."

"Our neighbor is Mildred Raines. I've heard some pretty bad rumors about her and her involvement in what happened with her sister. Was she involved?"

"I remember the case. It was one of the first ones I worked as a new deputy. You know it's a matter of public record if you'd like to look it up."

"I'm not really looking for all of the gory details. Mildred was here the other day and several people have warned me not to trust her."

"I wouldn't worry about Mildred. She was never under any suspicion. You know how it is with small towns where everyone knows your name. They want to know all about your business, and what you're not willing to share, they'll make up to suit themselves."

"That is so true. When my husband died, we lived on base and the entire neighborhood helped get me through the worst part. They took care of Christine, made sure she was fed, and had clean clothes. At the same time, they wanted access to my private life, and I had no desire to share that information. It's the biggest reason we moved here. John's parents live in Oakland, and I have no other family. This is a fresh start for both of us."

"You've done wonders with the place. Have you done all the work yourself?"

"What I could. I contracted out the rest. Eric Bowers has been taking care of the big things for me."

"He's a good man, installed our kitchen cabinets. Maggie insisted she fix him dinner afterwards. If we hadn't been together so long, I'd be jealous, but that's Maggie."

"She sounds like someone I'd like to meet. Do you have children?"

Paul shook his head. "Kids weren't in the cards for us."

"I'm sorry."

"That's all right. We've grown accustomed to a quiet house. Maggie drives a school bus and adopts every child that rides with her."

"Did you know the people who lived here before?"

"Bill Jenkins and I were friends. It's a shame what happened."

"What?"

"His son. I don't know if he fell in with a bad crowd or what, one day he took his own life. After that, the family fell apart."

"Oh my." Susan covered her mouth with her hand.

"I'm sorry, I didn't mean to frighten you, seems all I'm doing is apologizing. I did have another reason for stopping by."

"Oh?"

"We're working a case right now and I wanted to see if you or anyone else in the house might have seen any suspicious vehicles using the dirt road next to your house."

"What kind of a case is it?" Susan's curiosity was piqued.

Paul smiled as he shook his head. "Sorry, I can't share that information."

"I don't recall seeing any suspicious vehicles on the side road, I'm not here all the time. Sorry I can't be any better help to you."

"That's okay, it was a long shot anyway."

"I hope you're able to solve the case."

"So, do I. I better get going, I've taken up too much of you time as it is."

"Do you mind if I ask you another question?"

Paul took a drink from his mug. "As long as it's one I can answer,"

"I've heard rumors about a Witch coming back to take her due. What's that all about?"

"It's an old wives' tale. I believe every small town has their share of them. My mother used to threaten me and my brothers when we were kids, telling us if we didn't listen the Witch would come take us away in the night."

"That's terrible."

"They were simpler times. Nobody really believed the stories. You know how legends are."

"Is there any truth to the legend?"

"There's a spark of truth in every legend, I suppose. As for the Witch of Porter Mines, well, in the early eighteen hundreds an outpost stood on the ridge. After a bad winter, dysentery swept through the outpost, killing the weak, mostly children and the elderly. Those who survived believed the deaths were the result of witchcraft. They were simple, god-fearing people in a strange land, so it didn't take much to convince them that a witch was responsible.

"An old woman lived at the edge of the outpost. She traded with the local Indians and seemed to be prospering while everyone else was failing. It didn't take much for the crowd to get whipped into a frenzy.

"The story goes they bound her to a stake and piled dead brush around her. It's said that when they lit the brush, the woman cursed the members of the town, vowing to return every generation and take her due."

"Did she come back?" Susan rubbed her arms with her hands to chase away the chill that washed over them.

Paul smiled. "Of course not, it's a legend, an old wives' tale used to keep unruly children in check."

"Sounds frightening,"

Paul glanced at his watch and pushed himself to his feet. "I've wasted enough of your time spinning old tales. I better get going,"

Susan followed him to the door where he and looked around once again. "It's nice to see the old place fixed up again,"

"It was a pleasure to meet you. Don't hesitate to stop by again for a cup of coffee. I've always appreciated what law enforcement does for us."

"Well, thank you, ma'am, I'll keep that in mind. You have a good day." He turned and strolled down the driveway.

Susan watched him leave and when he was gone, she closed the door. It was becoming too much to wrap her mind around. Children killing themselves, old wives' tales, and a dangerous pond.

What would happen next?

37

His phone vibrated against the surface of the table and Eric lifted his head, scowling at it with a weary expression.

It was Susan.

Ignoring her call, he lowered his head and closed his eyes. Finding those openings in the forest around Fiddlers Pond had awakened old memories he'd fought to keep suppressed. Memories of his sister, and the sacrifice she made to give him the life he had. That wasn't enough. Not only did he have to witness her abduction by a creature that inhabited the night. She returned three nights later, or her spirit did, seeking entry to his warm bedroom, and the sustenance he could provide.

The phone vibrated again, and he glanced at the name on the screen, continuing to ignore it as he struggled against the overwhelming flood of memories that threatened to swamp him.

As he tried to keep the memories at bay, a notion emerged, one that filled him with an unrelenting shame. They stood in its path. Susan, and more importantly Christine, and what had he done to help?

Nothing. Nada. Zip. He ignored the situation like everyone else in Porter Mines. The nightmare he knew was not a nightmare. Christine's story about the dark place. Anyone who lived in the area for any length of time knew about these things, they'd grown up under their threat, once they got older, it was like they forgot.

It was human nature to forget your childhood and all the travails it entailed. The happy moments would stay with us until the day we died. In most cases, people tended to pack away all the bad memories, to isolate them from the good, and build a wall of forgetfulness around them.

Some memories could never be forgotten.

"Eric," his sister moaned from the past, and he was no longer sitting at his kitchen table feeling sorry for himself. He was back in his bedroom, only six, with the light of a full moon casting the skeletal shadows of the bare tree limbs against the shelf above his dresser. Blanketing the G.I. Joe action figure with a web of darkness. He wanted someone like G.I. Joe to come to his rescue, to save him from the terror that waited beyond his bedroom window, unfortunately G.I. Joe was make believe.

What wasn't make believe was his best friend Jacob standing on the other side of his bedroom window. He vanished the week before, falling victim to the curse of the Witch. Now he stood beyond the window, wrapped in an ebony cloak of shadows that fluttered in every direction around him. Eric was struck by the realization that it was Jacob standing before him, yet at the same time it wasn't, like he was nothing more than a disguise this creature wore.

Like the Halloween mask he'd worn the year before, with narrow slits for eyes that blocked most of his view, and nostril holes that proved too small. Behind the mask the scent of sweaty plastic was overwhelming. It was an odor that always brought back memories of he and his sister walking hand in hand down the street as they sought to fill their pillowcases with candy.

This memory was far from happy.

"I have a secret," Jacob said, his mouth moving in time with the words that echoed in Eric's mind. He was drawn to the window against his will, his feet moving of their own accord as his bladder emptied, and warmth spread down the leg of his Superman pajamas. At the window, he reached up to unlock it, to let this shadowy monstrosity into his room.

"No," his sister shouted, breaking the spell Jacob cast over him. She slapped his hand down, and pushed him to the door of his bedroom, shoving him across the room and into the hallway, closing the door behind him.

It was not the last time he saw her.

She came back, three days later, trying to get him to open his bedroom window to let her in. He'd fled to his parents' bed, burrowing into the blankets between their sleeping figures to hide from his sister's questioning expression.

He couldn't do this again. He'd faced the creature once before, and only survived because of his sister. Who could protect him now?

The memory faded and Eric stood at the kitchen window. The forest behind his house was filled with darkness. He'd spent his life immersed in the facts and figures of running a successful business, first in college, then in real life as he built his company into something he could be proud of. He was known for being fair, with a good head for business, and had earned the respect of other contractors who knew he could be counted on. He had achieved a good standing in the community.

Yet as he stood gazing into the forest behind his house, he realized it all meant so little in the greater scheme of things. He was a small cog in a vast mechanism that was the world around him. A world that did not always follow the ordered reasoning of a set of blueprints. Instead of straight lines and the sharp angles of a perfectly squared wall, real life was more fluid, curving and bending as needed to accommodate changes thrown our way as we lived our lives.

Movement drew his eye to the ever-present holly that formed a near-solid barrier between the ordered world of his back yard and the chaos of the forest. Something white glided into view and he realized he was looking at something that should not be.

Yet there it was, in his back yard. An errant memory from the past. A warning to stay out of it. To turn his back on the woman he'd fallen in love with.

A young girl stepped into view. Her face framed by a lifeless halo of black hair.

"You have no business here," that half-forgotten voice said as he stepped back from the window, afraid she might see him. He watched from the shadows as she vanished into the forest. Behind him his phone vibrated on the table and he turned to look at it as the girl's words repeated themselves in his mind.

You have no business here.

But I do.

He looked at the screen of his phone, the three missed calls from Susan lined up one atop the other.

What can I tell her?

The truth?

He didn't even believe the truth himself, and he'd seen it firsthand.

38

In an attempt to take Christine's mind off her recent loss, Susan accepted an invitation from Mildred's to help with an upcoming bake sale. The kitchen table was a mess of dirtied mixing bowls and utensils that lay upon a fine layer of flour. The counter was crowded with cooling racks filled with assorted cookies, brownies, and pastries. While Mildred and Susan worked, with Mildred playing the role of teacher, Christine moved along the counter, gazing up at the cooling racks that stood out of reach.

"Can I please have another, Mommy?"

"How many have you had so far?"

"Only a couple."

"More like a couple of dozen." Susan stepped around the table and joined Christine at the counter. "You do know you're eating Mildred's profits."

"Nonsense," Mildred said as she placed raw cookie dough on a sheet pan, "she's welcome to anything she would like. In fact, I'm going to send a couple of dozen home with you."

"You don't have to do that. We've intruded enough."

"You have not. It's not like I get many callers out here."

"Surely your family come to visit."

"Most of my family has passed on or moved away." Mildred said.

Susan wanted to ask her about her sister, to reassure herself that her instincts were right, and they had nothing to fear. She hesitated, not wanting to pry. She was the outsider here and Mildred was one of the few to make her feel like she belonged. Eric, Brenda, and most recently Sheriff Odenton also helped her feel like this was her home. Even after he reassured her Mildred posed no threat, the memory of Eric's words stopped her.

"Anything wrong, dear?" Mildred said.

"Not a thing. Why don't you go play, sweetie?" Susan told Christine in an effort to redirect a conversation that was beginning to skirt dangerously close to outright snooping. She was a guest and had no right to question Mildred about her past.

"I have something for you." Mildred placed her hand on Christine's shoulder. "Your Mommy told me about your special bunny. I have a special bunny too."

"Did you earn him?" Christine asked.

"What an odd thing to say," Mildred said as she knelt to Christine's level, one hand on the table to steady herself, "my parents gave him to me when I was a child."

"It has to be earned. That's what the man at the carnival said. For it to work it has to be earned," Christine answered.

Mildred looked up at Susan.

"It's a long story. Before John left for Iraq he won Puddles for Christine at a roadside carnival," Susan said.

"There are many things that have to be earned in life for them to work. But some things can be given with love and they are just as powerful. Just like your daddy gave you puddles."

"Can I see him?"

"Absolutely." Mildred pushed herself to her feet and vanished into the short hallway next to the kitchen.

Morning sunlight filled the kitchen, streaming through the row of windows facing east, filling the room with a warming glow that heightened its hominess. The counters matched the white purity of the appliances, a silver strip of metal wrapped around the edge, as was the style when this kitchen was last updated, more than fifty years before. One counter was dominated by a porcelain country sink that looked big enough to bathe in. An old gas stove sat against the opposite wall with a microwave, the only modern appliance to be seen, on a shelf above it.

A wide table with a natural wood finish dominated the center, around which eight chairs would normally be placed. They'd moved the chairs into the dining room so the surface of the table could be used for baking. Looking around, Susan felt at home in this kitchen.

"Here we go." Mildred emerged from the back of the house with a stuffed brown bunny whose floppy ears hung down the back of its head. In her other hand she carried a children's book. "Have you read The Velveteen Rabbit?"

"It's been years since I read that story," Susan said.

Mildred pulled a chair from the dining room and turned it around. "My knees aren't as strong as they used to be." She sat and motioned for Christine to come to her.

Christine hesitated, glancing at Susan, who nodded that it was okay.

Mildred held the rabbit out to Christine, who took it from her and wrapped her arms around its soft body.

"That's a very special bunny." Mildred opened the book on her lap. "There's even been a book written about it and everything."

"Really?"

"Absolutely, see," Mildred said, turning the book so Christine could see the pages. On the first page was an illustration of a stuffed bunny that matched the one in Christine's hands. "Do you like to read?"

Christine nodded and Mildred passed the book to her.

"What do you say?" Susan said.

"Thank you." Christine looked from the book to the bunny in her arms. "What's your name?" she whispered and lowered her head to place her ear next to the bunny's mouth.

"Why don't you go in the living room and read your new book while Mildred and I finish up out here," Susan said.

Christine nodded as she turned to walk into the living room. She stopped, turned back to Mildred, crossed back, and gave her a hug and a kiss on the cheek.

"Oh my," Mildred said, surprised.

"I think you made a new friend," Susan said as Christine turned and vanished into the living room.

Mildred pushed herself to her feet. "She's such a sweetie."

Mildred seemed to sense Susan's hesitance as she came around the table. She looked at her with understanding. "That's the problem with small town life."

"What's that?"

"I'm sure you know about my sister. Eric was a small boy when it happened but he's like all the others, spreading the same old rumors."

"I'm sorry, I don't understand."

"Come on, Susan, you can't expect me to believe Eric has not said a word to you about what happened." Her features held no anger, no excitement, only a weary acceptance of the facts.

"I believe he may have mentioned something in passing." Susan said.

"I'm sure he did," Mildred said with a weary smile. "My sister suffered from a unique problem that prevented her from living a happy life. It's called dissociative identity disorder. Some call it a split personality. When she was sixteen, she was raped by the handyman that worked here. Our father had already passed, and my mother had locked herself away to grieve, so the running of the farm fell to the three of us."

"There were three of you?"

"Me, my twin sister Margaret, and our older sister Jane. Margaret's alter ego killed the handyman for what he'd done but none of us knew that at the time. The same night the handyman vanished, so did Jane. I always assumed they ran off together.

"A month later we discovered Margaret was pregnant, she refused to tell anyone who the father was. It wasn't until seven years later that the truth came out."

"How did they find out?" Though Susan already knew the story, she knew if she didn't ask, Mildred would suspect she had been snooping.

"Margaret's daughter, Lindsay vanished. She was last seen at Fiddlers Pond, so the authorities dragged the pond and discovered the handyman's body wrapped in a canvas tarp along with the hammer she used to kill him. Of course, her bloody fingerprints were all over the handle. The cold waters of the pond preserved everything"

Susan shuddered at the idea of Lindsay in Fiddlers Pond. "Did they ever find Lindsay?"

Mildred shook her head. "Unfortunately, no. To this day we have no idea what happened to her. The only one who does is my sister, and she's not talking."

"Where is Margaret now?"

"The last I heard she was in a mental hospital downstate. When she was a child and they first discovered her problem, the doctors recommended that she be committed for her own good. Mom and Dad refused, deciding to raise her themselves as they would any of their other children. Sometimes I think it might have been best for everyone involved if they let them lock her up."

"Have you ever heard from your older sister Jane?"

Mildred shook her head. "She dropped off the edge of the world. I believe Margaret, or Candice as she called herself during a spell, had something to do with her disappearance, but no one has been able to prove anything."

"That is so sad," Susan said as she took Mildred's hands into her own.

"That's life." Mildred pushed herself to her feet and crossed into the kitchen. She slipped on an oven mit, opened the oven, and removed a cookie sheet full of chocolate chip cookies.

"There's more to it than that," Susan said as she passed a cookie sheet with a new batch of raw cookies over to Mildred.

"More to what, dear?"

"To life. Isn't fighting against things like that all a part of living?"

"It is, but sometimes it's best to leave the past alone. Like my Dad used to say, 'Let sleeping dogs lie.'"

Susan considered this as she recalled her own childhood growing up under her mother's strict rule. To let sleeping dogs lie would be a blessing. Unfortunately, the memory was an old wound that refused to heal completely. Something to pick at when she was trying to sleep.

Later, as they drove home, Christine in the back seat with her new bunny and book, Susan watched her in the rear-view mirror. With no traffic to contend with, she was able to focus her attention on her daughter.

"What do you think of your new bunny rabbit?" Susan said.

Christine held the stuffed animal up to her ear for a moment before replying, "I can't hear Daddy's heartbeat."

The despair in Christine's answer broke Susan's heart. Nothing she tried was working to pull her little girl from the depths of sorrow she'd fallen into. The only thing that would help would be to recover Puddles, but how?

She glanced again at her phone, noting that Eric had not answered any of her texts.

What is wrong with him?

What did I do wrong?

She turned off Fiddlers Pond Road into her own driveway.

39

As a rescue diver with the Maryland State Police, Brian was confident he had seen it all. Stationed on the Eastern Shore, many of his jobs had taken place in the Chesapeake Bay. Most involved the recovery of remains from boats that had flipped over, or the rescue of motorists who had plunged from one of the two major bridges that crossed the bay.

As he hung suspended beneath the surface of Fiddlers Pond, he came to understand how strange the world could be. Somewhere below lay the bottom, shrouded in darkness. The faint line of the rope he held vanished into the black depths as movement swirled in the deeper shadows.

Fish? He questioned as he gazed into that nighted abyss. As he watched the shadows swirl around the rope, he realized they were not the sea creatures he was accustomed to. They were not fish. Something was off about the way they moved. Instead of fluid movement through the water they jerked about in a wild waltz reminiscent of revelers dancing about a fire.

"We've hit four hundred feet." Officer Burton's voice crackled in his ear. Burton was on the boat on the surface above. At first they used a hundred-foot spool of rope, believing that was all they needed. When they reached the end without touching bottom, they switched to a thousand-foot spool marked in ten-foot increments. Attached to the end was an electronic device that would send a signal when they hit bottom. Four hundred feet with no signal.

It's not natural.

"Run out another hundred." Brian spoke into the microphone in the diving helmet he wore. In his line of work, it was imperative he be in contact with the surface as he was conducting a dive. Safety was a high priority when one worked beneath the surface of the water.

"Can you see the bottom?" Officer Burton said.

"Not at all. Can't go any deeper without changing my air."

"Anything at all that might help?"

"Nothing. From my perspective there is no bottom and there's nothing here." Brian glanced up at the silhouette of the boat on the surface. Between them the rope bowed out instead of following a straight line. A powerful current had surprised him as he followed the line down. Had it not been for the rope, he would have been swept to the sheer face of the cliff, and into the black maw of an opening ten feet beneath the surface.

He shuddered at the idea of vanishing into that cave. It looked big enough to permit his passage, and based on the strength of the current, it led to an underwater river that vanished into the mountain around them.

What's feeding the lake? He looked around, searching for another opening that would account for the flow.

"Let's move closer to the cliff face," Brian said, "check the crevices."

"Roger that."

Brian felt the tug of the rope as Burton guided the craft to the rocky face. When he was close, he saw plenty of places for a body to become lodged, and realized it was going to be a long day as he checked each one.

That was his job, bringing closure to the relatives of victims. The only way to do that was to recover the body. Seeing the remains would allow them to move on with their lives, putting to rest any doubts that might have haunted them if no body were found.

His neighbor across the street when he was growing up was an example of this. Her daughter vanished during a trip to Central America. The body was never recovered, and his neighbor clung to the belief to the day of her own death, that any moment her daughter was going to walk through the door.

"Is that good," Burton said in his ear.

"This will work." Brian glanced down at the emptiness below.

"Another five fifty to the end of the spool," Burton said as Brian flipped on his light and shined it into the space beneath a ledge of stone. He steeled himself as he did, preparing for the worst, as the underside of the stony ledge came into view.

A flash of movement startled him as a familiar crawling slithered through his belly. No matter how many times he recovered human remains, there was always that moment of hesitation. It was the one thing that kept him tethered to his humanity as he worked, and he knew the day he lost it, would be the day he hung up his flippers. Today it was only a fish that vanished into the shadows beneath him, fleeing his intrusion.

The rope slid through his hand as the spool unwound above him, his other held onto the stone ledge. He was more focused on searching the stone face than what was going on with the rope, unaware that it had begun to form a large loop in the water around his hand as his partner fed it out above him.

"Another twenty-five feet out. I don't think there's a bottom."

There had to be a bottom. Brian glanced again at the emptiness beneath his feet. His imagination stirring in response to that mysterious void. He tried not to think about what lived in those shadowy depths, preferring to remain ignorant of these things. His job was hard enough without adding that to it. In his line of work, it was better to not even consider the possibility that hovered at the edge of his consciousness.

From the rope came a soft vibration transmitted through the glove on his hand. As if they hit bottom, or something bumped into the rope in the black depths beneath him. He pushed the idea away.

He glanced at the rope that hung suspended around his hand, he'd have to straighten that out. As he was reaching for the rope, it was yanked through his hand fast enough to burn his fingers through the glove. The rope went taut before he could pull his hand free, trapping his hand in the loop.

Burton's shout of surprise came over his headset as he was dragged down into that black abyss. The depth meter on his wrist jumped from seventy to ninety feet instantly. The tension drew a tight knot around his hand, folding his knuckles over as pain shot the length of his arm.

He was trapped between whatever was dragging the rope down, and the boat above, the rope squeezing his hand until he was sure the bones would soon break. He struggled against his panic, remembering his training, as he fought to pull his hand free. The dial on his depth meter crept close to one hundred feet. It would still be manageable, if he went any deeper there wouldn't be enough air left to properly decompress as he ascended to the boat.

He pulled the diving knife from the sheath on his calf to cut the rope, bumping his elbow on a rock outcropping behind him. A flash of pain shot through his fingers, and the knife dropped from his hand. He watched as it vanished into the black depths, sparkling like a lost star fading into the featureless void of deep space.

The rope was stretched to its breaking point, trapped between whatever took it below, and the buoyancy of the boat above. Blood clouded the water as it seeped from the glove of his trapped hand. He glanced into the waiting abyss as the black depths rose up to envelope him. The sunlight grew distant as his air bubbles traced the path of his descent. The external pressure of the water felt like it was about to crush him, and he struggled to draw a breath from his dwindling air supply. He was not equipped for this depth, and if he didn't get loose soon, it would be all over.

Still he kept his panic at arm's length as he worked to loosen his hand. He'd been in worse places than this. On more than one occasion he'd gotten tangled in discarded debris littering the bottom. It was a matter of approaching the problem from a calm, reasonable, mindset.

The pressure eased on his hand as the rope below snapped. He untangled himself as the frayed end vanished into the empty depths below.

Untethered, he kicked out to ascend, propelling himself up the sheer face of the wall, using his good hand to pull himself to the surface. As he rose, he knew he needed to slow his ascent to allow his body time to adjust to the changing pressure. Unfortunately, the dial for his air tank had already breached the line between yellow and green. He didn't have enough air to properly decompress, which meant he would have to spend some time in the decompression chamber to normalize his blood.

Pulling himself up the face of the cliff he came to a deep crevice. He stopped when his light illuminated something huddled in the shadows near the back. Long black hair hung suspended in the water, framing a white face whose eyes were squeezed closed above a pert nose and a slack pair of lips. The flesh was perfectly preserved by the cold waters, untouched, which in itself was unnatural enough to cause a cold ball to form in the pit of his stomach. The tattered remnants of a dress clung to the small body, floating like a halo in the clear water around a small pair of outstretched arms that bobbed lifelessly against the top of the ledge.

He reached for the young girl as the edges of his vision darkened, and the air in his tank dwindled. Grabbing her wrist with his good hand, he was drawing her towards him when her eyes sprang open, and she pushed off from the face of the cliff.

He kicked back with a scream. Bubbles from his cry, expelled from the respirator, partially obscuring the scene. She emerged from beneath the ledge, her eyes as black as night as she came after him. He kicked out to propel himself to the surface, rising a few feet before icy hands closed around his ankle, and pulled him down into the shadowy depths. Beneath him, swirling shadows gathered in a feeding frenzy as reason fled in the face of terror.

Her features were twisted into animal-like fury as she pulled herself up the length of his body. He continued to kick out with his feet, struggling to push himself to the surface. He slapped at her with his good hand, the panic once caged now unleashed as his heartbeat thundered in his ears, and he noted, with a calm that resided like an oasis in the center of his panic, that the dial had moved from yellow to red on the air meter.

He was out of air.

With his uninjured hand, he unbuckled his weight belt and let it slip from around his waist. Unencumbered by the weights designed to give him near neutral buoyancy, he shot up through the water as his own natural buoyancy took over.

The girl clung to him until they reached the terminator, that point where the light could not penetrate the murky depths, a line of darkness that separated day from night. She fell back into the shadows as he shot towards the surface, holding his breath, aware that he had a long spell in the decompression chamber ahead of him.

He doubted he would be back. Fiddlers Pond had taken something from him this day. It had stripped him of his ignorance of those shadowy places. From this day on he would view the darkness with renewed fear, for it was within those depths real nightmares lived.

40

Donnie wasn't surprised to find the back door of Abner Fields's house unlocked. Porter Mines was a small town, and as such a locked door would have been the exception. It would not have slowed him down one bit. He stepped into a small kitchen lit by the faint glow of a night light above the counter.

A solid object brushed against his leg and he jumped, nearly shouting in surprise. A cat gazed up at him with luminous eyes. Kneeling, he scratched the cat's chin as it rubbed against his leg and purred.

Followed by the cat, Donnie crossed the kitchen and stepped into the living room. Here the shadows were deeper, and he stopped to let his eyes adjust to the gloom. Old fears stirred as he stared into the emptiness, touching him on a deep, primal level. Reaching from the shadows to caress his mind and awaken old fears he believed long vanquished.

As a child he'd always been afraid of the dark. Confident its unplumbed depths hid a multitude of horrors waiting their chance to pounce upon him. His friends filled his mind with tales of the Witch of Porter Mines and how she came in the night to lead bad children into the shadows where they would never see their loved ones again.

Later he learned some horrors lived in the cold light of day. Right under their noses. He saw his father, as he had that day, struggling against the noose as the mob pulled him higher into the air. He kicked and bucked against the rope, his face a contorted mask of agony as the flesh of his face slowly turned a deep blue.

In his final moments, with the last of his dying strength, he clawed at the soft tissue of his neck, opening the flesh, his spilled blood staining the collar of his shirt. With a final kick he became still as death claimed him.

The mob stood below his lifeless figure, silent, sated. Several of the faces becoming burned into young Donnie's memory. One belonged to Sheriff Odenton, who at the time had been a deputy. Donnie remembered him as the man who stepped aside to let the mob carry his father into the street. He represented all that was wrong with the world, an authority figure who dispensed justice to those he deemed worthy of receiving it. They were responsible for protecting his father, not handing him over to the mob without a fight, and they failed.

Donnie would have his justice. First, he would remove the aura of safety that permeated this town, then he would remove the sheriff.

Odenton would be the last, and afterwards Donnie would fade into the town's past as the Witch did after every appearance. Forgotten until the time came again for her return.

From the black corners of the house came the sound of someone fumbling with an object. A light came on at the other end of a short hall, and Donnie's next victim walked in a sleepy daze from the bedroom to what Donnie assumed was the bathroom.

Donnie started down the hall, stopping when a board groaned beneath his foot.

Abner, dressed in a pair of boxers, stopped in mid-stride, and looked up at Donnie at the other end of the hallway. Dazed confusion became fear and Abner spun around to race back to his bedroom. Donnie ran after him. The old man managed to get through his door and close it before Donnie could reach him.

Without hesitation, Donnie led with his shoulder and plowed through the flimsy door. Inside the bedroom Abner was on the other side of his bed at his dresser. He turned with a handgun in one hand, the muzzle aimed at Donnie.

"Hold it right there.."

Donnie raised his hands to shoulder height, watching Abner with a predatory gaze.

"Step back." Abner tried to sound commanding, yet failed, his hand with the pistol trembling. Donnie stepped back as Abner came around the bed to the telephone on the stand next to it. The muzzle wavered and Donnie smiled. It would be like taking candy from a baby.

Abner glanced at the phone. When he did Donnie closed the distance between them, grabbing the hand with the gun and pointing it straight up as he reached for Abner's throat with his other hand.

Abner squeezed off a shot, the sound deafening in the close confines of the room. A hole appearing in the plaster ceiling.

Donnie wrenched the gun from Abner's hand and tossed it on the rumpled bed.

"I'll give you anything you want," Abner said.

Donnie forced him to sit on the edge of the bed and held his hands before him as he wrapped them with the duct tape he'd brought.

"I have money, jewelry, anything at all, don't hurt me, please."

Donnie stopped and looked at him, recalling the younger Abner, who with Andy, were the first to confront Deputy Odenton, the raging mob behind them. He didn't seem so all-powerful now.

Without a word Donnie yanked him to his feet and forced him down the hallway.

Abner cried softly. "I'm sorry, for whatever it was I did, please, I'm so sorry."

They stopped in the kitchen, the cat twining between their legs, meowing for someone, anyone, to pay attention to him.

"You don't remember, do you?" Donnie finally spoke.

Abner searched Donnie's face, shaking his head. "I'm sorry. I don't."

Donnie's rage bubbled to the surface, the same rage that had gotten him into trouble every day of his life after he was sent to live with his mother.

"Please don't hurt me." Abner cowered from his rage. Liquid splattered onto the floor as the odor of urine assailed him. Abner pissed himself, and Donnie's disgust added fuel to his rage.

"You don't remember Adam Tasker? Or what you did to him?"

"I'm sorry, please, I don't know what you're talking about." Abner held his bound hands up to protect himself.

Donnie grabbed him by the front of his tee shirt, balling the fabric in his hand as he drew Abner's face close to his own. Gazing into the old man's rheumy eyes, he realized that Abner was senile. Of course, he didn't remember, his mind was gone. For all he knew, this was some twisted nightmare that had suddenly gotten out of hand.

Donnie's desire for vengeance faltered in the face of Abner's senility. What good was it to exact vengeance when the intended victim had no memory of what they did to deserve it?

Andy was different. He knew why Donnie was there. Abner was lucky to remember his own name between breakfast and lunch.

It had to be done. He'd made a promise to that sinister side while locked up in Chino. Imagining the look of horror on his intended victims' faces when they realized the past had come back to bite them in the ass. It was the only thing that kept him going during those lonely days in solitary.

"Please, don't hurt me." A faint smile played at the corners of Abner's lips. An attempt to make himself appear harmless, or a slip of the mask he was hiding behind to avoid paying for what he'd done. The latter stoked Donnie's need for vengeance.

He grabbed Abner by the back of his neck and spun him around to march him outside. He'd borrowed a car for the evening's festivities. The owner had no clue their '03 Cavalier was no longer in the driveway. He'd leave it at the scene, give them a real surprise when the police came calling.

When they got outside Abner's thin arms shivered in the cold night air, and a small part of Donnie, that which hadn't been completely brutalized by his past, felt a passing moment of pity for the old guy.

A pity that was quickly overwhelmed by his earlier rage as he led Abner to the waiting car, pushing him into the back seat before climbing behind the steering wheel. On the passenger's seat lay a coil of three-quarter-inch manila rope, fifty cents a foot at the local hardware store.

Pretty cheap considering what it was going to be used for.

41

Deputy Franke struggled to keep his eyes open as the headlights of his cruiser filled the empty road before him. The dark forest pressed in close on either side as he followed Jackson Hollow Road, a winding ribbon of blacktop that cut through the wilderness. It came to a dead end at Route Forty, the national road, a part of which served as Main Street for Porter Mines.

Drunk patrol was officially over. The only highlight of the night ended with the closing of the Wild Water Inn on Jackson Hollow Road. Only two people came out, the bartender being one of them. The other was Councilman Dodd, and though he staggered a bit, Deputy Franke didn't feel it was enough to warrant him spending the rest of the night filling out paperwork.

The members of the council were off limits anyway. His father-in-law made that clear when he'd gotten him the job at the Sheriff's office.

"Play your cards right," he told him, "and in a few years you'll be the new sheriff." Being the new sheriff was the furthest thing from his mind. His most immediate concern was a warm bed in the last cell on the right.

Turning onto Route Forty, he followed the yellow line for two miles before he entered Porter Mines proper when he passed the old post office on the right. Closed in '98 as a cost-saving measure, the building that once housed the post office now served as an extension office for the Maryland State Highway Administration.

Across from the SHA stood the old library. It too had been abandoned by the passage of time. Porter's Hardware was next to that, with a branch office of the First National Bank occupying the corner of Route Forty and Long Branch Road, where their satellite office was located.

The other side of Route Forty was filled by a row of old brick buildings whose architecture reached back to the eighteen hundreds. It was listed on the national registry of historical places. It did little to bring business to the small city center as a large percentage of the shops occupying the first floors were vacant. All that remained was a small bookstore that many suspected was on its last legs.

Walmart and Lowe's were mostly responsible for what happened to small town America. The problem began before they came onto the scene with the creation of the mall.

Porter Mines was no different than any other small town in the country. Its once vibrant Main Street reduced to a veritable ghost town by simple progress. In contrast, Porter's Hardware was thriving by virtue of the fact that most of its employees were old timers who could tell you how to wire a light switch and diagnose a problem with your hot water heater by listening to the symptoms. It was a degree of experience lacking in many of the big box retailers.

Another factor that kept Porter's afloat was old man Porter's great-grandfather started the business back in the eighteen hundreds. It owned most of the buildings on Main Street. Collecting lease payments that would keep the hardware store afloat for the next hundred years.

At the flashing yellow light where Route Forty and Long Branch Road met, Deputy Franke turned onto the narrow street where the satellite office was located. Pulling to the curb, he shut off the engine and climbed from behind the wheel. He was halfway to the front door when he stopped and turned to look across at the darkened streetlight. Something caught his attention as he walked by. At first, he couldn't make out anything in the deep shadows. As his eyes adjusted to the gloom, he realized something was hanging from the streetlight.

His desire for sleep forgotten, he stepped off the curb and crossed to the hanging object. A chill scrambled down the length of his spine as he got closer. The object slowly materialized from the shadows and he saw a pair of bare feet hanging six feet above the pavement. They slowly turned towards him, the toes pointed at the roadway, the hem of a pair of pajama bottoms showing above the ankle.

He looked up into the face of Abner Fields, whose bulging eyes stared back at him from his swollen face. His tongue protruded from a gaping mouth that would never take another breath of fresh air.

Deputy Franke whimpered when Abner's gaze fell upon him. He stumbled back as the whimper became a cry of terror.

42

One of the perks of being a receptionist for the biggest real estate office in the area was the contacts Susan had access to. Eric had done several jobs for the broker where she worked so it was easy to find his current job location.

Susan pulled behind Eric's truck sitting in front of a small frame house. From behind the house came the sounds of construction. Hammers driving nails, saws cutting wood, and carpenters yelling at one another.

She remained in her car, going over everything that happened since she learned Porter Mines was not the best place to raise Christine. Running away was out of the question. She'd already run enough when she fled the from west coast after john's death. The time had come to dig in her heels and fight back. If the witch wanted Christine, she'd have to go through her to get her.

When she first arrived, everyone she met had been so open and welcoming. Not completely she corrected herself. They failed to mention the legend of the Witch, and the belief that she was coming back to take her due.

Would she have believed them if they had?

She doubted it. Even now, she had a hard time believing the ghost of a woman who died hundreds of years before could be responsible for what was happening. Something else going on, something more plausible than a ghost, and when it was revealed everyone would say.

Why didn't I think of that?

Eric came around the side of the house and she climbed from her car to confront him. As she approached, she was struck by his haggard appearance. He'd always been clean-shaven, now it looked like he hadn't shaved for several days. The beard heightened his already handsome features that filled her with a desire to take him right there, in the side yard, for all the neighbors to see.

"Hey stranger." She tried to appear less desperate that she was. She didn't know what she'd do if she lost Eric. Christine loved him, and it wasn't fair for her to lose another man in her life while she was still so young.

Eric looked up, startled, then dropped his eyes as he mumbled, "I'm sorry." He changed direction to go around Susan.

She stepped into his path. "What happened?"

Eric stopped, looking down at her with an exhausted expression.

"Can we talk?"

Eric shrugged, and turned to the curb where he sat down. Susan followed, sitting down beside him.

"What did I do?" Susan said.

"It's not you," Eric said after a long pause in which Susan was certain he wasn't going to say anything.

She laughed nervously. "The ultimate break up line."

Eric turned to look at her, his haunted expression stirring an old fear in the pit of her stomach. She was reminded of the day at a farm pond when she was eight and nearly drowned.

She and her cousins had been diving from the end of a rickety old pier, the challenge being to touch the bottom with their feet. What they didn't know was someone had thrown an old mattress into the pond. Over the years the water dissolved all but the coiled springs inside.

When her turn came she leapt into the air and with her toes pointed straight down she plunged to the bottom of the lake. One ankle became tangled in a spring and when she pushed off the bottom to return to the surface she was pulled back down.

She saw her friends on the pier above, just beyond the reach of her outstretched hands as her lungs screamed in her chest and her heartbeat pounded in her ears. Near the end, as her lungs struggled in her chest, she had seen them. Dark shapes that slid through the water, gathering around her as death approached.

They were real, she realized. Inhabiting a place that existed on the other side of that veil of reality we kept securely wrapped about ourselves. Populating the shadows gathered along the edges of our well-lit world. The ghosts of the past clamoring for our attention as we went about our daily lives, coming in the night as sleep eluded us, filling our minds with the regret of goals never accomplished.

"She's real, you know," Eric said.

"Who's real?"

"The Witch. Mom and dad used to threaten us if we didn't listen, she would come and take us in the night."

It was no different than her mother threatening them with the closet if they didn't listen. The only difference being that for Susan, the closet was real. Was the Witch real? To Eric she seemed to be.

"I've seen her." Eric continued.

He was the second person to tell her this, and a chill wound its way down her spine.

"She came for me, and my sister pushed me out of the room." At this he dropped his head into his hands. "It should have been me," he finished.

"It shouldn't have been any of you."

Eric looked up at this. "You didn't grow up around here. You don't know what it was like. Me and my friends, we knew it could be any of us."

"What about your parents? Weren't they watching out for you?"

"Of course, by the time they had grown up they forgot that they once lived under the same threat. It was like a switch had been thrown, and everything they were afraid of as a child became make believe. The legend of the Witch was another old wives' tale used to help keep their kids in line."

Susan shook her head. "You said you saw her?"

Eric nodded and his hands trembled. "She came for me in the middle of the night, it wasn't an old witch. She looked like my best friend, Jacob. He had vanished the week before. It was as if the Witch were wearing my friend like a mask so I would let her in. My sister must have heard me because she came and pushed me out of the room. Then she was gone."

"They never found her?"

"They never found any of them. They vanished into thin air. As if they had never been. The police did everything they could to find her. We all knew they wouldn't. Me and my friends, we knew the Witch had taken her. My parents kept hoping she would be found. She never was and my mom died never learning if Jessica was alive or dead."

"How many?"

"How many what?" Eric said as he lifted his head.

"How many kids has she taken?" Susan was afraid that by voicing the question she would give the old legend, wives' tale, or whatever it was, more power over them. Like a fairy tale that could only be real if enough people believed.

"I only know of four, my sister Jessica, Billy Trembley who lived over on Woodcock hollow, Jacob Williams, and Lindsay Raines, Mildred's niece."

"Lindsay was taken by the Witch?"

Eric nodded as Susan placed her hand on his arm. "I'm sorry about your sister."

They fell silent, time ticking away as they sat on the curb. To anyone driving by it would look like they were a couple passing the time of the day.

Susan was the first to break the silence.

"Christine misses you."

"I miss her, I miss both of you. I'm afraid I'm not going to be able to prevent what will happen."

"What's going to happen?" Susan wasn't sure she really wanted to hear what he was about to say.

"She's going to get Christine."

It felt like the world had been yanked out from under her. She didn't know what she would do if she lost Christine. She was her baby, her only connection to the first man she every loved. When she looked into Christine's eyes, she saw a little bit of John looking back at her. She'd already lost John and couldn't bear the idea of losing Christine as well.

"Then help me," she said.

"Help you what?"

"Protect her, watch over her, be there for both of us." With the last she slipped her hand into Eric's. It made everything right with the world, and as she did, she realized she was long past getting on with her own life. The time had come to put some things behind her. To let the past lay where it belonged. Her daughter's life depended on it.

43

The sound of a car door slamming brought Donnie fully awake, and he glanced at Marie who was sound asleep, the sheets wrapped around her body. Swinging his legs over the edge of the bed, he pushed himself up, and crossed to the window where he peeked out along the side of the drawn shade. Three patrol cars sat in the driveway. He caught a glimpse of a brown-shirted deputy crossing the yard to the other side of the house.

At the opposite window he spotted two more deputies with shotguns slipping along that side of the house.

"Come on, wake up," he said as he retrieved his pants from the floor. He hopped across the room on one foot as he slipped on his jeans.

"What's wrong? What's going on?" Marie lifted her head from the pillow, squinting against the sunlight at Donnie. Her expression reminded him of his mother after a night of drinking and sex.

She had left his father and fled to the West Coast because he was boring. Her dream was to become an actress like the ones appearing in the weekly movies she watched. Instead she became a porn star, and not a particularly good one at that. Her addiction to cocaine ruled her life. When Donnie showed up, she tried to change with this added responsibility, yet old habits die hard, and by the end of the first week she was back to partying with anyone willing to trade a line of coke for a blowjob.

She OD'd on his sixteenth birthday, and the state stepped in to take him into the foster care program. The first night away from home he escaped, and never went back. Falling in with a group of other youths, he learned to live on the street. He became well-known to the local police, and for his eighteenth birthday he was given the gift of a five-year stretch in Chino.

He was at the junction of a crossroad, presented with a choice that had been made for him long ago. Down one path lay a life of security and comfort while the other led to this junction in his life.

The only man who could have saved him had not been protected by a system designed to protect those who could not protect themselves. It was why he came back. He had come to destroy them, and the institution that protected them.

"We know you're in there." A familiar voice came, amplified by a bull horn.

"Who's that?" Marie asked.

"I'm sorry." Donnie wished things could have been different. Marie had proven herself to be a good person and he felt bad for the trouble he'd drawn her into.

It wasn't her fault her father had been involved in his father's death. It was this realization that prevented him from carrying through with the next stage of his plan. That caused him to understand that even with all the bad that happened in his past, he was still a good person.

When he found out who she was, he decided to make it look like she killed herself. To bring the sorrow he'd known to her father before Donnie paid him a final visit. After Abner, with the realization the old man didn't even know why he was being persecuted, the steam had been let out of his anger. It was still there, smoldering beneath the surface, the rage it once fueled exhausted.

He came to realize, while driving away from Abner's hanging body, that a different path was open to him. One he could have followed if only he pushed aside the hate that ruled his life.

"What have you done?" Marie asked.

He shrugged, a small part of himself dying under her disproving stare. He could have made things different. He realized that now. He was in charge of his destiny. Not the state, not even a god, he himself was responsible for his actions, or lack thereof.

"You promised me," she said.

"I have to go."

"Are you going to give yourself up?"

Donnie shook his head. "I can't go back." And it was true, he couldn't. He wasn't the person he used to be. His anger had been spent, and if he went back now, they would eat him alive.

44

After slipping out the back door, Donnie surprised a deputy who was sneaking around the corner of the house with a shotgun in his hands. Before the deputy could react, he dropped him with a right cross to the chin. The deputy sagged against the wall, and Donnie eased him to the ground.

At his bike, he threw his leg over the seat and hit the starter button. The V-twin roared to life and he pushed back the kickstand as he dropped it into second and popped the clutch. A second deputy jumped back as he roared around the corner in a spray of gravel. Three patrol cars blocked the driveway, forcing him to skirt the edge of the drive, where thick brush threatened to pull him from his ride.

Reaching pavement, he gunned the engine and raced away with a squeal of rubber. No one was pursuing him, yet. But he knew he couldn't outrun a radio. He let the bike have its head as he raced along the winding country road. Leaning into the turns, his knees nearly scraping the pavement, as he wove back and forth.

Rounding a turn, he came upon a cruiser sitting sideways in the road. To the right was a dirt road that vanished into the forest. Without hesitation, he raced down the road, throwing up a rooster tail of dust in his wake.

The dense trees to either side kept him from determining where he was or where he was going. He was running blind, following the trail before him. Reacting to the obstacles thrown into his path.

The trees thinned on the right and he became aware of an opening in the tree cover. Maybe it was another road? He gunned the engine as the end of the path appeared before him.

He went up and over, expecting to land on solid pavement. Instead the sparkling black waters of Fiddlers Pond spread out below him, and he knew he was fucked.

Momentum gave way to gravity as he and the bike dropped, like a stone, to the water below. He pushed away from the bike, one becoming two, unwilling to ride it through the impact that was coming. The cuff of his jeans was tangled in the peg, and instead of separating fully he followed the bike's trajectory into the water.

Together they hit the surface, hard, his leg driven against unyielding steel. Pain flared in his ankle where the bone snapped from the impact. Down they went into the black depths, man and machine entwined as one while Donnie fought to release his pants leg and return to the surface.

As the sunlight dwindled, the darkness around him came to life with sinuous movement. He struggled to break free as his heart hammered in his ears, and a low roar blanketed all other sounds. Black shapes darted around him as he plunged deeper, following the trail of oily bubbles from his bike. He managed to get loose and tilted his head back to watch the surface as he rose to it.

Suddenly he was moving sideways, captured by a powerful current that swept him toward the blank face of the stone wall towering over the lake. With his lungs screaming for air he was driven to an opening in the stony face.

Then he was inside, his body battered against unyielding stone as he was pulled deeper beneath the earth. His lungs screaming in his chest and when he was sure it was all over.

When he'd reached the point of no return, and knew his body would soon betray him, he bobbed to the surface of a swift moving underground stream.

A stead roar came from the darkness ahead as he gorged on the musty air. He struggled to swim away from the sound, pain running the length of his shattered leg. He knew what the roar meant, the steam led to a waterfall, and if he allowed himself to be pulled over its side he might never see the light of day again. His prison would become the earth itself and no one would hear his screams.

His fingertips brushed against a smooth surface and he lunged forward, searching for a handhold in the slick stone as the swift moving current tried to take him. He managed to slip the fingers of his other hand into a narrow crack, jamming them in, tearing the flesh of his knuckles.

Searching with his hands, unable to see a thing in the black emptiness, he pulled himself onto a narrow ledge. Pain throbbed in his ankle as the cold air of the cave burrowed into his wet clothes, deepening the chill that enveloped his body. From his pocket he retrieved a lighter and tried the spark wheel. It was wet and no sparks issued from the small wheel. He blew on it, hoping his breath would dry it, and after trying several more attempts he was rewarded with a brief flash.

With the soft light from his lighter, he explored his surroundings. He lay upon a narrow ledge next to the black waters of a swift moving stream that vanished into the void with a steady roar. To his left was the sheer stone wall of the cave. Sitting up, he strained to look around, noting that the ledge he lay upon continued past his feet into the darkness beyond.

Working his way around, he followed the narrow path away from the steady roar that continued to nibble at his calm reserve.

If he had not caught himself?

The question surfaced and he shuddered at the only logical conclusion. Had he gone over the edge of the waterfall, if the fall had not killed him, he would have been lost forever beneath the earth. The ultimate solitary confinement. He'd been lucky to find the ledge, but luck was at times a double-edged sword.

With the faint glow from the lighter illuminating his way, he crawled along the path until it turned left away from the water and opened into a chamber large enough for him to stand.

Leaning against the wall to keep his weight off of his bad ankle, he shut off his lighter and waited. As his eyes adjusted, he became aware of a dim glow coming from somewhere above him. He looked up, searching for the source of the light, to find only a void.

"Mommy," a child's voice moaned in the shadows ahead and he shuddered at the terror filling that solitary word.

He flicked his lighter again, the flame weaker than before, offering little hope before it winked out completely. That faint glow returned as the school yard nursery rhyme from his childhood in Porter Mines whispered through his mind.

One, two, the Witch is due. The light ahead grew brighter as the air around him was fouled with the sweet scent of roasting pork. It was an odor that brought to mind a moment from his past, when he was a prisoner of the state of California. One of the prisoners was selling information to the guards to ease his time. As they were about to lock down for the night, several prisoners strolled by the snitch's cell. Two squirted him with lighter fluid, while the third tossed a lit book of matches at him as the cell door slammed shut. By the time, the Correction Officers were able to open the cell, it was too late.

Three, four, she's at the door. The chilled air was driven away by a hot wind that blew from the nether regions of hell itself. Ash and smoke filled his nose and mouth and he gagged.

Five, six, who will she pick? A scream shot through the air as the light grew brighter. Yellow, and red, orange, and white, crackling with the voice of an unleashed inferno.

Seven, eight, at night she waits. The air around him became thick with ash and he struggled to breathe. From the other end of the tunnel a shadowy form moved towards him.

Nine, ten, don't let her in.

"They are mine," a voice shrieked through the tunnel, and Donnie dropped to his knees, clasping his hands over his ears. The silhouettes of a line of children, back light by the glow of a distant fire, approached in single file.

When they were close, he lifted his lighter and spun the wheel. The small yellow flame illuminated the cracked and blistered face of an old woman whose eyes glittered with a harsh light. Behind her stood the children in various stages of decay. The first dressed in a pair of bib overalls.

Donnie recognized his face from the newspaper, Nathan, he was the second child to vanish this summer. Then Donnie knew no more as an inferno of pain washed over him.

45

While Eric was coming up the driveway Christine ran towards Brenda's waiting car, under one arm she carried the velveteen rabbit Mildred had given her.

"Where did you get the rabbit?" he said kneeling.

"Miss Raines gave him to me." Her voice lacked any enthusiasm, gone was the child-like joy of meeting another day, in its place was a dreary acceptance of the fate that awaited her.

"What's his name?"

"I dunno, he won't tell me." She whispered in the rabbit's ear before holding his face close to her own ear. Disappointment etched into her features. "I wish I still had Puddles. He could protect me from the witch. He has Daddy's heart."

"I'm sorry, sweetie, I'll try to get him back for you, I promise. I'll do everything I can to get him back."

"He's gone forever, Lizzie took him, and she won't give him back to me."

"Let's go Christine, gotta get you to school." Brenda motioned for her to hurry and Christine nodded.

"I'll try again," Eric said.

Christine gave him a fierce one-armed hug, a glimmer of hope in her somber eyes. "Thank you," she said before turning to run to Brenda's car.

Eric pushed himself to his feet and watched as she climbed into the waiting booster seat.

How can we protect her? He worried as Brenda waved before she turned to strap in Christine.

The fastest and safest thing would be to move away until everything blew over. Let the Witch take her due and go back to sleep for another thirty years. By then Christine would be all grown up.

Susan laid her hand on his arm. "I'm glad you came back."

"How does a person get a cup of coffee around here?" he said as Brenda pulled away and he turned to follow Susan to the house.

"I can put on a fresh pot." Eric followed Susan to the front door, hesitating at the threshold, aware that once he stepped through, he was committing himself to protecting them. He would no longer have only himself to worry about. If he were alone, he could stay away until everything settled down. He was tired of being by himself. He wanted someone to share his life with, his successes, his failures, his happiness, and his sorrow. He wanted Susan by his side and if that meant standing up to what was coming, so be it.

Susan retrieved Christine's tray from the living room. Her sweats pulled tight against her body, the sloppy tee shirt riding up to reveal her bare midriff.

Would she object to his advances? He doubted it.

She turned with the tray in hand, catching Eric staring at her. Her need written clearly on her face.

"I'm sorry, I didn't mean to stare."

"It's okay." She straightened her shirt, looking away, plucking at the hem with her free hand. She crossed to where he stood, her proximity caused his collar to become tight. He felt like a damned school kid.

"I'm just...I don't know...I'm sorry."

"Sorry for what." She leaned in close, looking up at him with questioning eyes.

He wanted to bend down and kiss her, wrap his arms around her. cradle her in his embrace. Instead he took a step back, afraid he might do something foolish. Disappointment flashing in her eyes.

The phone rang in the kitchen. Susan glanced in its direction, then looked up at him, her face a mask of conflicting emotions.

"I better get that," she said, breaking the spell. She pushed past him, brushing against his chest with an electric touch. Eric followed, listening to Susan's side of the conversation.

"I understand," Susan said, "no, that's all right, you take care of your mother. I'll work something out. Thanks for calling." Susan hung up the phone and looked across the kitchen with a worried expression.

"What's wrong?" Eric said.

"It's Brenda. Her mother had a heart attack and she's going to Baltimore to take care of her. Christine's in school. One of us will have to pick her up. She won't be able to watch Christine the rest of the week."

"You'll be here, won't you?"

Susan nodded, "After what happened the other day, I want someone to keep a close eye on her." She glanced at the newspaper on the table. "Especially now."

Eric had seen the paper that morning and understood her concern.

Susan searched through her pocketbook. "I know I put her number in here, she wrote it down for me."

"Who?"

"Mildred. Here it is." Susan dialed the number.

"You're not going to ask Mildred to watch her, are you?"

"Why not? You said she was a schoolteacher."

"Yeah, but..." Eric began, and Susan held up her hand to stop him.

"I've spoken to the Sheriff about her. He said there's nothing to worry about, she was never under suspicion."

"You spoke to the Sheriff? When?"

"The other day. He stopped to ask if I'd seen any suspicious vehicles on the side road. I told him no." Susan turned her attention to the phone. "Hello, Mildred. It's Susan."

Eric wandered to the laundry room. His gaze drawn to that dark opening. It's coming. He knew it as well as he knew the back of his own hand, and there wasn't a damned thing anyone could do about it.

46

Amber stood at her bedroom door, listening to the birthday party taking place below her.

It's not fair.

She'd been sent to her room for acting up during Tommy's party. Tommy was her older brother, and though she loved him with a passion, at times he could be a real turd.

She giggled at the idea. Turd. Poopy, ka-ka, brown submarines. The latter was what Tommy called them. *Another brown submarine has been sent on a secret mission.* He'd say upon leaving the bathroom full of a noxious odor.

Amber knew another word to describe brown submarines. One that would get her mouth washed out with soap. She learned the latter the hard way after Tommy taught it to her.

He and his friends were playing X-box in the basement, and they thought it was hilarious when she said the word. Her mom didn't think it was too funny when she took her new comedy act to the kitchen.

That single word cost her a day in her room and early to bed without dessert, topped off with the threat to wash her mouth out with soap if she ever uttered it again.

Amber wasn't sure what soap would taste like, but it couldn't be good. The few sips she'd taken of her bathwater had proven that point.

"I have a secret." The whisper came and she turned from the door to search her bedroom. It sounded like it had come from the closet and she crossed the closed door.

"I have a secret." That voice whispered again and this time she was certain it came from within the closet. With a touch of trepidation, she opened the door and peered into its shadowy depths. Her clothes hung in neat rows from the rod above. The floor below a mess of dirty clothes, pieces of games she'd lost interest in, and a few of her Barbie dolls.

Nothing hid in the shadows, so she swung the door closed and shrugged. Crossing to her bed, she climbed up and lay her head on the pillow next to Miss Pea, her favorite doll.

"I have a secret." That voice persisted, and Amber looked about her room, trying to locate its source. She wasn't sure if she was actually hearing the voice, or if it was in her head. The notion that it might be a ghost never entered her mind. She had been spared from ever learning about such things by an over-protective mother. Yet she knew what a brown submarine was thanks to her brother.

Without fear, she searched her small room for the origin of the voice. Wondering if maybe it was a small fairy speaking to her. Something like Tinker Bell from the book her mom always read to her. She searched through the pile of stuffed animals in the corner of her room.

Not there.

She turned her attention to her dresser, intent on searching every drawer, when from the corner of her eye she spotted movement beyond her window. Crossing her room, she gazed into the forest crowding close behind the house. In the yard below was the swing set she and Tommy would play on from time to time.

"I have a secret."

The voice was coming from the forest and Amber scanned its gloomy depths. At the tree line she spotted a young girl who was looking up at her. She wore a faded summer dress that was insufficient protection against the cold.

"I have a secret." Amber was certain it was coming from the little girl. She liked secrets. She even had a couple of her own. Like how she had broken Tommy's x-box after he refused to let her play a game. Or how she used her mommy's hairbrush to brush Wilson's shaggy coat.

She knew all about secrets. What was this girl's secret?

Opening her door, laughter came from the party in the basement. It was mommy and daddy, as well as Tommy and a few of his friends, having a good time without her.

It wasn't fair.

"I have a secret." She wanted to know what her secret was.

Carefully she tiptoed down the hall and down the steps. At the bottom, she stepped over Wilson, who lay sprawled in front of the heat vent, absorbing the warm air flowing from it. Wilson looked up at her as she passed over him, the tip of his tail wagged briefly before he lowered his head to his paws and stared at the heat vent.

In the hallway, she pulled her jacket down from its peg, and with Miss Pea tucked securely under her arm, she slipped out the front door, closing it quietly behind her.

Amber rounded the house into the back yard and spotted the girl standing in the tree line. She waved and received no reply. With a shrug, she crossed the back yard and entered the forest's gloomy depths.

47

Pete had not slept for three days, and the drugs they'd given him had done little to alleviate the problem. The cast on his leg conspired with the pain to keep him from moving freely. On the wall opposite, the television droned on, some late-night infomercial about a vacuum cleaner that could handle all your household chores.

Could it handle ghosts? The question came and he laughed, a dry cackle that held no merriment.

She's out there.

To the right of the television a picture window framed the forest. A scene that once held little threat to him. An avid outdoorsman, there was a time when he was more comfortable in the woods than anywhere else.

The girl changed all that and thinking of her made him feel like he'd become untethered from the world he knew. The drugs didn't help, and he struggled to cling to his sanity as the night moved slowly toward dawn.

The forest was full of mysteries. Old secrets that once discovered could never be unlearned. Though man thought he knew everything, his knowledge did not extend to those quiet places. Where the sun refused to shine, and the wind dare not disturb. Areas animals avoided, as if the soil itself was tainted by the passage of things living at the edge of madness.

From the kitchen behind him came the sound of movement, the soft whisper of bare feet across linoleum. A floorboard creaked, and he pulled his revolver from the cushion beside him. Gripping the handle in a death grip, his hand shaking, the muzzle danced a jig as he lifted the pistol from its hiding place.

He was ready for them, he thought.

In the picture window a reflection moved behind him. It had to be his imagination playing tricks on him. He was so tired he could barely keep his eyes open. Every time he closed them, he found her waiting for him. Watching him with that dead, featureless, gaze.

"Who's there?" He tried to turn around to see who it was. If it were Doug, he'd shoot the fucker for nearly giving him a heart attack.

The reflection moved as soft footsteps came from behind him. As it came closer, more details emerged. A shadow fell across him, cast by the light from the kitchen.

"Please," he moaned. The pistol forgotten.

An icy hand came to rest on his shoulder as drops of water fell into his hair. The musty odor of decay filled the room around him. In the picture window, a white oval surrounded by long strands of black hair floated above his head as another small hand came to rest on his other shoulder.

With her presence came memories that had been long suppressed. Memories of fleeing through the forest on his bike. Shadows filled the trees behind him, enveloping the path he was on, nipping at his back tire as he escaped from what he'd seen. A shattered bicycle, the frame twisted unnaturally, blood staining the handlebars that only moments ago his younger brother Jimmy had been holding onto.

Now he was gone, vanishing into the shadowy depths that pursued him. A day of swimming ending before it even began. Cut short by a child's cry that would forever haunt his dreams.

"Jimmy's waiting for you," a sinister voice whispered in his ear, dead breath tickling the short hairs on the nape of his neck, carrying with it the odor of rot.

"No," Pete whispered as a cold hand covered his own, wrapped around the butt of his pistol. Pete shook his head as his hand was lifted, the muzzle turned it was resting against his temple.

"Please," he whispered, tears rolling down his cheeks, his brother's cries echoed through his mind.

"He's on the other side, waiting."

Pete shook his head, overwhelmed with sorrow and terror that battled for control as he blubbered like a scolded child.

A single shot was swallowed by the night as Pete's terror ended abruptly, and his soul's torment began.

48

Susan sipped hot tea while Mildred worked on her knee. She originally wanted to pick up Christine and get back home to get supper ready. Mildred convinced her to let her take care of her injury. She'd taken a spill on the steps while carrying a few boxes to the attic. On the table beside her an old photo album was open to a page with several black and white pictures.

Susan pointed at the album. "Do you mind?"

Mildred nodded, and Susan pulled the album closer. One photo showed three babies all dressed alike, triplets. "Who's this?"

Mildred glanced at the photo. "That's me with my two sisters."

"Triplets?" Susan asked and Mildred nodded.

"You say you fell down the steps?" Mildred dabbed the cut with a cotton ball soaked in peroxide. It stung a little and Susan winced. Nothing like the medicine her mother used to use.

"Clumsy me, I was heading up to the attic with a load of boxes when I missed a step."

"These things happen. Would you like some more tea?"

Susan realized she had drained her mug and held it out to Mildred with a relieved smile. There would be plenty of time to get supper ready. Maybe she should take a moment to relax.

It wasn't that often she was pampered like this. Besides, it would give her time to get to know Mildred better.

As Mildred worked in the kitchen, Susan looked through the photo album. She came to one with an older couple and a young child, each holding one of the triplets.

"Who's the little girl?" Susan asked.

"That's my older sister, Jane." Mildred placed a mug of tea on the table next to Susan. "My dad is holding me, Mom has Margaret, and Jane is holding Michelle."

"Where's Michelle now?" Susan asked.

Mildred shook her head. "She died three weeks after the picture was taken. No one knew why at the time. One of those things that happens. We didn't know about sudden infant death syndrome back then."

"Such a shame. I'm sorry." Susan said as she flipped through the pages. The next set of photos was of Mildred and Margaret as children. They flanked their father, who stood behind a massive trophy. Each of the girls held a rifle with the butt resting on their hips.

"What's this one?" Susan asked.

Mildred looked over Susan's shoulder. "That's when we won the state shooting championship. Margaret came in first and I came in second. Dad always called us his M&M's."

"Shooting championship." Susan looked up at Mildred with a degree of respect. She had never like for guns herself, thought she had learned to use one, it was one of the things John introduced her to. He said it made him feel better knowing she could take care of herself if she needed to.

Mildred shrugged self-consciously. "Dad always wanted boys but got girls instead, so he raised Margaret and me as boys. Living on a farm, there's not much to do beyond chores. He got us interested in shooting when we were five."

Christine came into the room carrying a Barbie doll.

"Can I keep her, Mommy?" she asked.

It was the one toys Susan had fought to keep Christine from wanting to play with. She believed it sent all the wrong messages about body image and self-esteem. Yet it was such an iconic part of growing up it was heart-wrenching to tell Christine no when she asked for one.

All of her friends at Brenda's had one and Susan, who knew how cruel children could be, understood that her refusal to let Christine have a Barbie doll was having a detrimental effect. She could see it on her daughter's face. They had only recently moved to the area and she was already an outsider. It might explain why she created an invisible friend to play with.

"We've talked about this before."

"All my friends have them." Christine pleaded with her eyes.

"If all your friends had measles, I suppose you would want that too?"

"No."

"One wouldn't hurt, would it?" Mildred asked.

Susan glanced at Mildred with an expression she hoped would warn her to stay out of the conversation. It didn't.

"In fact, she can have that one. It belonged to my niece," Mildred offered.

Susan wanted to say more but kept her mouth shut. After all, Mildred had been hospitable to the point of taking in

Christine when Susan had no other choice. She decided they would deal with this matter later.

"Can I, Mommy, please?"

"Okay, only this once."

Christine gave her a quick hug before racing into the other room.

"I don't agree with the message those dolls send little girls," Susan said after Christine left the room.

"What message is that?"

"The need for a perfect body image. The misplaced belief that your looks will help you get ahead in the world."

"To be honest, I don't believe they even notice," Mildred said.

"Do you have children?"

"No, never had any, was always too busy with schoolwork or taking care of the farm to worry about such things."

"Then how would you know children don't notice those things?"

Mildred smiled patiently. "I taught third grade for over twenty years. I've had a hand in raising over two hundred children. As a teacher I got to see a side of them they hid from their parents. I'd still be doing it if it weren't for a nosy reporter that tied my sister and I together."

"I'm sorry," Susan said.

"It's all water under the bridge." Mildred settled into her seat. "What brings you to our neck of woods?"

Susan raised her eyebrow at Mildred's open attempt to pry.

"After all, I'm sure you know all about me, yet I know so little about you. Such as where's Christine's father?"

The question hit a sore spot and Susan's desire was to immediately deflect it. Instead she chose to be honest.

"He was killed in Iraq a little more than a year ago," Susan replied evenly as she struggled to control the sorrow unleashed by the statement. Having never properly grieved, she was overwhelmed by emotion, and lowered her head to keep Mildred from seeing her tears.

"I am sorry for your loss." Mildred placed her hand over Susan's on the table. "Do you have family here?"

Susan shook her head.

"Such a shame. What about in-laws?"

Susan nodded. "When they have time to visit."

"So, you've been dealing with this yourself."

Susan wiped away a tear and lifted her head. She had to be strong for Christine and she struggled to get her emotions under control.

Christine entered the room and crossed to Susan.

"Are you okay, Mommy?"

"I'll be all right, sweetie, you go play." Susan wiped away her tears and got herself under control.

"What's wrong?" Christine asked.

"We were talking about Daddy."

Christine turned to Mildred. "Daddy's in heaven where he can watch over us. Mommy still cries when she talks about him."

"I see," Mildred said.

Christine left the room.

"I'm sorry," Susan said, "most times I have myself under control. Every once in a while, they get the better of me."

"That's fine. It doesn't hurt to have a good cry."

"When I can find the time."

"Maybe you need to make the time. If it would help, Christine could stay here one evening while you have a good cry and get it out of your system. It's what you need. I see it eating at you. The way you looked at Eric when I was over the other day. You need to get past this so you can get on with your life."

"Are you always this forward with people?"

"Only those I like and want to help. You need help. Your sorrows on the verge of becoming self-pity, and it will poison everything else in your life."

"How do you know this?"

"Originally, I wanted to be a psychologist, majoring in grief counseling. I've seen what unresolved grief can do to a family. My mother suffered from it after the death of our father. She locked herself in her room and wouldn't come out. She gave up living. After working as an aide in the local elementary school I switched majors to primary education."

"What happened to your dad?"

Mildred shrugged. "He was killed in an accident."

"I'm sorry,"

"That was then, this is now. I've come to terms with my life. I stay active and involved."

Susan glanced at her watch and realized it was getting late.

"We better get going," Susan said as she pushed herself up from the table. "Thank you."

"You're welcome, I haven't done any more than anyone else would."

"You've done more than you realize." For the first time in a long time Susan found herself actually looking forward to the rest of her life.

Mildred had been on target with her assessment and the realization that someone else could see what she was going through forced Susan to stand up and face her sorrow. She knew it wouldn't be an easy road. Yet with a friend like Mildred to help her along the way, she was certain the burden would be lightened.

"Let's go, Christine. I have to get supper ready."

Christine came to the door with the Barbie doll in her hand. "Can I take her home with me Mommy?"

"I don't see why not."

Christine's face lit up and Susan's spirit lifted at the sight of her daughter's joy. Who said you couldn't let a kid be a kid?

By the time they reached the house, Susan had come to a decision. It was time she moved on with her life, and she wanted Eric to be a part of it.

49

With Christine securely tucked in, Susan turned in. It was time to move on. But first, she had to say goodbye.

Lying in bed, staring at the ceiling, she thought of John. She saw him as she had the last day. Waiting to board his flight to Iraq, surrounded by the other men in his unit and the families that had come out to see them off. Dressed in desert camouflage, his duffel bag leaning against his leg. That impish smile carried a hint of worry around the edges. They both worried about what his deployment meant. They'd watched the nightly news carrying grim reports of insurgent attacks, roadside bombs, and American deaths.

"I'll be all right." he promised the night before his departure. His words full of confidence though his eyes carried a hint of worry. They spent their last night together in each other's arms. She recalled how secure his touch made her feel, and the sorrow washed through her.

He was gone.

Tears slid down her cheeks as she clung to the memory of his arms around her. The feel of his chest against her cheek, the steady beat of his heart in her ear. As the sorrow filled her, she imagined she could smell him lying next to her. She reached out to wrap her arms around the extra pillow, pulling it to her chest, and wrapping herself around it as his scent tickled her nose.

Sorrow enveloped her as she cried into the pillow, adding her tears to his fading scent. She'd never washed the pillowcase after he left. Every night after his departure, she would cuddle it as she drifted off to sleep.

His year in Iraq passed slowly. They kept in touch with letters and phone calls. During Christmas they managed to speak to one another using web cams. Susan stayed busy helping out around the base. Volunteering at the local veteran's hospital where she saw first-hand the results of the war in Iraq. Soldiers missing arms and legs. She also saw the indomitable spirit of the American soldier.

She worked a part time job during the day, off post, to help with the bills, while Christine spent her days at base day-care. They made a calendar together they called Daddy's Countdown. It hung on the refrigerator and every night before bed, Christine dutifully marked off the day. At first it seemed they would never get out of the three hundreds. Before they knew it, it was down to two hundred and thirty days.

The marks on the calendar grew as the days between the present and their future reunion with John dwindled. Soon it was only a month, then a week, and before they knew it, there remained only a few days.

She and Christine spoke with John as he finished packing for the trip to the airport. Their voices full of joy, the conversation ending with the promise that the next time they spoke it would be in person.

It was the only promise John ever broke.

She reported to work as usual, knowing that in less than twenty-four hours John would be home. Afterwards she picked Christine up from day-care, and together they stopped for a special meal at McDonald's.

Susan remembered all of it with startling clarity. Christine had the nuggets kid's meal along with the Sesame Street figure. This time she got Cookie Monster and insisted that her mother buy them a chocolate chip cookie for dessert. Why not, she relented, they would soon be together.

Pulling into their driveway, Susan saw the green sedan parked in front of their house. Fear tightened her throat as Christine babbled excitedly that Daddy was home. Susan did her best to control her as they crossed the small yard to the house. A uniformed officer exited the car and approached them.

"Mrs. Anderson?" the officer asked.

"Yes," Susan replied. With the officer was a Chaplin whose expression told her everything she needed to know, and a female officer who kept her eyes down.

"May we come inside?" the Chaplin asked.

The bottom fell out of her world and she was left asking how?

They had spoken only a few hours earlier. He was coming home.

She sat on the couch in the living room as the officer spoke in comforting tones. The Chaplin next to her, holding her hand. The female officer had taken Christine out back to play.

"We regret to inform you that your husband was killed in action."

"He was coming home," Susan said.

"Yes, ma'am, he was enroute to the airport when his vehicle was ambushed."

"He was coming home." It was all she could think to say.

Susan cried as the memory of that day washed through her. Sorrow wrapped her in its embrace as images tumbled through her mind like the blocks of a wall crumbling. In a sense it was, after John's death she built a wall around the sorrow inside her. Isolating herself from it. She did all she could to ignore it. Believing for a time it was better to pretend it hadn't happened, and that John was still in Iraq doing what he needed to do.

With her sorrow came rage and she screamed into John's pillow.

Why. Why did he have to die? She knew the answer to that as well. It was one of the things that attracted her to him in the first place. His desire to do what was right, to help others who could not help themselves. He wanted to be a police officer or a fire fighter after he got out. First, he wanted to do his part to help the people of Iraq achieve the same freedoms he enjoyed.

In a letter to Susan after a particularly grueling day, he shared that he was there for his squad too. They had become brothers, and he would do anything for them.

The last was brought home to her when his best friend from Iraq, visited Susan upon his return to the States. He told her about John and how he was always willing to help with anything. He told her how he had saved one of his squad from certain death during an ambush by drawing enemy fire to himself while the medics pulled the wounded man to safety.

Until that moment, his medals had been nothing more than fancy decorations. Afterwards, she read the commendations that accompanied them, and learned a great deal about her husband, and how much of a hero he was to Christine, and the men he served with.

With the words of his friend from Iraq in mind, Susan drifted off to sleep. John was waiting for her with that same impish smile. She reached for him as the distance between them grew.

"No," she moaned in her sleep.

They grew further apart, and Susan realized she was falling. Below her an image came into view, small yet growing larger. With a burst of terror, she realized she was looking down upon Fiddlers Pond.

"No," she moaned as the black waters rushed up to meet her. Then she was in the water, sinking to the bottom as black shapes flitted back and forth around her.

She tried to swim back to the surface and felt icy fingers wrapped around her ankle. She struggled against it to no avail as a roaring filled her ears. Her lungs swelled in her chest as the last of her dwindling air escaped to the surface above her.

She could not escape her past that easily. Memories of her mother her brother, her father came. She was in the graveyard again, the headstones all carrying a single name, Porter. With it came the visage of a witch whose cracked flesh glowed with the fires of hell.

50

Susan sat up, gasping for breath. From the hallway came a child's giggle. The nightmare that awakened her slowly dissipated as her awareness grew.

"Christine, is that you?" No answer.

What is she up to now? Susan pushed herself out of bed and crossed to the door of her room. Looking around the corner, she caught a glimpse of Christine as she turned down the steps to the first floor.

"Christine," Susan said as she followed. At the top of the steps, she caught sight of her turning right, towards the stairs that led into the basement, and the laundry room.

"Don't go down there." Susan was afraid Christine could get hurt, or worse.

She takes all the bad little girls and boys.

She raced after her, a small part of her mind aware of the bone-numbing chill coming from the laundry room. She reached the top of the steps to catch a glimpse of a small pair of bare feet vanishing into the tunnel.

"Christine, don't, it's not safe."

Susan raced down the steps and stopped at the entrance of the tunnel.

"Christine," she shouted, her cry swallowed by the eternal stillness of the tunnel. Grabbing the halogen work light, she turned it on and shot the powerful beam of light down the tunnel in time to catch sight of movement as someone vanished around a bend.

"Christine, come back." Susan cried out as she entered the tunnel with the light. She ran past the pile of bottles, the light revealing a turn carved into the tunnel wall twenty yards beyond.

She was brought up short, and yanked on the light, pulling the extension cord from the outlet. The light went out, plunging her into near total darkness as a dank chill wrapped her in its cold embrace.

"Christine," she struggled to control the panic spreading through her stomach. From the darkness came the sound of movement, and Susan took a step back, afraid. Behind her, she saw the lighted opening of the tunnel, so close, yet so far away, and she cautiously backed towards it with the halogen light held out in front of her like a shield that would protect her.

"Mommy, where are you?" Christine cried out from the light behind her.

"I'm here stay where you are baby," she said as the unmistakable sound of someone breathing came from the emptiness before her. Their presence was a black void that reached out with a chilled caress to embrace her warmth.

"Mommy, please, I'm afraid," Christine said.

"I'm coming, sweetie." She took another step back and was aware that the darkness around her was becoming brighter. The pile of bottles on her right confirmed she was getting closer to the opening, and the safety of the laundry room.

Was it really safe?

Another step back and from the emptiness came an audible sigh.

"Please," she whimpered as fear slithered through her mind. She didn't belong here. This place was filled with the forgotten memories of a time long past. Of things that had no right to exist in the rational light of day.

The shadows grew brighter as she took another step back and she knew she was near the opening into her basement. An opening that would allow whatever inhabited the darkness of this narrow passage access to her and Christine. She realized that whatever had been following her, if anything had, was now gone and she breathed a sigh of relief as she stepped into her laundry room.

"Mommy," Christine cried out, wrapping her arms around her, "I was afraid the Witch had you."

"I'm okay, baby, it's all right, everything will be fine." She struggled with her terror as it slowly dissipated.

This wouldn't do. In the kitchen she snatched the phone from its cradle and dialed Eric's number. On the second ring, he picked up.

"Hey, what's up?"

"I need you to come over right away," Susan said never taking her eyes off the hallway leading to the laundry room.

"What's wrong?"

"Don't ask any questions, come over and close this tunnel."

"I'll be right over."

51

Paul shuffled through the folders on his desk.

Bobby Carr, Nathan Fraley, and now Amber Gardener had joined the ranks of the missing children that kept him awake. He was back at his desk after a restless night filled with glimpses into the terror each of these children must have experienced.

Accompanied by units from the state police K-9 division, his deputies were once again beating the brush as they searched for the latest victim. He took her photo from the folder. Red hair braided into a pair of pig tails that framed an innocent face. Freckles splashed across her nose. Smiling at the camera with a gap-toothed grin full of an innocent enthusiasm for the future that lay ahead.

There would be no future now unless the searchers turned up something. Dragging Fiddlers Pond had been a bust and the state police diver. Rumor was he'd be spending a week in the decompression chamber after he came to the surface too fast. An experienced diver didn't do that unless something forced him to surface.

He'd spoken with the FBI and they would issue a nationwide AMBER Alert detailing the young girl's physical description and anything else they could think to add, which wasn't much.

Paul didn't believe a national alert was going to do much good. He'd asked them to send a profiler and they agreed, but it would be two weeks before someone could get there. By then, he was confident, it would all be over.

According to her parents, Amber slipped out of the house while her brother's birthday party was being held in the basement. Everything at the scene bore this out. There were no signs of forced entry, or of a struggle, nothing to indicate she was taken against her will. Whoever came to the door was someone she knew.

What signs they could turn up pointed to the woods behind the house. He'd been forced to pass the search off to the state police who brought in their own K-9 units. Doug refused to let his dogs anywhere near Fiddlers Pond, or the woods around it. Claiming they had been affected and would no longer be any good for tracking.

Pete had taken his own life shortly after his accident. He called Doug before he blew his brains out, complaining that the girl he'd seen in the forest followed him home and was lurking in the wood beside his house.

Lurking? It was a hell of a word to use, yet it fit. Everything was falling apart, and it was only a matter of time before the other shoe dropped.

His secretary poked her head in his office. "Sheriff, Councilman Haynes is on line one,"

It appeared the other shoe was about to drop. He reached for the phone with a resigned sigh. He'd done all he could, *or have I?* It would be a question that followed him to his grave.

"This is Sheriff Odenton, what can I do for you today?"

"We need to get this straightened out, Paul, right now." Councilman Haynes dispensed with the formalities they'd grown familiar with over the years. It was not going to be a pleasant call.

"I've contacted both the state police and the FBI. The state boys have their K-9 units on the scene now. The FBI has agreed to send a profiler to help us sort this out, and they've issued a nationwide AMBER Alert." Paul said.

"Need I remind you that unless we see some results, the council is considering your replacement. We have a responsibility to our constituents to ensure their safety."

He'd had about enough of their shit. "You'll get no argument from me, unless you're aware of a step I've failed to take, this call will get us nowhere."

"Now, Paul, don't go getting defensive on me. We're only motivated by our concern for the citizens who elected us to office."

"Then get out of my way and let me do my job."

"Don't be getting testy with me. I'm on your side, and don't you forget that."

"If that was true, we wouldn't be having this conversation."

"I'm warning you, Paul, don't push me."

"I'd suggest you follow your own advice. I'm aware of the drunk patrol. How do you think your constituents would feel if they knew certain members of the council got free passes in exchange for a promised promotion?"

"What are you talking about?"

"You know damned good and well what I'm talking about."

"You wouldn't."

"Try me. Now if there's nothing else, I have a search to coordinate." With that he hung up. He'd played the biggest card in his hand, and he hoped it would give him the time he needed to make some headway.

Snatching the phone from its cradle, he dialed a number and waited. After the second ring it was answered by a woman with a high-pitched, nasally voice.

"Bradenour Investigations, how may I help you?"

"Is Tim in?" Paul said.

"One moment please," the woman replied.

"This is Tim, can I help you?"

"Hey Tim, it's Paul."

"Hold on a moment," Tim said, "Cindy, hang up the phone," Tim yelled. "How many times have I told you not to eavesdrop on my conversations?"

There came a loud click, then Tim was back on the line. "Sorry about that, Paul. Can't seem to find decent help these days."

"I heard that," Cindy yelled in the background and Paul chuckled. Tim was a private investigator he occasionally used for work beyond the scope of his deputies.

"What can I do for you?" Tim said.

"Could you turn up anything on Bowers?"

"You don't like making life easy, do you? Why did you give me a boy scout to dig into? The guy is cleaner than my own grandmother, of course that makes me want to dig deeper. I have found nothing. He has a master's in business administration yet chooses to stay in the area as a home improvement contractor. All of his licenses are in order, there are no complaints about his business practices. He drinks in moderation, hangs out with his friends, visits the gym regularly. Everyone I talk to praises the guy and that scares me."

"Do you think he's hiding something?"

"If he is, he's doing a hell of a job of it. I've had one of my guys on him for four days and nothing."

"What were his movements over the past thirty hours?"

"Hang on a second, let's see." The sound of paper rustling came through the receiver, "here it is. It's ten forty-five now, we need to go back to at least yesterday morning. Yeah, sleep, get up at five am, breakfast, shower, gym, work at seven. Lunch on the site with his guys, work till four. Wait a minute."

"What?"

"Looks like we lost him on the way back from work, accident caused a backup, my guy was too far back," more papers rustled, "we didn't reacquire him until, wow! Gonna have to talk to someone about this, it was nearly ten pm before my guy reacquired him."

"That's six hours unaccounted for." Paul reviewed the open file for Amber Gardener. Her family had noticed she was no longer in her room at around six pm.

"Has he done any work for the Gardeners?" Paul waited while the tapping of a keyboard came from the other end. They were getting close.

"A permit was issued for an addition last year. Bowers was the contractor of record."

"Can you get in his house?"

He paused. "Shouldn't this give you enough for a search warrant?"

"I want to be sure before I make an official move. Don't touch anything, don't remove anything unless it's absolutely necessary. I'm looking for trophies. If he's the kind of person I think he is, he'll hang onto certain objects from his victims. Report back to me, and only me."

"When do you need this done?"

"Weekend's coming. Can you get in during the day while he's at work tomorrow or Friday?"

"If he follows his regular schedule, I should have all day to do what I need to."

"I'll have one of my guys shadowing him. If it looks like he's headed home, I'll call you."

"Won't be able to help you tomorrow, so it'll have to be Friday."

"Sounds good. I'll be waiting for your call." Paul hung up and leaned back in his chair.

We're getting close.

For the first time in a long time, Susan felt refreshed, rejuvenated, restored. Mildred's suggestion had some merit. That, or she was ready to get back to work.

Either way she called John's parents and asked if they would like a visitor over the weekend. They were delighted to have their granddaughter stay with them, and the arrangements were made. Christine was thrilled with the idea and was looking forward to a weekend with her Pap. At dinner tonight, Susan would find out how Eric felt when she asked him to spend the weekend with her. She already cleared this through Christine, who liked Eric more than Susan realized.

Now, sitting in her car in the parking lot of the real estate office where she worked, her stomach was full of butterflies.

What if I failed?

The test had been pretty straightforward, the answers coming to her before she was done reading the questions. Yet that was no guarantee of success.

Gathering her courage, she opened her door and climbed from her car. It was now or never.

The first thing she noticed on entering the office was the air of celebration that filled the otherwise somber waiting area. Being the biggest Realtors on the lake had its perks, one being a waiting room in line with the type of clientele they sought. They sold vacation homes. High-end second homes designed to appeal to the creature comforts of those who could afford it. As such they had a certain image to maintain.

Crossing to Rebecca, the receptionist, Susan experienced a moment of doubt. She wanted to turn around and flee. The hell with whether she had passed her exam or not.

What if I didn't pass? What will I do?

"Hey, stranger," Rebecca said. It was too late. She couldn't run away now.

"Hey, Becca, how've things been?" Susan asked.

"You know what they say, same stuff, different day."

"What's going on? Is it somebody's birthday?"

"Oh, that. We've got a new agent starting today."

"Anybody I know?" Susan struggled to contain her disappointment.

Rebecca shrugged. "Who knows. Mr. Hawthorne did ask me to let him know the moment you came in. Said he wants to introduce you personally to the new agent."

Her spirits sank. Mr. Hawthorne was a kind, older man, a true gentleman. He probably wanted to let her down himself.

"I'll call him," Rebecca said.

Susan turned away and wiped her eyes.

I'm not going to cry! I'll take the test again and again if necessary. And keep taking the test until I pass.

Behind her Mr. Hawthorne entered the room. Wiping her eyes, and putting on her best smile, she turned to face him.

"Welcome back, Susan. How was your vacation?"

"It was busy, getting the house done and all that."

"And how's Christine doing? I bet she's getting big."

Susan smiled. Mr. Hawthorne exuded a genuine concern for his employees, unlike other bosses she'd worked for in the past. Her took the time to get to know them and their families. How her managed to remember it all was beyond her.

"She's getting to be a handful."

"I'm sure she is. So, are you ready to come back to work?"

"Absolutely. I need to get away from Spongebob and The Fairly Odd Parents and Jimmy Neutron."

"I bet you do. I have someone I'd like you to meet," Mr. Hawthorn held out his arm for her to lead the way down the hall where the agent offices were located. "A new agent I recently brought on board. Shows promise. I do believe we'll see an increase in sales."

"Did you get my test results back?" Susan asked.

"We'll talk about that later," Mr. Hawthorn replied.

She had put so much into passing that test. Right now, all she wanted to do was curl up and die. As they passed the other offices, Susan noticed the other agents getting up from their desks to follow. Not only would she have to face her own disappointment, it would be on public display for all her co-workers to see.

"Ah, here we are." Mr. Hawthorne ushered Susan into the office.

The first thing she noticed was the Welcome Back sign hanging over the vacant office chair. Then she saw her name on the name plate.

"Congratulations, Susan," Mr. Hawthorne said. "Let me be the first to welcome our newest agent. You passed your exam."

The other agents clapped as Susan picked up one of her business cards.

"I hope you don't mind. I took the liberty of ordering your first batch of business cards."

"Not at all." A tear slipped down her cheek. She wiped it away and wrapped her arms around Mr. Hawthorne.

"Thank you so much," she whispered in his ear.

"It was my pleasure, Susan. Now it's time to get back to work. We have houses to sell."

The other agents shook Susan's hand as they returned to their offices, leaving Susan and Mr. Hawthorne alone. She gazed at the Real Estate License framed and hanging from the wall of her office. She couldn't believe it was her name on the certificate. She had been so worried about failing. She could hardly wait to tell Eric and Christine this evening.

"To help get you started, Marie has agreed to let you have the Wilson contract. After all, according to her, if it hadn't been for you, we wouldn't have gotten it to begin with," Mr. Hawthorne said.

"Thank you, by the way, where is Marie?" Marie had been her friend, tutor, and mentor while she prepared for the test. Taking her under her wing on her first day.

"She'll be in later today." Mr. Hawthorne glanced at his watch. "You have a showing tomorrow night at eight with Barry Wilson. He's interested in the Timberland property. It's good to have you back, Susan. Don't forget tomorrow night." He pointed at her.

"I won't let you down, Mr. Hawthorne. Tomorrow night at eight," she said as she mentally ticked off what she needed to do to get done to be ready. "I'll make you proud."

"I know you will. Now I better get going. Mrs. Hawthorne is having her hair done this morning, so I have to sit with the kids."

The kids are a pair of Pomeranians his wife treated like children. They had no children of their own. In a way, aside from their dogs, everyone at the office was a member of the Hawthorne's' extended family.

"It's good to be back," Susan said.

Mr. Hawthorne nodded with a smile as he left, and Susan looked again at the certificate on the wall. It was as if a switch had been thrown and everything changed for the better. Maybe it had always been good, and she'd never noticed before because of her sorrow.

Twila watched the taillights of the car as they dwindled into the mist shrouded the day. It was the third one to have passed, none of them her mother. Rain beat a steady rhythm against her pink umbrella, the only spot of color in an otherwise dreary world.

The day matched her mood perfectly.

Mr. Tompkins, the bus driver, reluctantly left her at the side of the road after she assured him her mother would be coming along any minute. He wanted her to ride with him to the end of the route, promising he would return her to this spot. She convinced him that if she did, she would likely miss her mother. Mr. Tompkins relented, leaving Twila alone.

The low gray clouds deepened the melancholy compounded by a miserable day in school. She knew when the teacher called on her about a book report, she had yet to finish, it was not going to be a good day. At recess, to add salt to the wound, a group of girls she referred to as The Brat Pack, taunted her by making several derogatory references to her name.

"Tweetle Twila, weebles and wobbles, but never falls down." Marjorie's taunt whispered in her mind

She knew why her mother had chosen to name her Twila. At the time a child herself, she got caught up in the hysteria around the Twilight series. But that was no excuse to saddle a child with a name that would later be used to tease her. Another car came around the bend, and she leaned forward to watch as it approached. Disappointment adding to her bleak mood when it passed by.

Where's mom?

Probably still drunk from the night before, or she was already down the path to tonight's revelry. Such was life for Twila, who at twelve was forced by circumstances to grow up to look after herself and her little brother. Her mother wasn't going to do it. The only thing her mother was good for anymore was spreading her legs for her next fix.

A fourth car emerged from around the bend, its headlights sparkling in the rain, and she leaned forward hopefully as it came to a stop next to her. The driver's side window came down and LeAnn, who lived at the opposite end of the street from the trailer court, spoke to her.

"Twila Carr, what on earth are you doing standing in the rain, little lady?"

"Waiting on my Mom," Twila answered with a pained smile. It was no secret what her mother was like.

"Well, hop in, young lady, and I'll see that you get home," LeAnn said.

"I'm sorry." Twila recalled the last time she accepted help from anyone, and the resulting tantrum her mother threw. It was easier, and safer, to suffer the public degradation in silent misery. "I promised Mom I would wait for her."

LeAnn shook her head. "Someone needs to report that woman," she said loud enough for Twila to hear.

It wouldn't do any good. Twila understood this better than anyone else. She had been reported in the past, many times, yet no action was taken.

Social workers came to their single-wide trailer located at the back of the Whispering Hollow Trailer Court. There they had found a well-kept house. Clean clothes neatly folded in the dressers. Though her mother seemed out of touch with what was going on around her, it appeared she was maintaining a healthy home life for her children.

Little did they know it was Twila who made sure the beds were made each morning. That fresh clothes were readily available. That supper was made, dishes were washed, and the floors vacuumed each day before she did her homework.

LeAnn pulled away and Twila watched with longing. She couldn't wait until she was able to move out on her own. She would take her brother with her and care for him. Thinking of her brother sparked her sorrow and she wiped at her eyes.

She would have her own house, even if it were a single-wide trailer at the back of a decrepit trailer court. She would make a home and she would entertain. She would have dinner parties, movie nights, and game nights. She would have a life, and she would have friends.

She had no time for friends now. The only children she knew were in her class at school, and as a whole they dismissed her as unimportant.

"I know where your brother is." A whisper came from the forest on her left and she turned to the gloomy depths, made even darker by the dreariness of the day. The trees were full of buds that would become leaves to blanket the spindly branches in a coat of green. Drops of water clung to the branches, and as she gazed into the bleak depths, she spotted movement. Something lighter than the surroundings moved through the shadows towards her.

"I can take you to him." The voice came again, soft, carried upon a gentle breeze.

Twila glanced left and right as she searched for the owner of the voice. On her right, a young girl emerged from the forest and stood on the other side of a thorny barrier, watching her with wide, unblinking eyes.

"Who are you?"

"I know where your brother is," the girl answered, one finger held to her lips.

From the gloomy depths of the forest came a child's cry.

"Bobby?" She turned to follow the cry, stopping short of the narrow border of tangled brush that served as a barrier between the forest and civilization.

Something's wrong with the girl. Her eyes aren't right. Gazing into those fathomless depths, Twila realized with a shudder they contained no spark of life. The cry came again, so much like her brother. That couldn't be right. He was at home or should be. He had morning class at kindergarten, so the bus dropped him at the entrance to the trailer court every day at noon. It was after three so he should be home watching cartoons.

That wasn't right either. The night took him the week before.

The cry came again and this time she was sure she heard her name. The idea of Bobby alone in the forest filled her with a maternal rage.

"I know where your brother is," the girl whispered, and Twila was again struck by the odd emptiness in her eyes.

"Where is he?"

With a smile that failed to reach her eyes, the young girl turned and walked into the forest.

"Wait." Twila struggled to make her way through the thick bramble. Thorns pierced the flesh of her thighs in several spots. Fabric tore, and she knew she would be sewing tonight in addition to her other duties. She was wearing her only good pair of jeans. Every other article of clothing she owned came from the local Goodwill store. She bought the jeans herself with money she'd hidden from her mother. Money she earned by helping the older people in the trailer park with small chores.

Breaking through the line of brush, Twila ran into the gloomy forest. The girl had gotten ahead of her and she hesitated, afraid. It wasn't physically possible for her to have gotten so far. Twila watched as the girl vanished into a gathering of trees.

"Wait."

From the dense grove came the sound of a child crying, and Twila threw caution to the wind as she raced to the group of trees. Reaching the outer edge, she stopped and struggled to see through the screen of tree trunks. Nothing stirred on the other side, she spotted an outcropping of moss-covered stone, its surface slick with rain.

Pushing her way through, she came to an opening in the ground. *Mine sink.* She hesitated. They learned about these things in school. Unstable ground atop a labyrinth of interconnected tunnels. They were dangerous to stumble into as the ground could give way, sending the unwary traveler plummeting to their death.

Twila had fashioned a fairy tale around them, weaving the story that each mine sink led to a magical world filled with love and happiness. A place where it never rained. Where adults never raised their voices or threatened their children. Such a place did not exist. Twila knew this better than anybody. But it was fun to imagine what life would be like in such a place. An escape from the misery she knew all too well.

She stood at the opening, filled with hopeless despair deepened by the gloomy day around her.

From the black depths, her brother cried out. "Twila," he moaned, his voice floating up from the emptiness at her feet, awakening a primal need to protect him at all costs.

Without hesitation, abandoning her schoolbooks, she crawled into the narrow opening. Squirming through on her belly, the cold rain wicking into her clothes to chill her flesh, she squeezed into the cave beyond. Once past the opening, she found she could stand, and in the distance, shrouded by shadows, the young girl waited. From the behind the girl came her brother's cries.

Anger displaced unease and she raced down the narrow passage. Small openings in the roof of the cave allowed the muted light of the day to create spots of light. Under them, the cave floor was slick with rainwater. At the first one she nearly fell as her feet threatened to slide out from under her. She managed to catch herself and caught a glimpse of the young girl as she vanished into the floor.

Twila raced forward, brought up short at a narrow slit in the floor down which the girl had vanished. Every fiber of her being screamed for her to turn and run as she gazed into the opening. Ebony fingers of night reached up to caress her, as her brother's sobbing came from the void beyond.

"Bobby," she whispered, torn between her desire to protect her brother, and the terror awakened by the opening.

She stepped back and looked around, realizing for the first time how dangerous her position was. Her desire to protect her brother overrode her fear of the dark, and now she was trapped.

A faint glow pushed back the night, illuminating the floor of the cave that sloped down into the earth.

"Twila," her brother moaned.

She could contain herself no more. As the glow grew in intensity, she stumbled down the slope into a larger tunnel filled with a soft yellow light that came from everywhere and nowhere.

"Bobby," she shouted, her call echoing from the walls of the cave. From her right came an answering cry and she moved in that direction. A part of her in awe at the size of the tunnel, filled with the hope that her dreams of a magical place hidden beneath the ground had been true.

In the distance she spotted movement, a dark figure approaching fast.

"One, two, the Witch is due." Children whispered in a sing-song voice.

"Three, four, she's at the door," another answered.

"Five, six, who will she pick?"

"Bobby," she screamed as the shape grew larger and more detail came into focus. A stooped figure materialized, a tattered shawl wrapped about bony shoulders, threadbare tips weaving in the air like a multitude of snakes knotted together on her back.

"Seven, eight, at night she waits." A chorus of voices filled the tunnel around her.

The shape was less than twenty yards away, its presence a cold void reaching out to caress her with icy fingers. It was then she realized it was not the witch at all, but something much older, something alien that wore the visage of the witch like a mask.

"Nine, ten, don't let her in." The voices whispered around her and she backpedaled from the apparition. Afraid to turn and run for fear that if she took her eyes from this monstrosity, it would be able to reach out, and pull her back to its icy bosom.

The shadow loomed over her and she whimpered as it enveloped her, wrapping her in its chilled embrace, dragging her numbed body back to its lair, where in her catatonic state she saw the bodies of other children gathered around the walls of a massive chamber.

54

Bethany drummed the dash as she watched the empty road. Twila should have been waiting for her when she arrived.

She might have caught a ride with that busybody LeAnn again. Maybe not. Beth made it clear the last time how she felt about people sticking their nose into her personal business. As if LeAnn didn't have enough of her own business to meddle in, she found it necessary to dig into everyone else's.

If Twila didn't show up soon she was going to be late and Mr. Hampton already warned her once this week about her tardiness. She played with the radio, tuning through the stations, searching for anything to drown out the worry. She had two warnings already. This would be the last, and she'd be out of work, again. Begging for handouts from the county and state until she could find another dead-end job dealing with dead-end people.

Why does this always happen to me?

The school bus pulled around the corner and she slid out of her car to cross the rain-slicked street. "Is Twila on the bus?"

Mr. Tompkins shook his head, "I dropped her off earlier."

"Why did you leave her alone? She's only a child."

"She said you would be by any minute to pick her up. She was afraid to miss you."

Bethany turned and stomped back to her car. "I can't believe this shit."

Sliding behind the wheel, she slammed her door and pulled away, watching the side of the road for any sign of Twila. When that girl got home, she was going to get her ass whipped. She knew she had to come straight home after school to help with Bobby.

It was then it hit her with a force like a physical blow.

Bobby wasn't there anymore.

Her little boy had been taken, and for the first time since his disappearance, it sank in. She brought the car to a stop along the curb. Her hands shaking. She stared through the windshield as the wipers tapped out a steady beat.

Bobby's gone. She fell into a dark abyss of despair.

Where did he go?

Who took him?

Why?

The questions chased one another through her mind. She lit a cigarette, watching how her hands shook, as if seeing them for the first time.

God, what I wouldn't give for a drink right now.

Did he cry for her? A primal rage washed through her, shaking her to the core.

"They took my baby." She screamed, pounding on the steering wheel with her fists, stomping her feet on the floor, the car rocking back and forth on squeaky springs.

"Please," she shouted at the roof. Turning to a god she walked away from so long ago. "Please," she begged, hands clasped before her, "please," she whispered, "anything, I will give you anything if you send him back to me."

Then she lowered her head and cried.

55

From the darkened living room came the glow of the television. Robin Williams shouted, and Christine giggled.

Eric appeared in the doorway. "How about some popcorn?" He took a bag of microwave popcorn from the basket on top of the microwave, put it inside and hit the preprogrammed button. As he waited, the hum of the microwave at his side, he became aware of a faint tapping coming from the hallway behind him.

It grew louder, drowning out the sound of the microwave, and the sporadic popping that came from within.

He crossed to the hall and flipped on the light switch. The corridor filled with a comforting glow that did little to dispel his fear. An incessant pounding came from the laundry room. Chilled air enveloped him, his breath clouding before his face as goose bumps whispered across the flesh of his arms.

She's coming.

It had been the same way with Jessica the night she disappeared, and he felt like a child again. Watching from the safety of the hallway while his sister was led to her doom. Only this time he was an adult, responsible for another child. Yet, strangely enough, he didn't feel like an adult.

Adults weren't supposed to be afraid of such things as odd tapping sounds. They rationalized, and categorized them as the house settling, or a hot water tank cooling down. When you grew up you turned away from the dark possibilities that lived in every thump and creak that whispered through the night.

The tapping drowned out the sound of the popcorn cooking behind him. He followed the hallway to the steps leading to the laundry room. At the top he flipped on the light switch. A soft yellow glow pushed back the shadows. From his vantage point, he saw the laundry sink, and not much else.

"The popcorn's burning," Christine said from the hallway behind him.

He spun around, startled, the aroma of burnt popcorn invading his senses. He turned to go back and turn it off when the microwave dinged. Then he heard it, a child's soft cry. The pounding grew louder, becoming more frantic as the scent of something burning came from the laundry room. The sickly-sweet odor of roasting flesh overwhelmed that of the burnt popcorn.

He raced down the steps into the laundry room and came to an abrupt stop. Black ribbons of smoke spread out from the back wall. Emerging from around the edges of the plywood he'd put up to block the tunnel entrance.

"Go back to your room, Christine," he yelled over his shoulder. The plywood bowed out in the center as wisps of ebony night flowed out from its edges. The wisps that looked like smoke moved with a sentient purpose, with life, tentacles of night reaching across the laundry room for him.

He'd seen them before, behind his sister when she came to take him. The shawl the old Witch wore. Made of the smoke of her passing, the power of her hate, merging with the scent of roasting flesh as she burned at the stake.

The pounding intensified as Eric approached the opening. He had no idea what to do, or how he could counter what was happening. He only knew he had to try something. The creature had come for Christine, and he knew he would lay down his life to protect her and her mother. He'd never felt the way Susan made him feel, and he didn't want to lose that now.

A nail popped out of the plywood, shooting across the room like a bullet, impaling itself in the opposite wall. Another shot across the room, passing through the fabric of his tee shirt, grazing his flesh before continuing on to join the other in the wall. One almost stuck him in the head. He ducked at the last moment, and it hit the wall behind him a wicked thunk.

The sheet of plywood rushed him, faster than he could react, and slammed into him. Driving him against the wall. His head bounced from the plasterboard as stars shot through the emptiness behind his eyes, and he dropped to the floor like a rag doll.

The glow of an approaching fire illuminated the shadowy depths of the cave that now stood exposed. Living smoke billowed from the opening, heralding the arrival of a creature from the past, rising up to spread across the ceiling as a fine shower of ash fell to the floor.

56

Christine sat at the top of the steps, hugging the corner of the wall as Eric approached the opposite wall of the laundry room. She cried out when the plywood came free and slammed into him.

Emptiness leaked from the opening, ribbons of night twisted and turned in a blind dance as they groped along the walls, spreading out from the opening like a cancerous growth. A faint glow came from the depths of the cave. Steeling herself for what she was about to do, Christine took a deep breath and raced down the steps. She knelt at Eric's side.

"Please, Eric, wake up." She glanced at the cave as the glow illuminated rough-hewn walls. Long shadows danced against the wall behind her like ancient worshippers around a roaring blaze.

"Please wake up."

The glow intensified as ribbons of ebony night flowed from the cave, black tentacles that carried the sickly-sweet odor of roasted flesh. She gagged as ash fell to the floor, blanketing everything in a fine layer of gray.

She rocked Eric's shoulders back and forth, her heart hammering against the walls of her ribcage. His cell phone slipped from the case on his belt, and she snatched it from the floor as an image appeared in the center of that growing ball of fire. A shadowy shape surrounded by ribbons of night.

They reached for her and Christine jumped to her feet and raced up the steps. At the top, she stopped, and turned to watch. Drawn by the same curiosity that lured her into the forest the week before.

Yellow light filled the laundry room as the apparition approached.

It's your fault. A gravelly voice whispered in her mind and she clamped her hands over her ears, trapping a scream behind her teeth as some ancient thing invaded her soul.

Images from the past flickered through her mind. Surrounding her with hate filled faces that taunted her. The chilled air like ice against the exposed flesh of her bare arms bound at her sides. Stony-faced men piled brush around her legs. She struggled against her bonds as several men approached with flaming torches. The dry brush caught easily enough, and the scene danced on rising heat waves as the flames enveloped her.

Christine screamed, doubling over in agony, the flesh of her legs seared by an insatiable blaze.

"You and yours are responsible." The voice cut through her agony, clear and cold, icy.

The pain subsided and Christine looked up at the old woman who stood in the center of the laundry room, leaning heavily on a gnarled cane, her eyes burning with hellfire. Behind her the darkness pulsed with a life of its own. Ribbons of night twisted about her in a primitive dance, slithering over and around one another with wild abandon.

Christine became aware of the presence of another. Something much older, hungry, yearning for a sustenance that could only be birthed in the terror of the young. It fed on her fear, her agony, and her hate bubbled to the surface of her consciousness.

It's not fair! Why should daddy die? Her anger, suppressed for so long, flashed white hot, and the ribbons of night danced in delight. Her rage was short lived, dashed by a cold dose of fear when she realized she was being led to the laundry room, to the witch waiting at the bottom of the steps.

"No." She screamed, pulling away from the ebony ribbons slowly winding themselves about her. She turned and fled up the steps.

On the second floor she stopped, undecided, her head swiveling left, then right, as she sought escape. She turned to her own bedroom, then changed her mind and reversed course to slip into her mother's room. Rounding the bed, she dropped to the floor and scooted under, into the dust-filled shadows beneath.

She opened Eric's phone and searched for her mommy's number. Mommy wasn't listed. She fell back on the only option that was open to her, an act she and her mother had practiced in the past.

Dialing nine, one, one, she waited as the phone rang.

The operator came on with an audible click, "Nine, one, one. What is your emergency?"

"She's coming to get me," Christine whispered, her hand held over her mouth to mask any sound.

"Who's coming to get you, sweetie?" the operator said after a short pause.

"The Witch," Christine whispered as the door opened, and the sweet odor of roasting flesh filled the room as a perpetual storm of ash blanketed the floor. Christine closed the phone and scooted to her right as the presence moved around the foot of the bed.

The phone rang in her hand, startling Christine. A chilled caress brushed her arm as a ribbon of emptiness slithered across the floor towards her.

Christine scooted out from under the bed and slipped out the door, pulling it closed behind her as she raced down the hallway, and down the steps to the first floor. She didn't know where to go, where to hide. In the kitchen she crawled into one of the cabinets, squeezing behind the cookware piled inside.

The phone had stopped ringing and she opened it to search for her mother's number. When she again turned up nothing, she remembered it was Eric's phone. He wouldn't be calling her *Mommy*.

She found Susan's number and dialed it. The phone rang, beeping with an incoming call came from an unfamiliar number. She ignored it.

"She's after me, mommy," Christine blubbered as tears streamed down her face and the sound of movement came from the kitchen. She realized her mother's voice was a recording and hung up as it rang again. That unknown number appeared on the screen, and she ignored it as the sounds beyond the cabinet door became centered on her location.

Suddenly the door swung open and emptiness filled the void. She scooted away from its silent approach. Frantically crawling over pots and pans, making her way to the end, where she pushed out and rolled onto the kitchen floor. The air around her full of ash and the odor of roasted flesh. A chorus of voices cried out in a kaleidoscope of sound. The cries of the Witch's victims trapped for eternity in her blackened heart.

Christine raced from the kitchen into the hallway, a dead end. One door opened into the unfinished basement. Nothing more than a large room with no place to hide, unless she ventured outside, it was the last place she wanted to go.

That left her with only one option. As the cries of the dead swirled around her in a tornado of sound, she turned to the laundry room. Eric still lay where she left him, and she crossed to the washer, squeezing herself between the wall and the heavy appliance. She opened the phone and dialed her mother again.

This time she answered.

57

Susan led her client, Barry, through the downstairs of the three-story home. The rooms were large and spacious, with hardwood floors throughout, and nine-foot ceilings. Off-white walls trimmed in red oak lent the home a plain, yet stately nature. Since meeting him in the drive, she'd been conscious of the way she was dressed. She'd never given much thought to what she wore until she felt his eyes on her.

Barry, a developer from downstate, had a reputation for seducing women. Rumor was a female agent, not in her office, brought sexual assault charges against him. The charges were swept under the rug, the agent got a nice fat settlement, and nothing more was said about the matter.

Barry sauntered behind her, his hands in his pockets. If it was possible to undress a woman with the eyes, she was confident he was doing it as he followed her.

They'd completed the basement, and first floor, and all that remained was the second floor where the bedrooms were located. As they approached the stairs, she realized she didn't want to go up.

Never once during her training, or while studying for the exam, had she considered that being a real estate agent might put her at risk of being sexually assaulted. She knew what she would do if Barry made the mistake of trying to do anything.

A fist to the throat, a knee to the groin. She learned self-defense in California, in a class taught by an old gunnery sergeant on base. With husbands who could be called out at a moment's notice, they wanted to be prepared. John encouraged her to take the classes. Said he wouldn't worry about her as much if he knew she could defend herself.

At the bottom of the stairs she turned to Barry. "On the third floor are six bedrooms and four baths. One bedroom is the master with an attached bath."

"Well, let's go up and take a look, then." Barry winked.

"After you." Susan stepped back to give Barry room to get through.

Barry winked again. "Lead on, you're doing a splendid job, and besides, I prefer the view from back here."

"If you don't mind, I'd rather you went first, sir."

Barry shrugged as he sauntered by. "I like a woman who's not afraid to take charge."

"And I prefer a man who doesn't feel a need to use their position to get what they want," she replied evenly.

"I guess we understand one another, then." Barry climbed the stairs.

"I hope so."

In the master bedroom, Barry turned in a slow circle to take in the room. As he looked around, her phone rang.

Barry glanced at her as she tried to sneak a peek at who was calling. She saw Eric's number on the small screen and wasn't concerned. Probably wanted to know where something was. She'd call him back when they finished here.

"Do you need to take it?" Barry asked.

Susan shook her head. "No, it can wait."

"Good." Barry clapped his hands together loud enough to produce an echo in the empty room.

Susan jumped involuntarily at the sound.

"What do you think of a king-sized bed here?" He pointed at the blank wall before him. "Nightstands on either side, a dresser over there. Is there a walk-in closet?"

Susan crossed to a door and opened it to reveal the walk-in closet. Barry wandered into the small room and she waited. He emerged after a few minutes.

"They really put a lot of effort into this place."

"The builder is well known in these parts, has a solid reputation for quality work and standing behind what he does."

"That's unusual, of course we're talking about two different worlds here."

"Meaning?"

"Where I come from builders are in such a rush to get done, they're overwhelmed with work. Around here everything moves at a more leisurely pace. There's time to do it right. The builder is?"

"John Nemith, he's a third-generation builder, inherited the business from his dad, who got it from his dad. Nemith construction has been around since the mid-eighteen hundreds."

"Are they willing to make changes?"

"Within reason, I'm sure, we can get together tomorrow or the next day to discuss any changes you have in mind." She struggled to control her excitement.

"You have three other properties available?"

"I do." After their rough start she was sure he'd string her along to pay her back. Instead he appeared to be genuinely interested in the house."

"I'm planning on purchasing several..." Susan's phone interrupted him. "Please, answer your phone."

Susan pulled her phone from her purse, flipped it open and placed it against her ear. At first, all she heard was heavy breathing. Then Christine's terrified voice filled the receiver.

"Mommy. She's here. She's coming after me. She hurt Eric. Please, Mommy, I'm scared," Christine babbled.

Susan was overwhelmed by the flood of information.

"Put Eric on, now."

"I can't, Mommy, the Witch hurt him. Now she's looking for me." As if to lend weight to her statement she heard a commotion in the background. Someone yelled something unintelligible.

"Slow down, sweetie. Where are you?"

The connection ended, and she looked up at Barry, who watched her with mild interest.

"A little domestic situation?"

Susan tossed the keys for the house to Barry. "Please lock up after you're done." She left him standing in the center of the master bedroom. She might have thrown away her one chance of making a name for herself, but Christine and Eric were more important, and if they were in trouble.

58

Twila made four.

The notion lay heavy in Paul's mind as he made his way up the stairs to go to bed. One of his deputies responded to a disturbance at the Whispering Pines mobile home park to find Bethany Carr drunk and threatening her neighbor LeAnn Rish. During the subsequent interviews, they discovered Bethany's daughter, Twila, had vanished from the bus stop after the driver dropped her off.

Bethany blamed LeAnn for what happened and went after her in a drunken rage. They transferred her to the county jail while the state police and Paul's deputies searched the wooded area next to the bus stop. The dogs found Twila's scent and followed it to the area around Fiddlers Pond, where it vanished.

As he neared the bedroom, the phone rang, and he realized he had lost the will to continue the fight. After dedicating his professional life to solving that case, working on it long after reason dictated he should drop it and move on. It would remain one of the mysteries of the area.

In the bedroom Maggie sat on the edge of the bed, the receiver pressed to her ear.

"Who is it?"

"It's Carla, she wants to speak to you." Maggie twisted around and handed him the phone. She'd been crying. Carla worked in the county 911 dispatch office. A phone call from her did not bode well.

"Is it another one?" Maggie whispered.

"This is Sheriff Odenton," Paul said.

"Sheriff, we received a hang up from one of the numbers you have flagged. A child crying, claiming someone was after her."

"What number?"

"Two four oh, eight seven six, eight six, eight six."

Paul reached over to his trousers hanging from the chair and slipped his notebook from the back pocket. As he flipped through the pages, a renewed desire to keep going in the face of insurmountable odds filled him.

Maybe this is the break we've been looking for?

Finding the number, he felt vindicated when he noted that it belonged to Eric Bowers, the same number painted on the side on his truck.

They had their man.

"Thanks, Carla. I'll get someone on this right away. Paul hung up and reached for his pants.

"What is it?" Maggie said.

"A break, I hope."

"Not another missing child?"

"So far no, if it pans out, we'll be able to close this case for good," Paul buckled his pants.

Without lights or sirens to warn their intended target, a convoy of patrol cars followed a State Police Tactical van along the winding road leading to Eric Bower's house. Paul rode in the first patrol car with Deputy Reynolds driving.

"It doesn't make sense." Deputy Reynolds focused on the taillights of the black van ahead of them. A box truck, like those used by UPS to deliver packages. Only the cargo this van carried included a team of men whose sole purpose was to bring down barricaded suspects.

"It all falls neatly into place. Eric's family has lived in this area since it was settled. Hell, his great great-great-grandfather helped build the first trading post."

"I'm not disagreeing with that. It doesn't seem right that an entire family would do something like that. I can understand one or two individuals being involved, but to have something like this going on for generations?"

"Maybe it's some twisted religion that calls on them to sacrifice kids every thirty years or so."

"That's sick." Reynolds said.

Paul shrugged. "You'll get no argument from me."

The brake lights of the van flashed as they slowed to a stop. While planning, it had been decided they would approach the house on foot and not make any moves until everyone was ready. The tactical squad would enter the house at three separate points, front door, back door, and side entrance, at the same exact time. Since this was a state police operation, Paul and his deputies were relegated to observers. Paul would get his chance to question the suspect once he was in custody, for now they remained in their vehicle, listening to the radio as the operation unfolded.

"Lights are out at the house," a voice whispered over the frequency the state police established. They lent Paul one of their tactical radios so he and Deputy Reynolds could listen as the team entered the residence.

"Team one is in place,"

"Two's ready."

"We're almost there," a third voice whispered from the speaker grill. Then, "Three's set."

"On my mark, three, two, one."

The sound of breaking glass and splintering wood came from the speaker as the men breached the house. One by one they called clear as they moved from room to room.

"Local one, this is point one, over," a voice crackled from the radio in the dash of the car.

Paul took the mic from the dash and keyed it as he spoke into it. "This is local one, go ahead, over."

"It appears the suspect is not present at this time, over."

"Is his vehicle in the driveway? Over."

"Negative."

Paul had the sinking sensation that they had blown their one good chance of catching their suspect red-handed. In Paul's mind Eric had stopped being the handsome young man who installed their kitchen cabinets. He became another suspect in a long line of suspects he'd dealt with during his career.

"What are we gonna do now, boss?" Deputy Reynolds said, lending voice to what was already on Paul's mind, "he's gonna know we're looking for him. If he's the one, he'll go to ground for sure."

"I know. I blew it. I never believed he wouldn't be home, and never considered what to do in the event he wasn't. I should have told them to stay back until we confirmed his vehicle was in the driveway."

The van moved forward, and they followed as it turned up the driveway to retrieve the tactical team. They didn't need to be quiet now that they had entered the house to find it empty.

They still had the search warrant and would search the house. Paul was confident they wouldn't find anything. Eric obviously owned another place that wasn't under his name and now they were back to square one.

Blake, the senior State Police Officer on duty, crossed to Paul's window. "Looks like a bust." Blake knelt beside the window.

"My fault, had I thought about it earlier, I would have suggested we hold until his truck was in the driveway."

"Nothing to worry about. It happens. We'll run a detailed search of the grounds and the house. If anything pops up, I'll give you a call." Blake turned away, dismissing Paul and Reynolds as they took control of the situation.

"State paying for the damages too?" Paul asked.

"You know it'll be taken care of. Have a good night." Blake finished before walking away.

"I guess we've been dismissed," Reynolds said.

"It seems so. Let's get out of here. If they find anything that will stop these kids from disappearing, I'll be happy. That's all I ever wanted."

Reynolds shifted into reverse and they backed out onto Fiddlers Hollow Road. Paul was silent, deep in thought, as the black depths of the forest sped by on either side. Something tickled his memory.

"She said it was a young girl that called," Paul said as they approached Porter Mines Road.

"Who said?" Deputy Reynolds flipped on the blinker to turn right.

"The 911 operator said a little girl called."

"Okay, a little girl. What does that have to do with all this? A couple of little girls were taken."

"Go the other way." Paul sat up suddenly. He was getting old and had forgotten one little bit of info. Eric was involved with the woman who recently purchased the Jenkins place.

"Where are we going?"

"To the Jenkins place," Paul said, mentally kicking himself for missing what should have been obvious from the start.

60

The first thing Susan noticed when she entered the house was the assorted scents. The most prominent the stench of burnt popcorn. Beneath that the sickly-sweet aroma of charred flesh mingled with the sharp bite of burning wood.

"Christine," she shouted, crossing into the kitchen as the microwave dinged a reminder the food was done. From the darkened living room came the glow of the television, and she crossed to the doorway, hoping to find Christine and Eric asleep on the couch.

It was a short-lived hope that ran counter to the phone call she received. The living room was empty. The house carried an overwhelming sense of abandonment. Everything left as it was when they departed.

Where did they go?

She's after me mommy.

"Christine, Eric." She crossed through the kitchen, kicking a pot she hadn't seen. It skittered across the floor ahead of her. It's sound added to the abandoned feel. Other pots lay scattered across the floor, every door in the row of cabinets they once occupied stood open, revealing empty shadows within.

What happened?

The panic that had been slowly unwinding in the pit of her stomach ratcheted up a few notches when she reached the hallway. Light shimmered in a trail of wet footsteps in the center of the hall, originating from the laundry room, it crossed the kitchen to the cabinets where it vanished.

"Christine, Eric." Panic tightened her voice as she moved down the hall to the laundry room. Her heart clambered into her throat when she spotted a pair of legs on the laundry room floor. From this angle it was all she could see, and she raced down the steps to find Eric, lying unconscious.

"Eric." She dropped to her knees next to him and searched for a pulse. In addition to self-defense, she'd taken first aid training while living in California.

Finding the pulse strong and steady, she caressed his cheek, and pushed herself to her feet as a faint breeze came from the tunnel. The scent of decay assailed her, speaking of things that have lain long dead. Accompanied by the odor of wood char, and the sickly-sweet smell of burnt flesh. It was then she became aware of the fine layer of ash that covered every surface around her.

They burned her at the stake. Sheriff Odenton's words whispered in her mind. A faint cry echoed from naked stone of the tunnel. A child in distress.

"Christine." She approached the opening.

An answer came, indistinct, and she was confident it was Christine crying out for her.

She called 911 to report Christine's abduction and Eric's misfortune, took the flashlight from his belt, and crossed to the opening. There she stopped. Steeling herself to step into those shadowed depths as the memory of the last time she'd done so filled her with a quiet dread. The flashlight beam was swallowed by emptiness less than ten feet in and she was overwhelmed by the sensation of someone, or something, watching with hungry eyes.

From the bleak depths came a soft whimper. A child moaning in terror. The vocalization of her own fear. She had no choice. If she wanted to see Christine again, she'd have to find her, and save her.

61

The headlights of their cruiser cut a wide swath through the night. Paul rode shotgun as Deputy Reynolds carefully guided the powerful vehicle along Whispering Hollow Road. The trees of the forest to either side passed in a blur, bathed in the reds and blues of their emergency lights as their siren wailed.

They had to get there fast. A child's life hung in the balance. The car rocked as the roadbed rose and fell, the speedometer needle slowly closing in on one hundred miles per hour. They'd gotten the break they needed. Now if they could make it in time. Time. They had wasted so much of it at Eric's house Paul was afraid they might be too late.

"Patrol three, this is base, over," a static-filled voice came from the speaker mounted on the dash.

Paul grabbed the mic from its clip on the dash. "Go ahead base, this is three, over."

"We have a nine one, one, report from the occupant of one, one, eight, seven, three Fiddlers Pond Road of a minor in danger, over."

"Roget base, we're enroute, ETA four minutes, send back up, over,"

"Roger three, rolling back up, over."

"Roger base, this is three out." Paul hung up the mic and grabbed the handle above his head. All of them had taken high speed driving training, but it was still unsettling to be the passenger, relying on the reflexes and attentiveness of the driver.

Reynolds had taken the course a number of times, if it were possible for anything bad to happen, it would during a high-speed chase.

A pair of glowing eyes appeared at the far edge of the headlights and Deputy Reynolds drifted into the oncoming lane as they blew past an opossum so fast it had no time to react.

If it had been a deer. Paul pushed the notion aside. He didn't want to think about what would happen in a collision with anything at this speed.

With the turn off approaching, Deputy Reynolds began applying brakes. The heavy cruiser nosed down as he dropped the speed to a more manageable fifty miles per hour before hitting the turn. Tires squealed as the rear end fought to maintain traction, and they darted around the turn onto Fiddlers Pond Road. Here he had to slow down. A gravel road was not as forgiving as pavement when it came to high speed maneuvers.

Eric Bower's truck appeared in the headlights and they pulled in alongside it, coming up behind a Ford Focus whose driver's side door stood open. Paul recognized it as belonging to the owner of the residence, Susan.

Before the cruiser stopped, Paul was out the door and moving alongside the Focus with his pistol drawn. In all his years as a deputy, and a Sheriff, he'd never once fired his weapon outside the qualifying range. He hoped he wouldn't have to tonight, but if it came down to it, he was ready.

The headlights of the Ford illuminated the front door of the house. It stood wide open, the foyer beyond awash in a harsh light, the house filled with a sense of abandonment.

The Focus was still running. Reynolds stopped at the driver's door and turned the ignition switch off. In the resulting silence a screech owl's warning cry came from the forest, a sound so reminiscent of a child's scream that Paul was startled by an old memory.

His grandmother used to tell him that a screech owl's cry was really death calling to the one it sought. Among those who heard it, one would not awaken the following morning.

Is tonight my last night? He pushed the idea away, not wanting to follow it to its logical conclusion. His grandmother had been a woman of the hills. Some said she was a seer, blessed, or cursed as the case might be, by what they called second sight. She knew things others didn't, was attuned to the shadowy things that existed beyond the realm of reality.

She'd been one of the few to warn him away from Porter Mines when he first got the job as a Sheriff's Deputy. Telling him ancient things lived around Fiddlers Pond, in shadowed places far from the safety of the light.

He hadn't thought of his grandmother in years and he put aside the memory as they entered the house. He had to remain focused. Reynolds was counting on him, as he was counting on Reynolds to keep them safe.

Together they moved through the house silently, speaking only to let the other know it was clear to proceed as they moved in a rolling over watch. One with their weapon always trained on the area before them as their partner moved forward, each taking their turn at lead.

The first thing they noticed upon entering was the smell of burnt popcorn with another odor beneath, that of roasting flesh, mingling with the smell of old decay. Paul read the scene as they moved through the kitchen, having cleared the living room where Robin Williams fled an intrepid hunter from another time and place, while wild animals roamed freely through an unsuspecting town.

Down the narrow hall Reynolds led the way, staying to the right in order to give Paul a clear shot if needed. Reaching the steps to the laundry room, he motioned Paul forward and Paul reached the steps to see a pair of legs lying on the floor of the room below. A fine layer of ash covered everything. A single line of footsteps stood out in the ash.

On the floor of the laundry room Eric lay motionless, unconscious, otherwise unhurt. Deputy Reynolds checked his pulse and nodded that he was okay. A faint shout came from the tunnel on Paul's right and he glanced into those shadowy depths before removing his flashlight and crossing to the opening.

"Wait here for backup. I'm going in," Paul said.

"Not a good idea?" Reynolds shook his head.

"We can't afford to wait. It's going down right now, and I need to be there when it does. I need to know the truth."

Reynolds held his gaze for a second then nodded. Paul turned and vanished into the tunnel. It was a tight fit, but that didn't matter. The truth about what had been happening lay ahead. He was on the verge of closing the only case that haunted him since he was a deputy. The only question that remained was if he was prepared to face the truth.

62

Susan moved through an emptiness filled with the lurking monsters of unrealized nightmares. As her eyes adjusted to the dim light of the flashlight, she was able to make out more details of her surroundings. Jagged rock formed the walls of the tunnel and appeared to have been torn asunder in the distant past. The ceiling hung suspended between rough walls that spread outward in a vee, the floor narrower than the ceiling.

The stone above her was crisscrossed with narrow cracks through which the roots of the plants above protruded. They hung freely from the stone like the wispy strands of hair on the pate of a balding man combed over in modesty. Reminding her of spider webs, that made her shudder involuntarily as they brushed against her hair.

At the first bend, she peered around the corner into a narrow corridor that faded into a perpetual night. Beyond the faint edge of her flashlight's beam she detected movement, one shadowy shape moving across another.

"Please, don't," a voice cried out, and she was torn between her desire to save her child, and her own sense of self-preservation. Behind her lay the safety of the well-lit laundry room, while before her waited a hungry, bleak emptiness full of nightmares.

Her maternal instinct, that primitive desire to protect her offspring, even at the cost of her own life, was the only thing that drove her onward into the black depths.

Coming to a large chamber, she was faced with three openings, each going in a different direction. From the middle opening came a soft sob followed by an even softer slurping sound.

Christine? She cautiously entered the tunnel, following the flashlight beam. Deeper she plunged into that nighted abyss, the beam of her flashlight growing weaker with every passing moment, the emptiness nibbling away at the edges of the cone of light.

The cave grew tight around her, pressing against her shoulders, forcing her to stoop down in order to move forward. Ahead it shrank even more, and the sound of someone crying came from the darkness beyond the edge of the flashlight beam. The air around her was becoming stagnant, making it difficult to breathe.

The sound of crying came from ahead. Nearly on her knees, she plunged deeper into the darkness. An image appeared at the faint edge of light from her weakening flashlight. Gaining substance with every step forward, causing her to quicken her pace, certain she had found what she was looking for.

It looked like a little girl dressed in a white nightgown that reached the floor, long black hair hung down the center of her back. It was hard to tell in the dwindling glow of her flashlight.

It's not Christine.

"Who are you," she said, nearly panting from the exertion of moving through the cave. Thankfully, she had worn flats for her showing. In her panic she had no time to change her shoes. If she tried to follow the tunnel in heels, she would have broken an arm, or a leg, or worse.

She stopped as a chill washed over her, and goose bumps danced across the flesh of her arms. She reached out and steadied herself with one hand on the stone wall that was warm to the touch.

"Who's there?" Panic crept into her voice. The child ahead remained still. If she heard her, she would have turned at the sound of her voice.

Susan eased forward another step, the flashlight growing slick in her sweating hand.

If it's not Christine, who is it? One of the other children? What are they doing in the middle of this dark cave? The last sent a chill down the length of her spine. Whoever, or *whatever* it was, couldn't be good.

Christine had spoken of a friend that came in the night.

Is it her?

Is she a ghost?

Susan stopped, focused on the indistinct figure at the faint edge of the flashlight beam. She was torn about what to do. She couldn't leave the child here. Reason prevented her from moving any closer. That and a growing fear that she was confronting something beyond her understanding.

She had to do something.

Taking a deep breath, she eased forward, ready to turn and run if need be. Getting closer, more details came into focus, and she breathed a sigh of relief.

It wasn't a little girl at all. Only a jumble of rocks and roots that combined to create the image of a standing child. What she imagined was hair was in fact a shattered stone hanging down from the ceiling in front of a twisted mass of roots that formed what looked like a person standing with their back turned.

Which meant she'd gone down the wrong tunnel and Christine was still in danger, somewhere, behind her. She turned around to work her way back. She had taken several steps when the flashlight went out, plunging her into a nighted abyss.

Panic flared white hot and her knees became weak, threatening to leave her wallowing on the floor of the cave. Beneath the fingers of her left hand, the stone was coarse and warm, her only connection to the physical world as the emptiness called forth the nightmares of her past.

The closet under the stairs. Her mother's angry features. The doctor who performed her abortion, watching her over the edge of the mask covering the lower portion of his face. She relived the time of her near death at the bottom of a small pond as shadowy shapes swam around her, ready to lead her away into death. Robert's face materialized, his eyes open, staring sightlessly, bugging out, his tongue black and stiff, protruding from between slack lips. Hanging by his neck from one of the rafters in the basement, unable to endure his mother's relentless torture. His body hidden in shadows as it swung gently back and forth at the end of the rope.

A connection was made. Robert, Bobby. It was the name she and John had chosen when they learned she was pregnant. If the child were a boy, they would name him Robert in memory of her brother.

"Bobby's hungry, mommy," Christine whispered, and she whimpered as the images washed through her, trapping her between past and present as terror swelled up like an infected boil to be excised. Driving her to her knees where the sharp edge of a stone helped clear her mind and push away the nightmares of her past.

She had to keep moving. Christine was in danger. She couldn't stop now. Slowly, carefully, she blindly felt her way through the tunnel. Taking one hesitant step after another, her hands scrabbling along the stone walls to either side.

63

Throwing caution, and common sense to the wind, Paul followed the beam of his flashlight through the dark tunnel. He should have waited for back-up, but there was no time. The children were counting on him, and he didn't want to let them down, like the last time. Though he'd only been a deputy, to his way of thinking he was in a position of authority, and as such had to take responsibility for what happened.

Like he was responsible for Adam Tasker's death when he stepped aside to let Andy and the others take him. Which made him responsible for everything that happened to Donnie afterwards, up to and including his return. Pulling the trigger would have been justified. At the time he was too young, and too green to see that. One man would have died that day, but in the long run it would have saved three others.

The tunnel turned right, then left, and narrowed to the point where he had to turn sideways to slip through. For a moment, as he stood with his gut pressed against the opposite wall, he was afraid he might become stuck. When he was sure he would have to call for help, he slipped through into a wider tunnel whose ceiling provided ample headroom. From the emptiness beyond the light of his flashlight a child cried out.

He was getting close. Close to the truth. To saving the children and closing the only case tarnishing his career. It wasn't concern for his career that propelled him forward, but fear for the children that compelled to push on. He moved deeper into the tunnel with no concern for his own safety.

Focused on saving the children and putting an end to the legend of the Witch.

He stopped at a junction where three tunnels led in three different directions.

Which one?

In answer to his unvoiced question, from the opening to the right, came the sound of a crying child. He stepped through into an even deeper night and the ground slanted down abruptly, causing him to lose his balance. He managed to catch himself after staggering a few steps, imagining himself falling headlong down that narrow corridor. He might have broken his neck, and he shuddered at the idea.

Who would save the children then?

In the emptiness ahead he spotted a soft yellow light framed by a shadowy passageway. From the opening came the terrified cry of a child and he turned off his flashlight so as not to warn anyone of his approach.

Getting closer the scent of roasting flesh assailed him. A fine layer of ash covered the floor, like the ash in the laundry room. It filled the air around him, getting into his nose and mouth, burning his eyes as he struggled to breathe.

Reaching the opening the temperature spiked, and he believed he'd stumbled upon the doorway to hell itself. The bullet proof vest beneath his shirt quickly became soaked with sweat, its weight dragging him down.

He peeked around the corner with his weapon held low, ready to bring it up in an instant. The chamber beyond was wide and long with a low ceiling, illuminated by a yellow glow that had no discernible source. Dense shadows thick with menace filled the outer edges of the chamber.

From a circular opening in the middle of the floor, full of what looked like black water, a dense trunk of slender tentacles, twisted about one another like the strands of a wire, vanished into murky depths. Something moved beneath the surface, creating small ripples that lapped at the stone sides. The steady roar of rushing water came from somewhere beyond the chamber, eliciting the image of a subterranean river flowing through an eternal night.

Black tentacles snaked out across the floor from the opening, spreading out in a sunburst pattern, each fading into the deeper shadows along the outer edge of the chamber.

He pointed the beam of his flashlight into those shadows. A strangled cry of rage, combined with a touch of horror, escaped his lips when the beam illuminated a small figure sitting with its back against the wall.

The gun in his hand forgotten, he moved the beam of the flashlight from one child to the next. Their small bodies wrapped in burial shrouds of cobwebs that obscured their features. Movement drew his eye to the right, and he swung his beam around to illuminate a small girl who raised her hands to shield her eyes.

Amber, the name came to him as he pulled up a mental image of the photograph her parents provided. Next to her sat Christine, blinking in the harsh light. Beyond her sat Nathan, then Twila, who kept a protective arm wrapped around Bobby's shaking shoulders.

Who would do such a thing? His rage boiled to the surface and he stepped into the room. Looking around, searching for a target for his anger. Other than the children, the chamber was empty.

"It's okay, you're safe now." He crossed to the children. Amber cried out, pointing at the hole, as a dark shape rose from its unplumbed depths.

The smell of roasting flesh and ash thickened as a shadow blocked the yellow glow on his left. He turned towards it, raising his gun, when an ebony tendril of night slashed out. Though it looked insubstantial, it hit him with enough force to drive him across the chamber. His gun fell from nerveless fingers, clattering to the stone as a voice shrieked in his mind.

"They are mine!" With the voice came the image of an old woman's face, her lips twisted into an evil snarl, eyes burning with the fires of hell. The flesh of her face cracked and blistered, the yellow glow of an inferno raging beneath the shattered flesh.

Another presence emerged, older than the Witch. A creature that had lived in this place for eternity and would continue to exist in shadowed depths long after the sun was extinguished, and the planet became a ball of ice spinning around the dead ember of the sun.

It wore the Witch like a mask, drawing power from the fear this twisted old woman inspired. Feeding on their terror. It searched his mind, rifling through old memories with ebony fingers. Seeking the one thing that would give it power over his psyche. It wasn't long before it found what it was looking for and Sheriff Paul Odenton, a mountain of a man known to strike fear in the hearts of those who would do harm, found himself a helpless child.

The world was large and frightening as he moved with quick steps through the rooms of his grandmother's old house. Rooms full of old furniture and darkness crowded in shadowy corners. The surfaces were of polished oak and cherry that reflected the light coming though the only window.

He was looking for his grandmother and had become lost in the array of rooms in the house where his father was born.

Passing through the dining room, he stopped when a whispered word caught his attention, and he peered into the shadows beneath the sideboard next to the china closet. Something moved in the emptiness as a deeper shadow shifted.

"I ain't gonna hurt you," a sinister voice whispered as terror washed through him. Warmth spread across the front of his pants. The shadows reached for him, growing thick as he tried to back away. It blocked the light of day to throw him into a nighted abyss as the chill of an opened grave caressed his flesh, sending waves of goose bumps across his arms.

As the remembered fear washed through him, the presence fed on it, nourishing itself with the essence of his childlike horror. His fear held a purity that provided this thing what it needed to survive. A fear that could only come from a childhood memory, a memory unencumbered with the emotional reality of the world around them.

It was why it sought young children, their fear was raw and powerful, seasoned with a hint of innocence. Rolling over he pushed himself to a sitting position. His service revolver lay within reach, and he looked from it to the shadowy form towering over him. Darker shapes moved back and forth within the creature's essence as it shifted and shimmered, collapsing and rebuilding itself all in the same motion.

Could he even stop it?

He fell to his left, his hand slipping around the butt of the revolver, and he rolled away from the creature. When he came up to a sitting position, he held the revolver in a two-handed grip, sighting down the barrel at the beast that had trapped them.

"I'm taking them with me." Though he could be considered overweight, the sheriff was nimble enough to get to his feet with little trouble.

An ebony tentacle lashed out at him and he ducked, the muzzle of the pistol never moving from its target.

"They are mine." That voice cried out in his mind and he ignored it, keeping his eyes on the tentacles growing from the sides of the beast, coming together to encircle him in a lattice work of darkness.

The air was driven from his lungs and he was dimly aware of flying through the air. He slammed into the wall, fireworks erupting behind his eyes, and he slid down to the floor.

My fault. The accusation followed him into unconsciousness as the children screamed.

<h1 style="text-align:center">64</h1>

Susan's steps became more assured as the darkness grew lighter around her. She was able to make out more details as she emerged from that narrow tunnel. Returning to the chamber from which four tunnels spread out in four different directions. One, she knew, led back to her basement. The second was the dead end she had spent the past half hour working her way out of.

Which left only two.

From one came a soft yellow glow her flashlight masked when she passed through before. As she crossed to the opening a commotion came from the shadowed depths. A male voice shouted, children screamed, and the sounds of a scuffle propelled her headlong into those shadowed depths. With her attention more focused on saving Christine she failed to notice how the floor slanted down. With her second step it felt like she had stepped off the edge of a towering cliff. Her momentum threw her forward, and her hands grabbed at jagged stone as she fought for a hand-hold.

By the time her leading foot found solid ground, she was already overextended, and was thrown forward. Bright lights exploded behind her eyes as she slammed into the floor of the cave, several sharp stones cut into the flesh of her arm and leg. She lay for a moment, drifting between unconsciousness and awareness, breathing heavily as a singular pounding took up residence behind her eyes.

It would be so easy to lay down and let it all go. For a moment she did, her worry draining away as she struggled to cling to consciousness, pushing away the numbing darkness that offered a false security. A scream cut across her consciousness.

Christine?

She pulled her hands under her body and pushed herself to her knees. Using the wall of the tunnel to steady herself, she slowly regained her feet. Cautious now, she continued through the darkness that grew lighter with every step. Reaching an opening filled with a soft yellow light, she clung to the wall as she carefully peered around the edge. At first, she couldn't see anything, the persistent pounding behind her eye seemed to be clouding her vision. Slowly the world came into focus to reveal a wide stone chamber with a low ceiling.

She spotted Sheriff Odenton sitting with his back against the wall to the left of the opening. His head resting on his chest, his feet splayed out before him. For a moment she believed he was dead. His chest rose as he breathed, and she released her pent-up breath in relief.

On the floor beyond his feet an ebony tentacle led to a circular opening in the floor. It appeared to be full of water whose surface was disturbed by movement beneath. On the opposite side a thick trunk of twisted appendages rose from the water's surface and spread out in a fan of individual tentacles that vanished into the deep shadows crowded on the other side. Without the benefit of the flashlight Sheriff Odenton had used, she was unaware of the dead children sitting along the wall in the deeper shadows. A soft yellow glow came from nowhere and everywhere.

Carefully she eased into the chamber, on her hands and knees, crossing to Sheriff Odenton. She stopped as movement from the water drew her attention. A black form rose from the water, shifting and shimmering as its undulated, its sides glistening in the soft light.

Her attention was drawn to those sparkling lights and she imagined them to be stars glittering against the emptiness of deep space. She struggled against the allure of letting herself fall into those unplumbed depths. Understanding dawned and she realized she was on the verge of a tremendous discovery. Her curiosity compelled her to move closer.

A child cried out. The voice cut through her inner calm. She realized she was standing at the edge of the opening, staring at the emptiness towering over her. The stars she believed she had seen vanished as understanding dimmed, replaced by confusion.

The more she looked at it, the more it confused her. It had no rhyme or reason to its makeup. The essence itself, at first glance, was like a shadow cast on a sunny day. Upon closer inspection more details became visible. A hurried desperation emanated from this essence, the emptiness a blank slate upon which her nightmares, and fears, were played out.

The essence moved, revealing several children sitting around the perimeter of the small room. Knees drawn up to their chests, eyes wide with terror, crying softly as the ebony form moved from one to the next.

Susan watched transfixed. It had substance while at the same time it didn't. Terrifying forms emerged before fading into a churning cauldron of shadowy characters hinting at nightmare images better left undiscovered.

The shape moved to a small red-headed child who whimpered with terror as it knelt down in front of her. Tears sparkled in her eyes, tracing wet paths down her cheeks. A faint tendril of night caressed the child's face, accompanied by a soft slurping sound.

It's feeding on their fear. Nourishing itself with their terror, their tears.

Next to the red-headed girl sat Puddles, torn, and abused. One ear still clinging by a single thread, his body covered with a layer of mud from his travels in the tunnels.

On the other side of the red headed girl, *Amber*, she recalled. Christine gazed up at the shadowy shape with a terror-stricken expression. Fresh tears spotted her cheeks and Susan's heart climbed into her throat as that thing enveloped her daughter.

"Don't you touch my daughter," Susan shouted, "you leave her alone." Susan stepped around the edge of the pool as the shadowy form turned to confront her. An ebony wisp of night made a flicking motion, and Susan was flying backwards across the chamber. She slammed into the wall as several children cried out. Bright lights exploding behind her eyes as pain rippled across her back, and she struggled to catch her breath.

Her arms were pinned to the wall. Her hands trapped at shoulder height by bands of black emptiness. Where the ribbons of darkness touched her, an icy chill permeated her flesh.

Stunned by the impact, she struggled weakly as she fought to catch her breath. Getting herself under control, battling to contain the panic thundering through her. She managed to take several deep breaths that helped settle her fear.

"You leave them alone!" she screamed.

The essence towered over the children. She recognized them from their photographs in the paper. Bobby Carr, Nathan Fraley, Amber whose last name escaped her. Another child was present, a girl, older than Bobby, she sat next to him with her arm draped across his shoulders in a protective manner.

Bobby seemed to be in the worst shape, having spent the most time in this empty night, his flesh a pasty white, his eyes wide as sweat dripped from his brow. His gaze catatonic, his tears tracing filthy trails down dirty cheeks.

Christine carried a dazed expression. She didn't even recognize Susan's presence. Christine turned to look about as if she was seeing the room for the first time, and when her eyes settled on the muddy stuffed rabbit, she cried out. "Puddles," she shouted with joy as she pushed herself to her feet, and raced around that indistinguishable shape, snatching Puddles from his resting place.

"Where have you been?" she said, hugging him, "I've been so worried about you."

The nighted form turned to Christine and Susan cried out, "Leave her alone."

It stopped, regarded Susan for a moment before it crossed to her. As it got closer the dank chill of an open grave filled Susan with bitter remorse, and the forbidden knowledge of this creature's existence.

Its essence shifted and shimmered, billowing out, before collapsing upon itself. It lived in the hollow places between then and now, with no beginning, and no end. Existing as a stray thought that entered your mind at the most inappropriate moment. The cold chill you experienced when a dark cloud passed across the face of the sun, or a stranger walked across the ground that would one day be your grave.

Within shadowed depths lived the essence of nightmares, frightening things that slithered and crawled over and around one another in an endless dance to a god that ceased to exist before man walked upon the face of the earth. Clawed beasts that lived in the night, and corners of emptiness not as empty as they first appeared.

The Witch emerged, the flesh of her face cracked like fine porcelain, and beneath those jagged edges burned a raging inferno. Specks of black ash covered her face, and her eyes blazed with an unnatural light.

Susan realized the essence was attached to a twisting ribbon of night that vanished into the hole in the center of the chamber. She didn't know how deep the hole went but was confident it led to the hell her mother had spent so much money trying to avoid.

Her mother came into focus in that shadowy form. Replaced by Terry Blankenship, who got her pregnant when she was seventeen, and the doctor who took the baby, peering at her with piercing green eyes over the surgical mask covering the lower portion of his face.

The past, the present, and the future all came together, and all things became possible as that towering, featureless thing got closer. It was feeding on her terror, her fear, her anger, causing the emotions to drain from her body. Leaving her dazed and confused.

She slumped against her bonds, as drained as she felt when the base doctor prescribed her a little something to help her sleep after John's death.

No!

She had to fight it. She was Christine's only hope. There was no one else to save her. She struggled against the numbing cloud fogging her thoughts. Fought her way tooth and nail to full consciousness like a wild beast cornered. As the chamber came into view she noted the shadowy form had returned to the children.

A young girl emerged from the despair gathered at the center of the beast, she wore a simple white dress, her long black hair framed the pale oval of her face. Susan recognized her as Mildred's niece Lindsay. She stroked the creature with affectionate tenderness, yet her face hardened when she turned to the children, something glittered in her hand. "Who will be a part of my collection?"

"Leave them alone," Susan shouted as she struggled against her bonds. The flesh of her arms numb from the cold.

Lindsay crossed to Christine, who stumbled back, Puddles held close to her side, eyes wide with terror as Lindsay reached for her with one crooked hand, the other hidden behind her back. "I'm not going to hurt you," Lindsay whispered, and Christine shook her head as her thumb slipped into her mouth.

"Leave my baby alone," Susan shouted, struggling to break free of the emptiness that held her.

The girl spread her arms, the shadows swelling around her to block Susan's view. Christine cowered as the girl towered over her, and she was enveloped by shadows. Susan screamed as she yanked at her bonds.

From within the shadows came a muted cry of terror. Followed by a crackling sound like an electrical discharge. A faint blue glow shrouded the shadows as they parted. Christine emerged with Puddles in her arms.

The invisible bands holding Susan vanished and she rushed to gather Christine in her arms.

"I found Puddles, Mommy."

"Are you all right, baby?"

Blue sparks flew from the shadowy form, bouncing from the stone walls, to encompass everyone in a powerful blue light. Shrieks of pain came from the shadows that sank into the ground as the sound of a battle came from its ebony depths.

"Daddy's here," Christine said.

"What?" Susan asked, not sure she heard her daughter right.

"Daddy's back." Christine pointed at the shadow as a faint blue outline materialized from within those bleak depths. John emerged, dressed in the uniform he'd been wearing the day he died.

Susan's knees turned to water as tears streamed down her cheeks. Her sorrow, so long denied, washed through her. Their eyes locked and John nodded with a slight tilt of his head.

"I told you, mommy. Puddles had Daddy's love."

"Yes," Susan whispered as her misery lifted and the sorrow fled. She smiled at John, who reached out with one hand. Their fingertips brushed,. The past and present collapsed into one another. Images of their time together cascading through her mind, snapshots of joyful times that would remain with her forever. All of the bad things she'd endured fading away, overwhelmed by these joyous moments.

"I'm sorry," she said as he wrapped her in his loving embrace, "I didn't mean to be so upset with you."

"I know," he whispered and the weight she carried since the day he left was lifted.

"I love you," she said.

"I love you," he answered with a smile as he slowly faded from sight.

"No!"

"It has to be," he whispered in her mind, *"my time has come and gone, another's is to begin. I will always be a part of you, and I will always love you."*

Then he was gone, and Susan dropped to her knees as her sorrow overwhelmed her. Once again, she'd lost the love of her life, and as she knelt sobbing into her hands, a small hand came to rest on her back.

"It's okay, Mommy," Christine said, and Susan looked up as several children gathered around her. From the opening in the floor came the shrieking sound of the creature's death at the hands of her husband's ghost. His love having been sheltered and nourished by Christine, housed within the shell of a stuffed bunny earned at a roadside carnival.

"It had to be earned," she recalled Christine saying on several occasions and a chill washed down her spine.

Was it really dead? Could it be killed? The questions chased one another through her mind as the voices of their rescuers echoed from the tunnel beyond the chamber.

I hope so. She glanced at the opening in the floor as she pushed herself to her feet and crossed to check on Bobby and Twila. Her gaze turned firmly to the future

John's father accompanied Susan down the aisle, to the altar where Eric waited. Christine sat in the first pew with a clean and repaired Puddles on her lap. The stuffed rabbit was a connection to her first husband and a reminder that sometimes those old tales carried a hard kernel of truth at their core.

Though invited Sheriff Odenton was unable to attend, his vacant seat next to Christine a reminder that maybe it would be best if she tried to forget what she experienced that day. After all, what happened was now in the past, and as she was quickly learning, sometimes it was best to keep the past where it belonged.

She did attend Bobby's funeral, offering her condolences while secretly glad it was not Christine occupying the small silver coffin. The guilt she felt at the notion was short lived. After all, wasn't it natural for a parent to feel that way?

Only a few mourners were present, unlike the family members who turned out to celebrate her wedding. She'd become something of a celebrity after her name appeared in the paper as one of those responsible for helping solve an ages old crime. She helped put down a myth that held a small town in its grip.

Everyone turned out to celebrate her union and afterwards, at the reception the three of them would have time to connect with the extended family she'd forgotten she had.

In the basement of the First Presbyterian Church, three streets over from the church where Susan was being wed, another meeting was taking place.

They came from all walks of life, rich or poor it didn't matter. Employed, out of work, or retired, they all shared a common curse. Armed with cups of strong coffee to take the edge off, they came together to offer encouragement and solace to those who continued to fight their solitary battle.

In the parking lot of the church, Bethany sat behind the wheel of her battered Cavalier, her gaze fixed on the side door that led to the basement where the meeting was taking place. The only thing she could see was a small silver coffin. It was an image that would haunt her the rest of her life.

Bobby had been the only one not to survive. At first she clung to the hope that she would see him again but as the story unfolded and she, along with the parents of the other missing children, were brought by the police to the entrance of the tunnel in Susan's basement, she suspected she had been called upon to face her toughest test yet.

A test she was far from able to face.

The preacher gave her information about today's meeting, along with a promise that no one was there to judge anyone else. That each of them was facing the same demons she was.

To go in would require a change on her part, something she was far from capable of doing. No, it was better to face one's demons alone, she decided as she twisted the key in the ignition, and the engine roared to life with the clatter of worn lifters. She drove from the parking lot, turning right towards town and the only real home she'd ever known, the Wild Water Inn, the tavern where she worked.

Paul could finally close the cases that hounded his career. While he could not officially identify the person or persons responsible for the abductions, after all how would he even begin to describe what he'd seen, to his way of thinking it was case closed. If anything, he'd come away with a better understanding of the power of old wives' tales, legends, and ghost stories.

Sometimes they were grounded in fact.

As far as the state police and the council was concerned, those responsible for the abductions were still at large. None of the rescued children offered any clues that made sense. They spoke of a young girl in the forest who lured them to the caves with a promise of revealing a secret. Paul knew the curse everyone lived under had been lifted, and in time the council, along with the state police, would forget about everything that happened.

Rescuing the children also earned him renewed respect from the county council that secured his position until the day he chose to retire. Yet it was a win that was bittersweet. As that small silver coffin was lowered into the ground he watched from a respectful distance, hoping Bethany would be able to move on after her loss.

He found he couldn't. At night, when the house was quiet, and the only sound was Maggie's steady breathing as she slept beside him, he would lie awake, staring at the ceiling as he worked over the only conclusion he could find any real solace in.

It had been too easy.

Evil did not die that quickly.

With this in mind he'd peer into the shadowy corners of the room searching for clues to what was coming next. Evil would always be a part of life. It was a malignant force that found its voice in those who believed it was easier to follow the path of least resistance.

Alone it had no power. But among people who blamed everyone but themselves for the bad things in their life, it would find safe haven. There to nurture the hatred and fear it needed to survive. Anywhere people gathered, evil would find a voice to sow dissent, and spread discord, for that was the nature or man.

This was an intermission. A break between battles, and he hoped the next one would be fought by someone other than himself.

He was too old to go through all that again.

The End

Richard Schiver August 2018.

Curious about Mildred, Margaret, and Lindsay? Grab a copy of my novella to get the whole story.

"Reprisal: Vengeance knows no boundary."

About the Author

Richard is the author of eight novels, two novellas, and a collection of short stories. His most recent works are A Call To Arms, book four in his post-apocalyptic coming of age series, This Lawless Land, and Not Of Us, a WWII creature feature published by Severed Press.

During his life he has played a series of roles, husband, father, son, and lover, but his favorite by far is grandfather. He and his wife of twenty plus years have raised four children and helped raise eight grandchildren. They provide a secure home to a yellow lab named Max.

His wife, Dena, has experienced firsthand the exasperation of living with a writer whose mind tends to wander at the most inappropriate times. Yet she manages to keep his feet firmly planted on the ground.

Richard can be found online at:

Facebook: http://www.facebook/RichardSchiver

Bookbub: https://www.bookbub.com/authors/richard-schiver

Written in Blood is Richard's personal blog where he shares his writing, and whatever else might strike his fancy. http://www.richardschiver.com

He can be contacted directly at rschiver@gmail.com and would be delighted to hear from you.

www.ingramcontent.com/pod-product-compliance
Lightning Source LLC
Chambersburg PA
CBHW051212190726
48288CB00006B/1926